# "Where...whe

Emily knotted her fingers together until they bloodless. This was the difficult part. Now she had to tell Jackson what she'd done.

"I was so scared," she began in a trembling voice. "I tried and tried to reach you. Then my mother found out I was pregnant and she was furious at my stupidity. It was pure hell, and I didn't know what to do. In the end, I did what my parents wanted."

"What was that?"

"I—I gave her up for adoption."

"We had a daughter?" he said in a hoarse voice.

"Yes, but I never saw her. I only heard her crying. I asked to hold her but they wouldn't let me."

He got to his feet, his body rigid. "You gave our daughter to *strangers*? How could you do something like that?"

"I was seventeen, alone and scared!"

"You just wanted to get rid of it as fast as possible so you could get on with your life, your big career."

Emily rose to her feet, her eyes huge with the emotions that consumed her. "How dare you! You weren't here, so don't tell me how it was. You didn't have to live through the horror and pain of hurting your parents. And you have no idea what it was like to give birth all alone and have that child taken from you before you could even see her face. So don't stand there and act holier than thou—because you are *not* blameless."

Dear Reader,

I'm sure you noticed the wedding gown on the cover. Isn't it spectacular? It's the winning design in Harlequin's 21st Century Wedding Gown Contest, which was open to young designers this past year. Over 400 entries were received and 28 finalists chosen. But it was this French-couture-influenced design by Sophie Sung of New York that won the judges over with its textured roses and fabulously feathered layered veil. I'm excited to have my heroine wear it in *Emily's Daughter*. And by the way, the Harlequin wedding gown will be available for home sewers through The Simplicity Pattern Company Holiday catalogue.

*Emily's Daughter* takes place on the Texas Gulf Coast. My husband and I go there at least a couple of times a year. He fishes and I write. We stay in Rockport, Texas. It's a small commercial and sport fishing town separating Aransas and Copano Bays. We love the friendly people and tranquil landscape and the hometown atmosphere. On one of our visits I was trying to think of new story ideas. We met a mother and daughter who rented rooms to tourists. They looked like sisters. We only talked for a little while, but that conversation stayed with me and I knew what my next book was going to be about—a mother and a daughter. Then I had to come up with a situation that would make the story interesting. Eventually *Emily's Daughter* took shape and now you'll read all about Emily and her long-ago lover and their quest to find their daughter.

Hope you enjoy it.

*Linda Warren*

P.S. I love hearing from readers. You can reach me at P.O. Box 5182, Bryan, TX 77805 or e-mail me at LW1508@aol.com

# Emily's Daughter
## Linda
## Warren

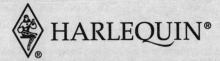

TORONTO • NEW YORK • LONDON
AMSTERDAM • PARIS • SYDNEY • HAMBURG
STOCKHOLM • ATHENS • TOKYO • MILAN • MADRID
PRAGUE • WARSAW • BUDAPEST • AUCKLAND

ISBN 0-373-71016-X

EMILY'S DAUGHTER

Visit us at www.eHarlequin.com

**Printed in U.S.A.**

To Paula Eykelhof, my editor, for her faith in my writing and in me. Thanks, Paula. It means more than you'll ever know.

A special thanks to the friendly people in Rockport who answered all my questions with such patience and enthusiasm. The characters in *Emily's Daughter* are fictional and any errors you find are mine.

# CHAPTER ONE

*PLEASE. STOP. PLEASE.*

The little girl paid no attention to Emily Cooper's plea. As she ran away, long dark hair blew behind her and a white cotton dress whipped around her legs. Her bare feet made imprints in the sand along the deserted beach.

Emily's lungs were tight and she could barely breathe. She had to keep going, though. She had to catch her. Her sanity depended on it.

*Please stop.*

Just when Emily thought her lungs would burst, the little girl stopped and slowly turned toward her.

*Yes, yes, yes, now I'll see her face.*

Emily caught her breath and waited, but before the little girl could make the complete turn, Emily woke up. She was bathed in sweat and breathing heavily.

"No, no, no," she cried. "Not again." Why couldn't she see her face? Just once…that was all she wanted.

The darkness didn't have an answer, and she slipped out of bed and walked into the bathroom. She switched on the light, then filled a glass with water. Taking a couple of gulps, she stared at herself in the mirror. Her dark brown hair hung in disarray around her shoulders and her eyes were groggy.

"You'll never see her face," she told the woman in the mirror. "You don't deserve to. You gave her away the day she was born."

She took another drink of water and went back to bed. Curling into a fetal position, she cried herself to sleep. Something she hadn't done in a very long time.

THE NEXT MORNING Emily drove into the doctors' parking area and glanced at her watch. Ten past nine. Damn. Her first appointment was at nine, which meant she was already late. As a geriatrics specialist, she was very conscious of her patients needs. Some of them were in a fragile mental state and could tolerate no disruption in routine, no unexpected upset.

She grabbed her purse and reading material and got out, slamming the door of her Lexus. She hurried into the building and toward the elevators. She'd worked with a group of doctors at this busy medical center in Houston for the past four years, and she prided herself on her punctuality—not only for herself, but for her patients. Now she'd have to do some juggling and explaining.

She'd overslept because she'd had a restless night. Why did she have the dream? She hadn't had it in so long. Why *now?* she wondered again. There was nothing different in her life—hospital rounds, seeing patients, consultations with other doctors. And of course her personal life was nonexistent since she'd broken up with Glen. Was that it? she asked herself as she stepped onto the elevator. Was she subconsciously mourning the fact that she'd never have another child? At thirty-five her conscience should have gotten use to that.

Glen was also a doctor and they'd dated for more than a year. Everything was fine until he started pressuring her to get married. The more he pressured, the more she resisted. Glen was divorced and had two children. At first, she told herself that was the reason—she wasn't prepared for a ready-made family. But she'd finally had to admit that she didn't love Glen. If she did, she would have told him her secret, but she'd never even come close to sharing that with him.

She enjoyed being with Glen, but she didn't have those blinding, passionate feelings she'd had for— No. She refused to think about him. Not today...not ever.

Before she could make it to her office, Harold, the office manager, stopped her. "Dr. Cooper, do you have a minute?"

Emily took a quick breath and turned to face him. She shifted the folders she'd taken home to her other arm. "I really don't. I'm running late," she told him.

Harold checked at his watch. "By God, you *are* late," his said, his blue eyes enormous behind his thick glasses. "You're never late. Is something wrong?"

"No." She looked down at the bundle of case files she held. "Just too much reading and not enough sleep."

*And too many painful memories.*

Harold shook his head. "You're the most dedicated doctor I've ever met. Your patients are lucky to have you. Your forgotten ones—that's what you call them."

Yes, she did. Children, no matter what age, had a hard time dealing with their parents when illness struck. They had lives and usually the old people were relegated to a nursing home where they were completely forgotten. It was a sad reality, but one she saw all the time.

"When I get old, you're going to be my doctor," Harold smiled.

Harold was in his mid forties and she could have told him she had patients his age with Alzheimer's, but she didn't want to frighten him.

"Thanks, Harold. Now I've got to go," she said, and started to leave.

"Oh, Dr. Cooper," Harold called after her. "I just wanted to remind you about the eleven o'clock meeting."

She stopped. "Meeting?"

"Yeah, about the new computer system we're installing. Didn't you get the memo?"

Frowning, she said, "Maybe. I'm not sure—I've had so many memos this week. I'm sure Jean or Sharon will take care of whatever needs taking care of."

"No, no" was Harold's quick answer. "The staff and nurses have already had their instructions. This is for the doctors. The head of the computer company is flying in as a favor to Dr. Benson. He's speaking with the doctors personally. It's an amazing system and it'll make life so much easier."

"My schedule's already backed up and—"

"You have to be there," he interrupted. "Dr. Benson expects *everyone* to be there. Half an hour or so—that's all it'll take."

Dr. Benson was head of the group and he'd been talking for a while about a new system. She didn't have time, but she should probably learn something about it. She hated the business part of her job. She only wanted to treat patients, but she had to admit that improved computer skills would benefit her *and* them.

"Okay, Harold," she said in a resigned voice. "I'll be there."

She went in through her private entrance and laid her papers on her desk, then shrugged on her white coat and walked into her bathroom to check her appearance. She hadn't had time to do anything about her hair so she'd pulled it back and clipped it behind her head. It made her look older, more mature, and that was fine. Her face was blotchy, though, from lack of sleep and too many tears. Her patients wouldn't notice, she was sure.

"Dr. Cooper?" her nurse called from the doorway.

"Yes, Jean," Emily answered, coming out of the bathroom.

"Thank God." Jean let out a sigh of relief. "I was getting worried."

"I'm here now, so let's get started," Emily said. "I suppose we have a full morning."

"Sure do. All the exam rooms are occupied." She smiled brightly. Jean was a lovely young woman in her late twenties with a calm, sunny disposition that was invaluable to Emily's patients.

Emily took the folder Jean was handing her. "Do you know anything about this new computer system?"

"Yes, we've had classes for two days now." At Emily's puzzled expression, she asked, "You didn't read your memo, did you?"

"No." Emily glanced at her desk. "I remember Sharon giving it to me, but I must have put it somewhere."

Jean raised her eyes toward the ceiling. "You're hopeless when it comes to interoffice communication. The memo was all about the system, the computer company— all sorts of information."

"Well, I'll learn about it later. Right now I have patients to see." She walked to the first exam room. "Remind me that I have a meeting at eleven."

Emily was busy for the rest of the morning, and even though she tried to make up time, it was a lost cause. Her patients didn't like to be rushed and they liked lots of attention. When she finished with her last appointment for the morning, she realized that it was almost noon. Oh, no!

"Jean, you were supposed to remind me about the meeting," she said, hurrying into the corridor. She might be able to catch the end, the question-and-answer part.

"I'm sorry." Jean's apologetic voice followed her.

She quickly made her way to the conference room. Opening the door, she stepped inside, but it was too late. The meeting was over. Doctors were standing around talking.

Harold immediately approached her, and he didn't hide his grin. "Forgot, huh?"

"I'm sorry, Harold, the morning got away from me."

"Well, at least you can still meet the head of the company. He can answer any questions you might have."

Questions? How could she have questions about something she'd never even seen?

He took her arm and led her to a group of men. "Mr. Talbert, I'd like you to meet our geriatrics specialist, Dr. Emily Cooper."

A tall man in a dark business suit turned around—and Emily's world came to a complete stop. Jackson Scott Talbert. She'd know him anywhere. He hadn't changed all that much from…God, how long had it been? Eighteen years and five months. Funny how she remembered that exactly. And he looked the same, just older. Same lean build and honed masculine features. Same dark blond hair that curled slightly, although now there were streaks of gray. Same deep green eyes that haunted her dreams. All these things registered as Emily shook his hand.

His clasp was warm and strong, another thing she remembered about him. Her pulse quickened and she had trouble breathing, but she heard herself talking. She had no idea what she was saying. All she knew was that she had to get out of the room and fast.

Within seconds she was in the hallway, almost running to her office. Why hadn't she read the memo? she chastised herself. Then she would've known. She would have been prepared. She rushed into her bathroom, closed the door and leaned heavily against it. Pushing away from the door, she sat on the toilet and buried her face in her hands. Why now? Why did Jackson have to come back into her life now? Especially after last night. The dream was still vivid in her mind. Did her daughter—no, she corrected herself, *their* daughter—have those deep green eyes? She'd never know and neither would Jackson because she would never tell him about their daughter.

She stood up and glanced in the mirror. She looked like hell. She smoothed a hand over her dark hair and tightened the clip at the back of her head. Opening a drawer, she took out some makeup. She powdered her face and applied lipstick, but it didn't help; she still looked hollow-eyed and tired. Jackson probably hadn't even recognized her, she thought grimly. Very little of the happy, laughing teenager he had known was left.

She hadn't lost her composure like this in years. Seeing him, so suddenly, so unexpectedly, was a shock, and it had blown her professional persona completely to shreds. Jackson must think she was some babbling idiot, and Dr. Benson would demand an explanation of her rude behavior.

What if her colleagues knew the truth? What if they knew her secret? Would they look at her differently? Of course not, she told herself. They were professionals like herself and they would understand. During their years in the medical profession, they'd frequently seen teenage pregnancies. Everyone made mistakes; adoption was a legitimate way out. It gave the mother a second chance and it gave the baby a loving family. But things weren't always that simple, especially for the birth mother. No matter what age, giving away a child wasn't easy. She knew that firsthand. After all these years, she still couldn't justify her actions. Guilt was always with her. Looking back, she knew adoption had been the wrong choice for her. Right for many other girls, but wrong for her. So many times she wished she'd stood up to her mother because now she knew that her parents would have eventually come around. Even though they abhorred the idea of her having a baby out of wedlock, they would've supported her. She could have managed to get her education and still keep her baby. If only... Hindsight was twenty-twenty, as people always said, and it didn't help the way she felt about herself. She had given away the most precious part of herself—her child—and nothing would ever make that right.

She'd blamed her mother for years and their relationship was still strained. But in her heart she knew it was her own fault. She'd gone along with everything her mother had planned for her future—and that future did not include a baby.

It was so long ago, yet it seemed like yesterday. She grew up as an only child in Rockport, Texas. She was pampered and protected, and she was happy. In school, she was at the head of her class. The kids called her brainy, but it didn't bother her because she recognized that their teasing was affectionate. She was friends with everyone. Then, in her senior year, Emily's life started to fall apart.

At forty, her mother discovered she was pregnant. It was a shock to everyone—especially Emily. She was so naive that she'd never thought about her parents having sex; she couldn't even imagine them doing such a thing. They were too old, she kept telling herself. Inevitably, the kids started to tease her about her sexy parents and it became an embarrassment. For seventeen years, she'd been a model daughter, but the new baby changed her whole attitude. She grew rebellious, staying out late and arguing with her parents.

Then Jackson Talbert came into her life. Her father was a fishing guide in Rockport, a small town on the Gulf coast. Jackson and his father had come down for two weeks of fishing after Thanksgiving. Her parents had cottages they rented to tourists during the peak months. During the winter season, if a person wanted a fishing trip and also asked for accommodations, her father always rented the back room. The cottages were closed until March, so it was easier for her mother to have everyone in the house.

When Emily had first seen Jackson, she thought he was the handsomest man she'd ever seen, with his blond hair, green eyes and charming smile. He was tall, with a trim, athletic body. She was sure he'd played football, and later he told her that he had in high school. Football players usually ignored Emily. She wasn't the cheerleading, pompom-shaking type, so she couldn't help feeling excited when Jackson took an interest in her. He was older and much more mature than the boys she dated. He seemed a balm to the misery she was experiencing over the new baby.

It started with smiles and innocent flirting, then sitting on the front porch talking while their parents sat in the kitchen planning the next fishing trip. She knew her mother was watching her and that made her angry. She was old enough to do what she wanted. Her parents didn't consult her about *their* lives, so she wouldn't consult them about hers.

Emily groaned now, a sound of pure disgust. It echoed her feelings about the way she was back then—spoiled and selfish. She left the bathroom and sat in her chair, staring into space. She could remember it all so clearly, could remember sneaking off to the beach to be alone with Jackson. It was wintertime, but they hardly noticed as they laughed, held hands and talked about their lives. He'd just graduated from college and was working in his father's hardware store. He had a degree in computer science and hoped to work in the computer field, but his father wanted him to take over the family business. He was torn between his family and his dream.

She told him about her plans to become a doctor and how it was all she'd ever wanted to be. Before she knew it, she was head over heels in love and Jackson seemed to feel the same way. She told him things she'd never told anyone else, and making love seemed a natural conclusion to all the tumultuous feelings inside her.

Late at night they would grab a blanket and steal away to the beach to make love and to be with each other. Jackson always used a condom. They knew it was important to be careful, but the night before he left, they made love more than once and used the same condom.

She was so young she didn't even realize how unwise that was. She only wanted to spend every possible moment with him. That night she cried because he was leaving, but he promised he'd call and he'd come back as soon as he could. *Famous last words.* She sighed in disbelief at her own innocence.

Of course he never called and he never came back. Every day she'd rush home from school and wait for the phone to ring, but she waited in vain. By the end of January her body began showing signs of something she didn't even want to think about. She bought a pregnancy test kit and her worst fears were confirmed—she was pregnant.

She didn't know what else to do, so she called the Talbert Hardware Store in Dallas. Jackson would help her, she kept telling herself. The man who answered the phone said Jackson wasn't in and claimed he had no idea when he'd be back. She called again the next day and the day after that and always got the same answer. Finally the man, irritated with her many phone calls, told her Jackson had left and wasn't expected to return. She got the feeling he was lying to her and it hit her that a lot of girls probably called the store looking for Jackson. She realized just how stupid she'd been. Jackson wasn't going to call and he had no intention of coming back. It was all a line—a line guys used on naive girls like her. Facing the truth was hard, and it was the first grown-up thing she'd had to do in her life.

Her mother was having a difficult time with her pregnancy and had to stay in bed. Emily struggled with how to tell her that she was pregnant, too, but her mother noticed the changes in her. She confronted her one day in the bathroom and Emily admitted she was.

Her mother yelled at her and called her stupid and ignorant, but in the end relented and said she'd take care of everything. Emily didn't have to worry, she said; an unwanted child wasn't ruining her life. She went on to say that Emily would have to give the child up for adoption. It simply wasn't possible for her to keep the baby with college and med school ahead of her, and her parents wouldn't be able to help because they had their own on the way. Emily had made a mistake and now she had to do the right thing.

She was appalled at what her mother was suggesting, but when she appealed to her father he said she couldn't upset Rose any more than she already had. There was a chance she might lose her baby. So Emily felt she didn't have a choice. She couldn't cause her parents any more misery. Dealing with that cold, hard truth was the second adult thing she had to do. She thought of running away, but she'd heard horrible stories of what had happened to girls who'd left home on their own. She became like a robot going through the motions of everyday life and letting her mother take over completely.

Her mother forced her to stay in school. With her grades she would graduate as valedictorian of her class and receive scholarships for college—and she did, just as her mother had planned. Even though Rose grew enormous with her own pregnancy, Emily gained very little weight and was able to hide her expanding waistline with loose-fitting clothes. No one guessed she was hiding a secret.

After graduation, her father whisked her off to San Antonio to live with her mother's aunt and to wait for the arrival of the baby. She wanted to stay home because her mother's baby was due in a couple of weeks and she wanted to be there for the birth. But Rose said that Emily was getting too big and people would start talking and Emily needed to be in San Antonio where they'd arranged for the adoption to take place.

She hated living with her great-aunt, who quoted scripture to her so she could see the error of her ways. She spent a lot of time in her room, reading and talking to her child. As the baby grew inside her, so did her motherly instincts. Everything was set for the adoption, but somehow she never really believed it. She just kept hoping she could find a way to keep her child, which only made it harder for her in the end.

Her mother delivered a girl the first week in June and her father called to say they weren't doing well. Emily pleaded to go home, to be with them, but her parents refused. Her resentment over the new baby had vanished in the wake of all the turmoil in her life, and she wanted to see her new sister. Instead she sat by the phone waiting for news. She felt banished by her parents and knew she deserved everything that was happening to her.

Her mother had a heart murmur and the birth had further weakened her heart. The months of June and July were rough for Emily because she didn't know what was going on at home, but her father said not to worry. Everything would be fine.

Emily's baby was due at the end of August, but due to stress the baby came early. She lay in a hospital bed in excruciating pain, giving birth—alone. They told her she'd had a girl and Emily begged to hold her, just to see her, but the nurse said it was best if she didn't. The baby was given to a couple who was waiting to love her and to raise her as their own. The nurse told her she'd done the right thing and in time she would see that, but she never did. Not a day had gone by that she hadn't thought about her daughter in some way or other.

When her father arrived, he found her in a fetal position, crying. He, too, told her she'd done the right thing. All she could think about was going home—to forget and to be with her family. Again her father refused, saying her mother wasn't well and she had her hands full caring for the new baby. Emily said she could help, but her father said she needed to regain her strength and make plans for college. That was what her mother wanted for her. She felt as if her parents had washed their hands of her and she cried and cried…for herself…for her baby…for so many things.

In September, her father took her to the University of Texas, where she was enrolled. Again there was no talk of going home. Her mother had sent her some pictures of her new sister and she clung to those like a lifeline. During Thanksgiving break, she was finally able to go home and see her sister for the first time. She was tiny and precious and Emily spent most of the week just holding her, talking to her, trying not to think about her own baby. Those memories came at night when sleep would elude her and she'd ache for a glimpse of her daughter's face. Would she look anything like her? Or would she favor Jackson? On and on it went over the years and still she had no answers. But she prayed her daughter was healthy and happy and with people who loved her.

She hadn't known, when she left to have her child, that she'd never be home for any length of time again. She only went home to see her sister, and she was grateful they had a good relationship. Her mother said she spoiled Rebecca and that was another bone of contention between them, but if she could afford to give Rebecca the things she wanted, then she intended to. The arguments with her mother that followed were never pleasant.

Emily slid lower in her chair, sighing deeply. Memories seemed to be weighing her down, smothering her. After all this time, she should be past the pain, but she wasn't—that was why seeing Jackson so unexpectedly had thrown her. God, she'd made a fool of herself. Now what? Forget about him, she told herself. She was good at forgetting Jackson. She'd spent years doing it.

IT TOOK JACKSON TALBERT about ten seconds to recover, then he made an excuse about getting something from his briefcase and turned away. Emily Ann Cooper. He couldn't believe it. She was half woman, half child when he'd known her, but today he could see she was all woman and there was not a glimmer of recognition on her pretty face. Could she have forgotten him? Or did she just prefer not to acknowledge him?

He didn't like either of those possibilities. He had felt they'd shared something out of the ordinary once and he'd always regretted not going back to the coast to see her, but his world had been turned upside down with an aspect of life he was ill-equipped to deal with. And later his life had gone in so many different directions that Emily Cooper became merely a pleasant memory.

She looked great, he thought, and she'd become a doctor

just as she'd wished. He was glad for her and he wondered if she was married. Her name was still Cooper, but that didn't mean anything. It might just be her professional name. Anyone as intelligent and beautiful as Emily had to have someone in her life.

He kept thinking of the young Emily with her warm, bubbly laugh and seductive dark eyes. She'd been a breath of fresh air after the experienced college girls he had dated. He grew warm just remembering their nights on the beach that long-ago winter....

He closed his briefcase and tried to recall what she'd said. Something about *busy, patients, had to go*. He didn't catch much else because he was in a state of shock and too preoccupied with staring into her eyes, which were somber and professional. There was no laughter or mischief in their depths. They were serious—maybe a little too serious.

What did he expect? he asked himself. A giggling teenager? He was sure he had changed, too. There was gray in his hair, lines around his eyes and a whole lot of living on his face. But still, she should've recognized him. Why hadn't she said something or, for that matter, why hadn't he? Well, he planned to rectify that. She worked here, so it should be no problem finding her. And this time they would talk.

THE RINGING OF THE TELEPHONE startled Emily back to reality. It was her private line, so it had to be family.

She picked up the receiver. "Hello."

"Em, she's driving me crazy!" The frantic words of her sister resounded in her ear.

Emily took a deep breath, not certain she was in any shape to handle another argument between Becca and their mother. "What is it, Becca? What's Mother done now?"

"She said I have to be home by ten o'clock from the prom and I have to wear one of my old dresses. Tommy and I had been nominated for prom king and queen, and I have to have something nice and I'm not leaving at ten o'clock. Everyone'll laugh at me. I can't take it anymore! If you don't come home, I'll run away."

Emily took another breath. "I told you I'd buy you a dress for the prom, and I'll talk to Mom about the ten o'clock business."

"Mom said you can't buy me anything else."

"I'll talk to her."

"In person, okay? She always lightens up when you're here."

"I can't. I'm too busy."

"Yeah, yeah, I get the message. You're always too busy for your own family."

"Becca, that's not fair."

"You haven't been home for ages. Admit it, you can't get along with her any better than I can, but I'm stuck here."

"It's not that bad, and you know it. You can't get your way so you're angry right now, but I'll talk to Mom and we'll work this out."

"You promise?"

"Yes, I promise."

"*Please* come home. Just for a little while," her sister begged.

Emily closed her eyes, Becca's plea was getting to her. She didn't go home much; it was too stressful. She and her mother couldn't get through a visit without Rose making some reference to the past. Becca had never been told about any of it, so she didn't understand. But Emily knew that her mother was making Becca pay for Emily's mistake. Becca didn't deserve that.

"Okay, I will, and we'll go buy you a dress for the prom." Emily heard herself giving in.

"Great, Em! I knew you wouldn't let me down."

"Just let me handle Mom."

"Don't worry." Becca laughed, then more solemnly she added, "She hasn't been feeling well lately. Maybe that's why she's so grouchy. Dad even leased the cottages to the Hudsons next door for the season because Mom can't take care of them anymore."

Emily straightened. "What's wrong?" she asked, knowing that if her mother had given up the cottages, it had something to do with her health.

"She gets out of breath so easily, and last night she had trouble breathing. Dad was up with her most of the night."

"Did she have her oxygen?"

"Of course. She says it was my fault because I upset her so much."

"It's not your fault," Emily told her. "Mom had a heart condition long before you were born and any upsets she brings on herself."

There was a long pause, then Becca asked, "She's not going to die, is she?"

"Don't say things like that. As soon as I can clear my schedule, I'll come and check Mom over."

"Thanks, Em. I can always count on you. Love you."

"Love you, too," she replied, but before she could say anything else the phone went dead.

Emily hung up and ran both hands through her hair, loosening the clasp. God, she didn't need this today. The past seemed to be looming over her and she couldn't escape it. First, the dream, then Jackson, and now the old problem with her mother. What else could happen?

## CHAPTER TWO

THE AFTERNOON WAS JUST as rushed as the morning, and at six o'clock Emily said goodbye to her last patient and headed into her office. Jean followed.

"That's it, thank God," she sighed. "I'll file the charts and finish up for the day."

"Okay," Emily said absently, leafing through some notes on her desk.

Jean made to leave, then turned back. "Did you meet the computer guy?"

Emily blinked. "What?"

"The computer guy," Jean repeated. "All the women are talking about how fine-looking he is."

Emily glanced back at her notes, trying to remain detached, trying not to react. "I didn't notice."

"*What?*" Jean shrieked. "You're hopeless. Absolutely hopeless. If it's not an old man, you're not interested." Realizing how the words sounded, Jean quickly backpedaled. "That came out wrong. I meant—"

Emily stopped her. "Don't worry about it. I know what you meant."

"Thank God." Jean rolled her eyes. "I'd better go before I get my foot completely stuck in my mouth." At the door, she couldn't resist adding, "I just think you need to get out more, have some fun."

"I appreciate your concern, but most likely the computer guy's married."

"Oh, no." She walked back. "He's divorced."

Emily's eyes widened. "Really? How would you know that?"

Emily was sure Jackson was married and had a family by now. He probably had another daughter...a daughter who—

"I talked to Dr. Benson's secretary who talked to Dr. Benson's nurse, who had all the juicy details."

"The grapevine," Emily groaned.

"Yeah, it comes in handy sometimes."

"And sometimes it's totally inaccurate," Emily pointed out.

There was a pause, then Jean asked, "Are you interested in him?"

"Heavens, no," Emily was quick to deny. "I'm just curious."

"That's how it starts," Jean said with a laugh.

Emily ignored that remark. "I'm not on call this weekend, am I?"

"No," Jean answered. "Why?"

"I'm thinking about visiting my family."

"Okay." Jean nodded, and left, returning to the filing area.

Emily went back to her notes, blocking out Jackson Talbert's face, blocking out the past and everything else— everything but her work. She had to get over to the hospital, to check on Mrs. Williams. She flexed her shoulders and stood up. It had been a long, exhausting day, not to mention humiliating, and now she needed a hot bath and some sleep. She removed her white coat and hung it on a peg.

She massaged the back of her neck, trying to ease the ache starting at the base of her skull.

"Had a hard day?" a familiar voice asked.

She swung around, her eyes huge in her pale face. "Jackson," she whispered.

He was leaning against the doorframe, hands shoved in the pockets of his gray slacks. He had lost his tie and several buttons on his lighter gray shirt were open, revealing the beginning of dark blond chest hair. Her stomach tightened uncontrollably as she relived the sensation of running her fingers through...

"You remember my name," he said, and pushed away from the door.

She stared at his face—the lean lines, defined cheekbones, straight nose and green, green eyes. Everything was the same...except for the tiny lines around his eyes and mouth and the gray in his blond hair. Jean was right; he *was* fine-looking, even more so than she'd recalled. And he was now a man instead of the boy she had given herself to.

Seeing that he was waiting for an answer, she collected herself. "Of course I remember you."

*I'll never forget you.*

"Earlier you acted as if we'd never met, never..."

He let the unfinished sentence hang between them, and to stop the nervousness in her stomach she slowly took the stethoscope from around her neck and placed it on her desk. She chose her next words carefully. "I didn't think my colleagues would be interested in my girlish infatuation."

"Infatuation?" He raised a dark blond eyebrow. "Wasn't it more than that?"

*To me, it was.*

But the words that came out of her mouth were "No, I don't think so. You left and never came back and I got on with my life." She hated that she couldn't disguise the bitterness in her voice.

He knew she was lying and trying to hide it. He remembered that about her. She had a hard time lying, especially to her mother. He used to tease her about it. But through the nervousness, he could hear the hurt in her voice. He should've gone back. He'd never wanted to hurt her, but he'd gotten so caught up in his own turmoil that he could only think about himself. Looking at her, he regretted that.

He couldn't help asking, "Did you wait for me?"

*Every minute, every hour of every day.*

"Of course not," she denied emphatically.

She was lying again. He could tell by the way she ran her hand along the edge of the desk. He was making her nervous. Why? He just wanted to talk.

The terse chitchat was disconcerting her. She felt as if her emotions were in a blender and someone had pushed the high button and any minute she was going to explode all over the room.

"I've got to go," she said abruptly, reaching for her purse. "I'm expected at the hospital."

Jackson was taken aback by her sudden departure and he was thinking of ways to keep her talking a little longer. He saw a picture on her desk. He walked over and picked it up. It was a family portrait of her parents, herself and another young woman. Her mother had been pregnant all those years ago, and this had to be the baby. Emily had so many problems with her mother's pregnancy, but judging by their smiling faces everything had obviously worked out.

"This must be your sister," he said.

"Yes, that's Rebecca. We call her Becca," she replied, and swung the strap of her purse over her shoulder.

*Why didn't he leave? She didn't want to talk to him.*

"She looks like you when you were seventeen."

"Yes, everyone says that," she found herself saying.

"But her hair is lighter and our personalities are completely different. Becca's very outspoken and direct. She's always talking and laughing and getting involved in things that my parents disapprove of. She's constantly arguing with my mother and—"

She stopped, unable to believe she was telling him all this. For a moment, it seemed like old times when she used to pour her heart out to him.

"Sounds as if she's a lot like you," he said, and carefully placed the picture back on her desk.

"In ways I guess we are," she admitted, knowing that Becca was stronger than she ever hoped to be. Her mother would never be able to force Becca to do anything against her will. Becca was strong-willed and stubborn, and she had her own views on everything. Emily had never been that opinionated or unyielding. She was weak...weak and...

*Don't think about the baby. Don't think about her now.*

"I've got to run," she said in a detached voice. "Is there something you wanted to see me about?"

Again he was thrown by her coolness. She clearly had no interest in talking to him. Had his callous behavior almost two decades ago destroyed any chance of their having a normal conversation?

"Yes," he said quietly. "I wanted to talk about old times. Maybe take you to dinner."

A paralyzing fear gripped her, and she fought to maintain her composure, her control. Jackson Talbert wasn't getting to her again. Talk? Dinner? Absolutely not! She had to escape from him as quickly as possible.

"I'm sorry, I'm too busy, but it was nice seeing you again," she lied, moving resolutely toward the door.

"Emily?"

Against her will, she halted. It was the way he said her

name—soft and persuasive with a deep, husky nuance. It was the same way he always used to say it on the beach, before his lips claimed hers…before he'd kiss her into oblivion…kiss her into forgetting everything but him. How could a voice, a sound, obliterate years of pain, years of hating Jackson Talbert? She didn't know, but just like that, she felt herself being pulled toward him.

"Aren't you curious about why I never came back?"

Those words held her spellbound and suddenly she desperately wanted an answer. She turned slowly around.

"Yes, I am," she said, and she wondered if that low, aching voice was hers.

He smiled and her stomach tied into a painful knot of pure need—something she'd never experienced with any other man. What was she doing? she asked herself. Walk out that door and don't look back.

*Go. Go. Go.*

But her feet didn't move.

Something stronger than herself kept her rooted to the spot. All these years she'd believed that he'd simply used her for a good time, a vacation fling—but maybe he hadn't. Maybe he'd had a reason for not returning to her, for not calling. She needed to find out—for her own sanity. She needed to justify what had happened back then. If she could do that, maybe the dreams would stop…. Maybe she could let the memory of her daughter go.

"Good. There's this little Italian restaurant I go to when I'm in town," he was saying. "It's not far from the medical center." He checked his watch. "We could be there in less than twenty minutes."

She gripped her purse strap, knowing she was about to take a step that could change so many things. Was she ready? She swallowed. "I really have to go to the hospital

first," she told him. "I can meet you there in two hours."
To her surprise, she made the decision quickly and easily.

"Two hours?" He frowned. "That long?"

"Yes," she replied. "I don't rush my patients. I try to be attentive to their needs."

"The dedicated doctor." He smiled again.

She didn't respond.

He reached for a pen and pad from her desk. He scribbled on a piece of paper and handed it to her. "That's the address and my cell phone. Just in case you get tied up."

"Thanks."

"I'll see you at the restaurant," he said, and walked through the door.

She stared at the paper and began to question her decision. She didn't need two hours at the hospital. Seeing Mrs. Williams wouldn't take that long. She wanted to go home and shower and change into something more feminine, more... She was having dinner with Jackson Talbert, Emily reminded herself with a sense of panic. The father of her child. She couldn't help wondering how he'd say her name if she told him *that*. She shuddered. It was her secret, and after tonight she'd never see Jackson again.

She'd only accepted his invitation because she had to hear his version of the past, his explanation for disappearing from her life. Then she could put Jackson out of her heart forever. As long as she remembered that, she'd be fine.

SHE SPENT LONGER at the hospital than she'd planned, and barely had enough time to shower and change. She went through her closet repeatedly before she decided what to wear. For someone who was seeing Jackson only once and only to hear about the past, she was a little too excited, too eager. She tried to curb those feelings, without success.

She felt seventeen again and she knew that tonight was a bad decision, but it was too late to do anything about it. Or was it? She could just not show up and let him get a taste of what it was like to wait for someone who was never coming. Oh, yeah, that would be sweet revenge. She chewed on her lip and had to admit she wasn't out for revenge. She'd gotten beyond that, thank God. Now she just needed answers…about the past.

She gazed at herself in the mirror. She had on a pale pink vest with turned-up collar and a long maroon skirt that whispered around her ankles. Her dark hair hung loose to her shoulders and her makeup was simple—some mascara and liner, a slick of lip gloss. With her olive complexion she didn't wear much, but in the evenings a little helped. At least it eased the tiredness in her eyes.

Noticing the clock, she realized she had to hurry. She slipped on a pair of sling-back heels and headed for the door. Traffic was a nightmare, as always, but she made it on time. Jackson was already there and she was shown to his table. The restaurant, which was unfamiliar to her, was small, but had a warm, pleasant atmosphere with its linen tablecloths, candlelight and soft music. Wine bottles and glasses seemed to be everywhere, and green plants adorned the nooks and crannies.

Jackson stood as she reached the table. She saw that he too, had changed. He now had on a dark blue suit and a crisp white shirt that emphasized his lean good looks.

He smiled, taking in her new appearance. For a moment he was speechless. He had known the young, enticing Emily, and today he'd met the professional Emily, but now he was staring at Emily, the woman. *Wow* was all he could think. She was dressed to perfection; even her makeup was flawless. He remembered she'd rarely worn it back then.

With her coloring she didn't need adornment, but tonight it was perfect, setting off her beautiful face and dark eyes.

Those glorious eyes—he never tired of gazing into them. They used to be tantalizing and bright, but now they held shadows, shadows he knew nothing about. Maybe her life hadn't been all that rosy. His certainly hadn't. A lot of things had happened in the intervening years.... But none of them would be discussed tonight. They—

He pulled himself up short. He was reacting as if he and Emily had a future. After tonight they'd probably never see each other again. Somehow he didn't feel good about that.

He wanted to tell her why he hadn't come back and she wanted to listen. He was aware that she had ambivalent feelings about him and, if nothing else, he had to set the record straight. She still might not understand, but at least she'd know the truth.

"I ordered wine," he said. "I hope that's okay."

"Sure," she answered as the waiter handed her a menu.

She inhaled deeply, trying to gather enough strength to get through this.

Jackson approved the wine, and the waiter poured it into glasses that sparkled in the candlelight. "Are you ready to order, Mr. Talbert?"

Jackson put down his menu. "House salad and linguine for me, Carlo, as always, but the lady might need a moment."

"No, no," she said promptly. "I'll have the green salad—vinaigrette on the side. Roasted garlic chicken breast with pasta—no sauce."

"Yes, ma'am," the waiter responded, then took their menus and walked away.

Jackson stared at her. "You eat healthy, don't you?"

She folded her hands in her lap. "I try."

He leaned back in his chair. "A doctor, Emily. You made that dream come true. I bet your parents are proud."

She took a sip of wine. "Yes, my mother loves telling people about her daughter, the doctor."

"Having met your mother, I can imagine that."

She tilted the glass to her lips once again. She'd talked endlessly about her mother to Jackson. She'd confided her innermost secrets, her struggle with her mother's pregnancy, her strict morals and unreasonable discipline. Jackson knew all about her problems with Rose, but he didn't know the worst part.

"Evidently you didn't go into your father's hardware business," she said, deftly changing the subject.

"No," he murmured, "I didn't. That's what I—"

Before he could tell her anything, their salads arrived and conversation was interrupted.

Sprinkling vinaigrette over hers, Emily asked, "Do you come to Houston often?"

"Maybe once a month. We have a lot of customers here. Our new program cuts down on work, and on the expenditure of time and money. It's been very successful and it keeps me traveling."

"Everyone at the office is raving about the program you installed for us."

He wiped his mouth with a napkin. "You haven't tried it?"

She glanced up. "No, but I will. I just hate taking time away from my patients to learn technical things."

He leaned toward her, his eyes sparkling with enthusiasm. "It'll make your life so much easier. Simply by hitting a key, you can pull up a patient's history, his drug chart, his last visit, your recommendations and diagnoses. Then you speak into a headphone to update any chart. The computer will recognize your voice. This will save tremendously on paperwork. The hardest part is getting all the information into the computer and keeping it current, but I'm sure you have people to do that.''

She was mesmerized by the glow in his eyes, which clearly revealed how much he loved his work.

The waiter removed their salads and their food was brought out.

They ate in silence for a while, then Jackson asked, ''How's your chicken?''

''Fine,'' she replied, swallowing a bite. The food was delicious and she was hungry. Having skipped lunch, she was very conscious of that.

''Next time you should try the linguine. It's the best I've ever eaten,'' he said.

*Next time. There would be no next time. At least not with Jackson.*

He asked if she wanted dessert and she refused, but asked for another glass of wine. She felt she needed it.

Jackson twisted his wineglass, watching her, and his thoughts drifted. He was seeing Emily on the beach with nothing but the moonlight on her soft, smooth skin. So many things about her surfaced—things he'd thought he'd forgotten. Her uninhibited smile, her sharp intelligence and the incredible beauty she was so unaware of.

His gaze heated her senses and she rushed into speech. ''You were going to tell me why you didn't come back.''

Engrossed in his memories, he was startled for a second. He took a deep breath and tried to find the words. ''When I left Rockport that winter, I was unsure about my life,'' he began slowly. ''My parents were pressuring me to come into the hardware business, while I wanted to go out on my own and start a computer company. I had a friend who was interested in the same thing.''

''You told me that years ago,'' she reminded him.

His eyes caught hers. "Yes, I told you a lot of things about myself."

She looked away and carefully placed her napkin on the table. "We both did that."

"Two kids eager to become adults," he sighed.

"You were an adult," she said. "I was the kid."

"I guess you were," he admitted, feeling guilty because he'd taken advantage of her young spirit. "But you were so delightful, so—"

She cut in. "Why didn't you go into your father's hardware business?"

He studied her for a moment, then answered, "The decision was made for me."

Her eyes didn't waver. "By whom?"

"My parents."

She lifted a dark eyebrow.

This was the hard part. "My father took me on that fishing trip as a way to prepare me for what was to come," he said. "The day after we got back to Dallas, my parents said they wanted to talk to me. I assumed it was about the business, but..." He stopped and swallowed before continuing, "My mother told me she was dying of pancreatic cancer. My father was supposed to tell me on the trip, but he couldn't. They gave her three months to live. I couldn't believe it. I was stunned—in shock. My mom was always so active, so full of energy. It wasn't fair, and I hit back at everything and everyone in sight. But not at her. I didn't want her to see my pain. I intended to be there for her. She was very brave right up until the end. She died January 30."

"I'm so sorry," she immediately offered, feeling the pain that was obviously still with him. Then something clicked in her mind. January 30? That was the day she'd found out she was pregnant. She remembered it vividly.

She'd borrowed her mother's car and driven into Corpus Christi to buy a pregnancy test. She went to Corpus Christi because she didn't want anyone she knew to see her buying such a personal item. It would've been all over Rockport in minutes. She hurried home to take the test. Even though she'd suspected what the result would be, she was in shock. At the same time, Jackson was dealing with another kind of trauma.

"After that, I was restless. I couldn't concentrate on anything," Jackson was saying. "My aunt was spending a lot of time with my father, and I told him I had to go. There were too many reminders in the house, at the store. He said he understood, and I hit the road trying to outrun the pain."

That was why he wasn't at the hardware store when she'd called. He was trying to deal with his mother's death. It wasn't what she'd believed at all.

*Why didn't you come to Rockport?*

As if reading her mind, he went on. "I thought about coming to Rockport, but I knew your mother would eat me alive. She didn't like me much." He paused for a second. "That wasn't the real reason, though. I was a mess. All I could think about was *my* life, *my* grief, and I couldn't drag you down with me. You were young, finishing high school, getting ready for college. You didn't need an albatross around your neck."

*Oh, God, if he only knew.*

"I traveled around for a while, then headed to San Antonio to see my friend." His words froze her thoughts.

*Had he been in San Antonio when their daughter was born? Had he been there when she'd given their daughter away?*

She licked dry lips. "When did you go to San Antonio?" she asked in a tight voice.

He frowned. "I went that spring and I stayed for about a year and a half and— Emily, are you all right? You look pale."

"I…ah…" She couldn't answer as she tried to grapple with this twist of fate. He'd been there when their daughter was born. So close, yet so out of reach. "It's just hot in here," she lied. It was the only excuse she could invent for her strange behavior.

"Would you like some water?"

"Please."

He called the waiter and a glass of ice water was placed in front of her. She held it with both hands, letting the coolness soothe her shaky nerves.

"Better?" he asked as she took several swallows.

"Yes, thanks," she said. "You were saying?"

"Oh." He tried to remember what he was talking about. "My friend, Clay, and I started the computer company in San Antonio. It was slow that first year, then it took off like a rocket. Later, we moved the business to Dallas and it's still doing very well, although Clay's not with me anymore. He fell in love with a school teacher from Alaska, sold his share to his brother and moved up there."

After a strained silence, he said, "I promised to call and come back, but do you understand why I didn't?"

*No, I never will,* she immediately thought. But he'd had his reasons. He'd loved his mother and he'd coped with her death in the only way he could. He didn't know about Emily and the baby. He'd no cause to think that she might be pregnant; after all, they'd been so careful. Sadly, his love for her hadn't been enough to bring him back, and she was the one who'd had to suffer.

Her fingers played with the linen napkin. "I used to rush home from school to wait for your phone call," she admitted in a near whisper.

"Emily, I can't tell you how sorry I am," he said, his voice deep with emotion. "That first night I was home, I couldn't sleep because I kept remembering our nights on the beach. Later, after the pain and fog had cleared from my mind, I wondered if you were seeing someone else. If you'd forgotten me."

*No, Jackson, I never forgot you. You left a reminder that stayed with me and will stay with me forever.*

Her eyes challenged his. "But you forgot me rather easily, didn't you?"

He looked embarrassed, and she was glad he wasn't going to lie about it. "Yes, I guess I did. With my mom's illness and the computer company, I didn't have time for much else. I'm not proud of that. We made a lot of promises under the stars and I should've called and let you know what was happening. I regret my lack of concern for your feelings, but I couldn't talk about my mom's death to anyone—not for a long while." He stopped for a second. "*I'm sorry* sounds too contrived for my actions, and my only excuse is that I was totally unprepared to deal with the death of someone I loved." He stopped again. "When I saw you today, I realized I hadn't forgotten a thing about you. I remember all the little details and—"

She broke in. "Please, Jackson, let's not dredge it all up."

He swallowed some wine, his eyes never leaving her face. "Okay, but I want you to know that time meant a lot to me."

*But not enough to bring you back.*

She clasped her hands in her lap, thinking maybe that was all she needed to hear…now. Back then, she'd needed a whole lot more. But it really didn't matter any longer. "What happened to your father?" she asked, trying to get out of dangerous waters.

Her shift in conversation didn't escape him, but he let it go. She'd made it clear she didn't want to talk about the past. "My father sold the business and retired. He bought a cabin on a lake and spends his days fishing and playing dominoes with his buddies. He still misses my mom, but he's a survivor."

"He never remarried?"

"Nope, he's more interested in catching that big fish than catching a woman."

"I'm sorry about your mother," she said again.

"Me, too, Emily," he responded readily. "And I'm sorry I let my grief overshadow everything in my life—even my word to you."

She bit her lip; they were moving onto dangerous ground again. "Did you get married?" she asked abruptly, then wished she could take the words back.

"Yeah, a few years later I decided to settle down. My wife, Janine, was a…"

His voice trailed off as he saw the look on her face, and he quickly added, "I'm not married anymore. I'm divorced."

"Oh," she murmured weakly. It wasn't the fact that he'd been married that startled her. She already knew that. But when he'd said *my wife,* an odd feeling came over her. Until that moment, she hadn't realized she'd always seen *herself* in that position. Which was crazy, completely crazy.

"I'm sorry," she said.

"Don't be," he told her. "It was one of those marriages that should never have happened, and it didn't take us long to figure out we were wrong for each other. I wanted kids and a family. She didn't."

"Why not?" slipped out before she could stop it.

"She's a lawyer and works for a big law firm in Dallas.

Her total focus was on advancing her career. I understood that. My career was important, too, and we both put in staggering hours. After about two years, I asked her to take some time off and have a baby. She refused, saying she wasn't ready.'' He paused for a sip of wine. ''She has two sisters who'd given up careers to raise their children. She said she wasn't doing that. After four years, I realized she wasn't going to change her mind, and by that time we'd grown so far apart that the marriage was basically non-existent. We both wanted different things from life and we mutually decided to call it quits.''

''You wanted children?'' she asked quietly.

''Sure'' was his quick response. ''I was an only child and I planned to have at least two kids, the big house, a dog—the whole nine yards. I just forgot to mention those things to Janine.''

*He wanted kids.* She didn't know why she was having a hard time grasping that. Maybe her guilt was spiraling out of control.

''I guess I was looking for what my parents had—a home filled with love and laughter.'' He drank more wine. ''But I don't see that in my future now. I'll soon be forty and I've resigned myself to being a fatherless bachelor.''

*You're not. You have a daughter.*

The words burned in her throat and she ached to tell him. But what good would it do? Their daughter would be eighteen in August—a grown woman with a life of her own, which didn't include them.

He interrupted her disturbing thoughts. ''How come you never married, Emily?''

''How do you know I'm not?''

He grinned. ''I asked someone.''

*So did I. So did I.*

''Well?'' he persisted.

She shrugged. "I was busy with medical school, then establishing a practice. I guess I never had time to develop a lasting relationship."

"But there were men?" He couldn't prevent the question.

Her eyes met his. "Yes, but no one ever overshadowed my career."

*Or you.*

He raised an eyebrow. "So that's what a man has to compete with?"

Emily suddenly noticed that the restaurant was almost empty and it was getting late. She could feel herself yearning to tell him about their daughter—but she couldn't. She had to get away from him. "I really have to go. I've got an early day tomorrow."

Jackson reached into his pocket and pulled out his wallet; he laid a credit card on the table. The waiter immediately took it and disappeared. Within minutes he was back, and Jackson and Emily got to their feet. They left the restaurant in silence, stepping out into a pleasant May evening. The night sky was clear and bright, and the traffic made a loud humming sound, but Emily was hardly aware of her surroundings as she walked to her car. Jackson followed.

She opened her car door and turned to face him. She didn't know what to say. So many conflicting feelings surged through her.

"I enjoyed seeing you again," he said.

"Me, too," she replied, and meant it. Certain questions had been answered, certain issues resolved—and yet she recognized that the past would always be with her. There would be no absolution. After hearing Jackson talk about kids, that was clearer than ever.

"I'd like to see you again."

She shook her head. "I don't think that's wise."

"Why not?"

"Because we can't recapture our youth..."

Her words trailed away as he stepped close to her—so close she could smell his aftershave and feel the heat from his body. He cupped her face in his hands, and her heart pounded in her chest in anticipation of what she knew was coming.

His lips gently touched hers, then covered them with a fierce possessiveness she remembered despite all the years that had passed. He didn't touch her anywhere else. He didn't need to. Her lips moved under his and she kissed him back. She couldn't help it.

"I don't think we have to recapture anything," he whispered against her lips. "It's there. It's always been there. Ever since I first saw you in your mother's kitchen."

He was right. The feelings were still alive. Oh, God, they were. Her body was on fire and she hadn't felt this way since...since those winter nights on the beach. But she couldn't give in to this. She wouldn't.

"Jackson—"

"I'll call you tomorrow."

"No, I—"

"Yes," he asserted, and she got into the car without another word. Just before he slammed her door, he said, "Tomorrow, Emily."

EMILY DIDN'T REMEMBER much of the drive home. She kept hearing Jackson's words. "Tomorrow, Emily." Over and over they echoed through her head, her heart, and she realized she'd crossed a dangerous line between the past and the future.

Now she was older and much wiser, and the words shouldn't affect her so intensely, but they did. Had she learned nothing? Yes, Jackson's explanation for not coming back was a good one, but still… If he'd loved her as much as she'd loved him, nothing would have kept him away. Instead he'd managed to resume his life without her and she had dealt with hers as best she could.

She'd made bad decisions, and nothing she did now would change that. She sensed that seeing Jackson again was another bad choice. It was probably best to leave the past where it was—in the past. She couldn't handle anything else.

As she climbed into bed, she decided there would be no tomorrow for her and Jackson. She'd call him and make an excuse. Having settled that, she felt better. Surprisingly she fell asleep easily.

Except that she had a different dream.

And Jackson was in it.

She didn't wake up crying or trembling. She was actually smiling, and that shook her. She tried to understand this new dream. She and Jackson were on the beach and they were holding a little girl. Their daughter. Emily kept saying "I'm so glad I told you," and he kept saying "Thank you."

She pulled her knees up to her chin, trying to still the joy inside her. She didn't have to look far to grasp the meaning of her dream. She wanted to tell Jackson about their daughter.

She closed her eyes, trying to collect her thoughts. The dream was also about guilt—her guilt. It was consuming her, and it had become more voracious since yesterday. Since his return. Her subconscious had clarified what she had to do and why. She would tell him. He deserved that much; he believed their time together was innocent and beautiful, but it was marred with so many ugly things.

She would tell Jackson about their baby…and the adoption. She wasn't sure what his reaction would be, but he had a right to know. Beyond that she didn't want to think. But she had to.

Whatever the consequences, she'd pursue this unaccustomed urge, this need to tell him the truth. Maybe it was the love in his voice when he talked about having kids. Maybe that had triggered her dream. Or it could just be plain old selfishness. She wanted to tell him because she had a desire to share her precious baby with someone. She'd never done that. She'd never spoken of her daughter or the adoption and the grief she'd experienced, and she desperately needed to. She wanted to talk about all of this with her baby's father...Jackson.

She curled up in bed. If she told him, there would be disbelief in his eyes, along with hatred and anger and disgust. She would see herself through his eyes. Could she endure that?

Grabbing a pillow, she held it tight. "Yes," she said into the darkness. Right or wrong, she would tell Jackson about their daughter.

## CHAPTER THREE

WHEN JACKSON REACHED the hotel, the first thing he did was call his friend and partner, Colton Prescott.

"Hey, Jackson, I'm glad you're home," Colton said before Jackson could speak. "I'm dealing with the Conley contract, but they want to talk to you."

"I'm not home. I'm still in Houston."

There was a pause, then, "Problems with the system?"

"No, everything's running fine."

"Then why aren't you back?"

"Because I've met someone and I'm staying for a few more days."

This time there was a very long pause. "Met someone? You mean a woman?"

Jackson laughed at Colton's disbelieving tone. After his divorce, he'd tried to date, but it became more trouble than it was worth. Every woman he got involved with wanted to rush him to the altar, and he wasn't ready to tackle marriage again. These days he spent time with his dad and at the company. When he went out, it was strictly for pleasure and he made that clear up front.

"Yeah, a real live woman."

"Damn, those women in Houston must be a helluva lot better-looking than the ones in Dallas."

Jackson laughed again. "It doesn't have anything to do with looks. She's someone I knew a long time ago."

"O-o-oh."

From that drawn-out exclamation, Jackson knew what Colton was thinking. "It wasn't some one-night stand. This woman means a lot to me." As he said the words, he realized that he cared a lot about Emily—probably always had.

"Really. Well, that sounds interesting."

"I'll let you know when I plan to return."

"Wait a minute." Colton stopped him before he could hang up. "What am I supposed to do about Bill Conley?"

"Use some of that Prescott charm on him."

"But he wants the system in by the first of the month. That's pushing it and I refuse to do that. Fast work creates glitches that take much more time to fix."

"I'll talk to Bill in the morning. Will that help?"

"It sure will. He treats me like a twelve-year-old."

Jackson smiled. At thirty-two, Colton had a youthful exuberance, but there wasn't a thing he didn't know about computers. Once their customers recognized that, everything went smoothly. "See you next week," he said, ending the conversation.

"Oh, Jackson, your dad called."

A knot formed in his stomach. "Did he say if something was wrong?"

"No, he just wanted to talk to you."

"I see," Jackson said slowly. He'd spoken with his dad last night and everything was fine. So why had he called again? Eager to get off the phone, he added, "I'll talk to you tomorrow."

As soon as he'd hung up, he dialed his father's number. Six rings. Seven... Finally the phone was picked up. "Hello," a sleepy voice said.

"Dad, it's Jackson."

"Jack, my boy, why are you calling so late? Are you okay?"

"Yeah, Dad, I'm fine, but Colton said you called the office. Thought it might be something important."

"No, not like you mean. I was just mad and upset, and I wanted to talk to you."

"Why were you upset?"

"Because of that damn aunt of yours. You'll never believe what she did. She came to visit and brought a woman friend with her. A friend she assumed I'd be interested in. How many times have I told her to stop matchmaking? But does she listen? No. She doesn't hear a word I say. She wanted me to go dancing with them. Can you imagine? *Dancing!* I told her in no uncertain terms what she could do with that idea and she got angry. I figured she'd be calling you and complaining about her mean old brother."

Jackson took a patient breath. It was the same ongoing argument between his father and aunt. Aunt Maude was lively and sociable, and his dad was happy being by himself, fishing or doing whatever he pleased. Aunt Maude didn't understand his attitude and Jackson had a hard time with it at first. But he'd finally realized his father had spent years in the work force and after his mom's death, just wanted some peace and quiet.

"She worries about you," Jackson told him.

"Well, if she worries so damn much, she can come over here and cook me a meal every once in a while."

"As a peace offering, why don't you take her out to dinner? Someplace nice."

"You know Maudie. She'll want to go someplace where there's drinking and dancing."

"Dad," Jackson sighed. "Aunt Maude's always been there for you and it won't hurt to humor her."

A pause followed. "All right, all right," he said irritably. I'll take her out to eat. But if she brings another floozy over here, I'll—''

Jackson cut in. "Just tell her how you feel—politely."

''I do, but I think she has a hearing problem'' was the wry answer. "Why didn't you come home today?"

Jackson didn't miss the quick change of subject, but he was glad. He'd rather not talk about Aunt Maude and how she got on his dad's nerves. He preferred to discuss Emily.

"I was going to, but I met someone."

"Really? Of the female persuasion?"

"Yes, Emily Cooper. Remember her?"

A pause. "Don't think so."

"Sure you do. Owen Cooper's her father—a fishing guide on the coast. We stayed at their home that November before Mom died."

"Yeah, I remember now. A pretty thing with big brown eyes. You were crazy about her, weren't you?"

Jackson didn't answer that. His father knew he'd been a lot more interested in Emily than in fishing. Instead, he said, "She's a doctor now and works at the clinic where we installed the computers."

"You don't say."

"Yes, and I had dinner with her tonight and I'm planning on seeing her tomorrow."

"Life is strange," his dad remarked.

"Sure is. I've got to go. Be nice to Aunt Maude."

"I will, and you have a good time. Lord knows you deserve it."

As Jackson hung up the phone, he planned on doing just that—enjoy his time with Emily.


THE NEXT MORNING Emily waited for Jackson to call or show up at her office, but by noon she began to get a déjà vu feeling. When she finished with her last patient for the morning, she asked Sharon if she'd had any private calls. Sharon said no, and a discomfort settled around her heart. She didn't think she'd misjudged his sincerity, but then, she didn't really know Jackson Talbert at all. Of one thing she was certain, she wasn't waiting for him. She wouldn't put herself through that again. But now that she'd screwed up her courage to tell him about the baby, she desperately wanted to…needed to. Maybe it wasn't meant to be.

She ordered a take-out salad for lunch and was busily writing notes in patients' charts when Sharon buzzed her.

She pushed a button on the intercom. "Yes?"

"There's a Mr. Talbert on line two. Says it's personal."

Emily let out a deep breath. "Thanks, Sharon."

She stared at the phone for a second, gathering her thoughts, then picked up the receiver. "Hello."

"Hi, it's Jackson."

Her heart fluttered involuntarily at the sound of his voice.

"Yes, I know," she said simply.

"What do you want to do tonight? You name it and we'll do it."

She bit her lip, remembering all the promises he'd made and remembering that he'd kept none of them. That didn't matter. She had to talk to him; that was the important thing.

"I'll probably get away from here about five-thirty and then I have to stop by the hospital. I won't get home until around seven."

"You work long hours."

*Yes, it's what I need to keep the memories at bay.*

"It's part of my job," she said lightly.

"You'll be tired. Why don't I pick something up and we'll eat at your place and talk?"

She felt a moment of joy at his concern, but it vanished

when she realized Jackson was probably hoping for a lot more than food and pleasant conversation. And he'd get it, but not the way he was expecting. Instead, he was going to get the biggest shock of his life.

"That'll be fine," she agreed, thinking it would be best if they met somewhere private instead of a public place. At least she'd be in her own surroundings.

"What would you like to eat?"

"Surprise me."

There was a noticeable pause. "Okay, but remember you said that." She could hear him smiling.

She gave him her address and they hung up, but Emily was still with him, still hearing his voice. Still experiencing the way he'd always made her feel... Oh, God, she had woven so many dreams around Jackson Talbert, and to her dismay, she found she could easily do it again. So many years, yet she could remember his touch, his smile, his energy, as if he'd never hurt her...never broken her heart. But he had. The past stood between them like a brick wall they couldn't scale or tear down. Tonight, though, she'd make an attempt to dismantle the barrier brick by brick, and when she was through there'd be nothing left but the truth. A truth that would be stronger than any wall ever built, separating her and Jackson forever. She was preparing herself for the worst.

The rest of the day, between patients and rounds, she kept rehearsing what she had to say, but nothing seemed right. How did you tell a man he had a daughter he'd never see? She didn't know, and finally decided there *were* no right words. She just had to do it.

They'd agreed to meet at eight. She drove into her garage a little before that and hurried inside, hoping she had a chance to shower and change before—

The doorbell stopped her halfway up the stairs and with

a deep sigh she went to open the door. Jackson stood on the threshold with a large bag and a charming smile.

"Delivery, ma'am," he joked.

He was dressed in khaki pants and a green plaid shirt that emphasized his beautiful eyes. That old familiar ache circulated through her stomach and she quickly curbed it. She couldn't let sexual feelings sway her thinking.

She stepped aside and he entered her home. "I'm sorry," she apologized. "I'm late getting in."

"I know, I saw you drive up," he said as he set the bag on the kitchen table. He turned to gaze at her. Her hair was clipped at the nape of her neck, and she wore a brown suit with a cream silk blouse. Her dark eyes were enormous and fatigued, but held a sultry welcome he remembered well. His heart thumped loudly in his chest, and he thought she was the most beautiful woman he'd ever seen. He'd felt that about her years ago and that hadn't changed.

She ran a hand nervously over her hair and he could tell she was tired—that was obvious. "If you'd like to freshen up, go ahead," he offered. "I'm in no hurry."

"Thanks, I will," she said, and started up the stairs. She was grateful for this reprieve. She desperately needed some time to collect herself and to bolster her courage.

When she'd left, Jackson glanced around the condo. There were hardwood floors throughout and the living area was done in creams and greens with touches of mauve. Everything was orderly, elegant—*perfect*. Just like Emily.

He removed the food from the bag and arranged it on the table, then searched for plates, forks and knives, an easy task since Emily was so organized. He found wineglasses, too, and uncorked the Chardonnay he'd brought. As he poured it, he had no idea what the evening would bring but felt it could only be good. They'd both matured and could now enjoy the fruits of that process.

He only hoped she understood about the past and had forgiven him for his selfish behavior. He couldn't believe he'd let someone as rare as Emily slip away, but then at twenty-one he hadn't been thinking too clearly. If she let him, he planned to make it up to her. Oh, yes, he planned to do just that.

EMILY RUSHED INTO HER ROOM and stripped out of her business clothes. She grabbed a pair of ivory lounge pants and a tank top and put them on. She intended to be comfortable. After unfastening the clip, she brushed her hair vigorously and stared at herself in the mirror. Her eyes were troubled. She could see that. Could Jackson? She carefully laid the brush on the vanity. It didn't matter, she told herself. She had to tell him. She had to say the words she'd never said to another person. She had to say them out loud.

*I was pregnant. I gave our daughter away.*

A lump formed in her throat as the impact of those callous words tore and gnawed at her heart. She'd lived with that feeling for so long and now...

Turning toward the door, she forced herself to stop thinking about the revelation she had to make. She actually wanted to talk about their daughter with Jackson, but once she did, he might not want to see her again. That was a risk she had to take.

As she entered the kitchen, she stopped short. The table was set with candles and wine and she stared openmouthed at the poached salmon, angel hair pasta and spinach salad.

"Jackson! How did you manage this?"

Jackson was busy taking in her new appearance. Her breasts were pressed invitingly against her sleeveless top and her hips were slim and... Her figure hadn't changed in all these years, except that her breasts seemed fuller, and he ached for her with an intensity that astonished him.

"Jackson," she said again to get his attention.

He shook his head to clear it of pleasant memories. "I'm very creative." He said the first thing that came into his mind. "After your long day, you need more than fast food."

If she knew all the trouble he'd gone to, she'd probably laugh. He wanted tonight to be special and he'd spent most of the afternoon making sure it would be just that. He'd found a restaurant and a chef who agreed to do everything he'd asked. He'd even bought serving dishes because he didn't want the food in plastic or paper.

"That's so thoughtful." She couldn't squelch the joy that rose inside her. This was something she hadn't expected.

"I'm a thoughtful guy. Don't you remember?" he asked teasingly as he held out a chair for her.

She did. He was kind and caring, too. When he'd learned she was a virgin, he hadn't wanted to make love to her, but she had pressured him, convinced him otherwise. At seventeen, she'd enjoyed the power she had over him. Those feelings—the passion, the companionship, the excitement—had made her forget the bitter things about her life, but they'd created so many more problems.

They ate in silence, simply savoring the delicious food. Finally Jackson asked, "Is your father still a fishing guide?"

"Oh, yes. If he can't be on the water several times a week, he goes a little crazy."

"And your mother—how is she?"

"Having Rebecca weakened her heart, and she has a lot of bad days. Of course, at her age, having to deal with a seventeen-year-old stresses her out and she loses her patience, which triggers other problems.''

"I don't think age has anything to do with it," he remarked. "She didn't have much patience with you, either."

"No, she didn't." Emily ran her finger along the rim of her wineglass. "But as I told you in my office, Becca's very outspoken and that causes a lot of heated arguments."

"Whereas the only time you rebelled was with me," he said, and saw the conflicting emotions shift across her face.

"Yes." Her eyes caught his with a fierceness he didn't understand.

He reached over and took her hand, wanting to reassure her about their time together. "You didn't do anything bad, Emily. What we shared was something rare and special. That doesn't happen too often."

She freed her hand slowly, his touch stirring emotions she couldn't face at this moment. He was being so compassionate, so gentle…everything she remembered him to be. She couldn't face that, either. She had to tell him, had to see this through. And when he knew, those recaptured emotions would crumble into nothingness. Dammit. Dammit. Dammit. This was harder than she'd ever imagined.

Suddenly, she got to her feet. "I'd better clean up," she said nervously, and began to carry dishes to the sink.

Jackson watched her with a puzzled expression, then stood to help her. They cleaned up the dishes without saying a word and carried their wineglasses into the living room. Jackson sat on the sofa; she sat beside him, twisting her glass with such force that he feared she was in danger of breaking it. Uneasiness darted along his spine.

"I need to talk to you," she said quietly, still working the glass.

"I can see that."

"This isn't easy."

"I can see that, too," he answered. He placed his hand over hers to stop the agitated movement.

She drew back. "Don't touch me, please."

That uneasiness knotted into a hard ball in his stomach, and he didn't know what to say. He wasn't prepared for this. They were getting along so well. He tried to think of what he'd said to upset her, but nothing came to mind that would cause this reaction.

She set her glass on the coffee table. "You think those days we spent together were special, and they were—until you left and never came back."

Oh, God, that was it. She still hadn't forgiven him. He should've known.

He turned to her but didn't touch her. "Emily, I'm so sorry. I tried to explain. I thought you understood."

She didn't seem to hear him. "I waited and waited for you to come back, but you didn't. I waited for a call, a letter, but I didn't get one of those, either. It was like you'd disappeared off the face of the earth. I needed you terribly, but…"

His chest tightened at the ache in her voice. He never imagined he'd hurt her so deeply, but she had such a passionate nature. They'd confessed their love and made vows to be together—vows he'd broken. It was clear he'd also broken her heart. He cursed himself for his callow youth. Somehow, he had to rectify this.

"Emily, I—"

"No." She held up a hand. "Let me talk. I have to tell you."

"Okay." He settled back on the sofa and everything in him strained to hear her next words.

She clenched her hands in her lap, gaining courage, gaining strength. "After you left, I discovered I was…"

The word stuck in her throat and she couldn't finish the sentence.

After a moment, he asked, "Discovered what?"

She gulped in a deep breath and forced the words from a mouth that felt dry and bitter. "I discovered I was pregnant." There…the words were out. Now they had to deal with them.

Absolute silence followed. Jackson shook his head. Had he heard her correctly? No, he couldn't have.

"What did you say?" he asked warily.

Her eyes jerked to his. "I said I was pregnant."

He shook his head again and tried to assimilate the words. But they didn't make sense. "No, that can't be true. We were so careful. We used a condom every time."

"That last night we ran out and used the same one more than once. It must have weakened—must have torn—and we didn't notice."

"Oh, God." The blood drained from his face. "It's true. You were pregnant?"

"Yes," she murmured in a low voice.

He raked an unsteady hand through his hair as he tried to grasp the situation. His eyes delved into hers. "Did you have an abortion?" The words seemed to come from somewhere outside him.

"No," she whispered.

He swallowed hard. "You had the baby?"

"Yes."

"Where…where is it?"

She knotted her fingers together until they were bloodless. This was the difficult part. Now she had to tell him what she'd done. And she had to do it before she lost her nerve.

"I was so scared," she began in a trembling voice. "I tried and tried to reach you to no avail. Then my mother found out and she was furious at my stupidity. It was pure hell and I didn't know what to do. In the end, I did what my parents wanted.''

''What was that?''

''I—I gave her up for adoption.''

The room spun crazily, then righted itself. So many emotions shot through him, each deep and cutting. *I gave her up for adoption.* He struggled to concentrate on Emily and her words. Her cruel words. But one thing was torturing his mind.

''We had a daughter?''

''Yes, but I never saw her. I only heard her crying. I asked to hold her, but they wouldn't let me.'' She spoke matter-of-factly, and that angered him.

He got to his feet, his body rigid. ''You gave our daughter to *strangers?*''

''Yes.''

His eyes narrowed. ''How could you do something like that? How could you? She was our flesh and blood. Didn't that mean anything to you?''

''Do you think it was easy for me?'' she snapped, her control slipping. ''I was seventeen, alone and scared.''

''You weren't alone. You had your parents.''

''My mother was having problems with her own pregnancy. They couldn't help me.''

''That's bull and you know it,'' he shouted. ''You just wanted to get rid of it as fast as possible so you could get on with your life, your big career.''

She rose to her feet, her eyes enormous with the emotions that consumed her. ''How dare you! You weren't here, so don't tell me how it was. You didn't have to live through the horror and pain of hurting your parents. And you have no idea what it was like to give birth all alone in a cold, sterile room and have that child taken from you

before you could even see her face. I live with that agonizing memory every minute of every hour of every day.
I hear her crying and I ache to hold her. So don't stand
there and act holier than thou—because you are *not* blameless.''

He paled under the attack and sank onto the sofa with
a shattered expression. Emily wanted to say something, but
any words she could have spoken were trapped between
her need to console and her own desire for some sort of
comfort from him.

Jackson thought of all the years he'd wanted a child and
all along he'd had a daughter. A daughter! He had a daughter. The words went around and around in his head until
he was dizzy with a sensation of loss and despair. He
wasn't blameless, just as she'd said, and that intensified
the feeling until he was afraid he might be ill.

''Jackson?'' Emily found her voice.

Slowly he raised desolate eyes to her. ''How could you
give her away?''

She bit her lip, striving to explain, but the only thing
that came out was ''It's something I bitterly regret.''

''Then why, Emily, why?''

She turned away, unable to answer. She had asked herself that same question so many times and never found a
reason, an excuse, that gave her any peace.

''Why are you telling me now? Is this some sadistic way
of getting back at me for what I did?''

She whirled around. ''No! I never intended to tell you
at all. But last night, when you talked about having kids,
I, ah, I wanted to tell you that you had a daughter. I
couldn't do it. Then later the feeling grew—and I have to
admit it was purely selfish.'' She drew a shuddering breath.
''I have this need to share her with you. I've never done
that with anyone.''

Jackson raked both hands through his hair. "God, Emily, I'm having a hard time taking this in."

She knew that, and there was nothing she could say to ease his pain.

"Why didn't your parents help you?"

"Remember, my mother was pregnant, and it was a difficult pregnancy. When she found out I was pregnant, too, she went into a rage, and the doctor said if she didn't calm down, she could lose her baby. I was devastated. I didn't want her to lose Rebecca." She paused. "Later, she said I'd shamed and disgraced the family, and adoption was the only answer."

"Oh, my God."

"I was torn between my child and my parents. When I couldn't reach you, I—" She choked back tears. Right now, those emotions seemed as real as ever.

"So you agreed to give the baby away?"

"Yes."

He stood and knew he had to go. This was something he didn't know how to handle and he was struggling to keep his temper.

"I came here tonight hoping we could salvage something from the past. But there's nothing left except a deep, ugly void that keeps growing by the minute. I'm trying to understand, but I'm not there yet. I don't know if I'll ever be."

He swung toward the door, then stopped. "Do you know where our daughter is?"

"No. The adoption was confidential."

His expression tightened. "I'm sorry, Emily, but I have to get away from you. I just…I can't accept this." With that, he disappeared out the door. And out of her life.

# CHAPTER FOUR

EMILY WALKED CALMLY upstairs to her bedroom. She lay across the bed and stared at the ceiling. Slowly the tears started, running unchecked from her eyes. *I have to get away from you.* Over and over the words kept torturing her. It was what she'd expected—the hatred, the disgust and anger. All the things she felt about herself, she recognized in his eyes. But the impact of actually seeing and hearing those emotions was much worse than she'd ever imagined. It was horrible and incapacitating.

Sobs racked her body and she turned over and curled into a ball. She shouldn't have told him. She shouldn't have. Now Jackson was hurting like she was. That had accomplished nothing; it had only made matters worse.

She had wanted to share her daughter with him, but she couldn't share something she'd never had. She saw that now. Telling Jackson had been a big mistake and opened doors she couldn't close. She had to find the strength to go on. She had before, and she would now. She kept telling herself that, but all she could hear was *I have to get away from you.*

In the early hours of the morning she fell into an exhausted sleep.

JACKSON DROVE STRAIGHT to his hotel and packed his bags. He'd flown to Houston, but he couldn't wait for a flight. He had to leave *now,* so he rented a car and headed home to Dallas. He took I45 North, and as he drove through the night all he could hear was *I was pregnant. I gave her up for adoption.* Sweet, caring Emily had destroyed everything he'd held dear about life. She was pure, innocent, good—that was what he'd foolishly believed. She had shattered that illusion into so many parts he'd never be able to piece it together again.

Had he ever really known her? Was what they'd shared merely sexual? Had he confused sex with other emotions? He shook his head; he didn't know anymore. His hand hit the steering wheel in anger. He *wanted* to understand, but other, deeper feelings kept getting in the way.

No wonder Emily was nervous when he'd first seen her in the boardroom. She had good reason to be. "How could she do it? How could she give our daughter away?" The words echoed in the car, but there was no answer and he felt there never would be.

Rain splattered the windshield and he flipped on the wipers. The steady to and fro movements seemed to calm some of his anger. To and fro, back and forth—the effect was almost hypnotic. He turned northeast off the freeway just before Dallas, and by four o'clock he was sitting on his dad's deck, gazing across the peaceful lake. George lived on a privately owned lake, away from the noise and pollution of the big city. The water glistened silver with moonlight, but Jackson didn't even notice.

*I have a daughter.* He would never know who she looked like, her personality, her likes or dislikes. He would know nothing about her—just that she'd been born. Being a man was lousy, he decided. A man should have more rights. He had a right to know his own child. The thought swept through his mind and certain ideas began to take shape. Before he could respond, a light came on in his father's bedroom; George was an early riser. When a light shone through from the kitchen, Jackson stood and tapped on the back door.

"Dad, it's Jackson. Let me in."

The blind opened a crack and his father stared at him with a puzzled frown, then the door swung in.

"Jack, what are you doing here?" George Talbert wore navy-blue pajamas. His gray hair was tousled and he had a worried look in his eyes. "What's wrong?"

"Just let me in and I'll explain."

George moved aside, still frowning.

Jackson could smell coffee perking. "Coffee," he sighed. "I need coffee." He walked to the pine cabinets, grabbed two cups and filled them. Bringing the coffee to the oak table, he handed his dad a cup and sat down.

George scratched his head and took a seat.

Jackson sipped the strong, black coffee and wondered how to tell his father. That was the reason he was here. He had to tell someone.

The kitchen, dining area and living room all looked out onto the lake and Jackson sat for a moment, enjoying the tranquillity.

Finally George said, "You came all the way out here for a cup of coffee?"

"No," Jackson answered, but said nothing else. He'd always been able to tell his dad anything, and he valued that bond. Now he had a hard time finding the right words.

"Why aren't you still in Houston with that girl, Emily?"

The question whirled around in his mind, and he had to admit he'd hoped they'd be wrapped in each other's arms this morning, discovering new and— What a fool he'd been.

"Are you going to tell me or just sit there with that

gloomy expression? You know I'm not getting any younger.''

Jackson glanced at his dad. At sixty-four, he was active and in good health, and Jackson was grateful for that. He couldn't stand to lose another person he loved—although there were no guarantees in life. That was a reality he'd learned a long time ago, but now he'd lost a daughter he hadn't even known about, someone he'd never even had a chance to love.

"Jackson, talk to me, son," George begged.

He took a sip of coffee. "I'm not sure where to start," he said frankly.

"Does it have to do with Emily?"

"Yes, she told me something and I...I..."

"What?"

He swallowed painfully. "This isn't easy."

"Just say it."

"She said that after I left Rockport, she found out she was...pregnant.''

George's eyes opened wide. "Pregnant?"

"Yeah."

"My God. A baby? She had your baby?"

"Yes." His hand gripped the cup; he could crush it if he just applied pressure and he wanted to. He wanted to break something badly.

"Where is this child? Where's my grandchild?"

Jackson looked up at that word—*grandchild*. His father had always wanted grandchildren, but after his divorce from Janine, George had finally accepted that wasn't going to happen. But all along, there'd been a girl out there who belonged to them. His daughter. His dad's grandchild. A child they would never see.

"Jack." His father waved a hand in front of his face to get his attention. "Where's our child?"

He released a tight breath and said the words that felt like acid in his throat. "Emily gave her up for adoption."

"My God, no!" George cried out.

"Yes, Emily gave her away. I don't know where she is, and neither does Emily. Strangers have my daughter."

"A girl, you have a daughter." A softness came over George's face. "Sarah would have loved a granddaughter."

At the mention of his mother, Jackson had to stifle tears. He ran both hands down his face in a weary gesture. "I don't know what to do. I'm so hurt and angry inside, I can't think. All I can do is feel and I don't like what I'm feeling."

George stood. "I'll get you another cup of coffee."

Jackson started to protest, but he realized his father was giving him time.

Placing the cup in front of him, George said, "From what I remember about Emily, she was a pretty, sweet and caring girl. Owen and Rose were very protective of her. They kept a tight rein on her—especially Rose."

"Rose hated my guts," Jackson spit out.

"Well, she probably knew what you were doing with her daughter." George sat down and looked directly at his son.

Jackson met that look squarely. "Did you?"

George shrugged. "I knew something was happening. You couldn't take your eyes off her, and I saw all those secret glances at the dinner table. One night I woke up and you weren't in the room or in the bathroom. It was a couple of hours before you came back. I figured you were with Emily, but I didn't do anything about it. Hell, you were twenty-one and a man. There was nothing I *could* do."

"We were so careful…. Neither one of us was ready for a pregnancy."

"Did you love her?"

"What?" he asked, but he'd heard the question. He just didn't want to answer it.

"Did you love Emily?" George repeated.

"Yes," he admitted slowly.

"Did you promise to go back and see her?"

He wanted to block out the truth, but he couldn't. "Yes, but then you and Mom told me about her illness and I couldn't think about anything else. Later, I just had to get away."

George patted his arm. "It was a difficult time for all of us."

He raised his hands in a helpless gesture. "I just can't understand how she could do that—give up our baby."

"I'm sure she didn't do it without a lot of pain and suffering. It couldn't have been an easy decision. Why didn't her parents help her?"

"When Rose found out, she flew into a rage and there was some danger of her losing her own baby."

"Oh, yeah, I forgot about Rose's pregnancy."

"Emily said she did what her parents wanted."

"What did she mean by that?"

"Her parents were hurt and embarrassed by the situation and they insisted that the only thing to do was give the baby away so no one would ever find out. They had their own child to worry about and I suppose they weren't interested in raising Emily's bastard." He couldn't keep the bitterness out of his voice.

George shook his head. "Emily was alone, scared and probably didn't know what to do. Why in God's name didn't she call you? She knew where you lived."

"She did," Jackson said in a low voice. "She called

the hardware store and the house, but I was too upset about Mom to take any calls, so she never got through to me.''

"Oh, my God." His father sounded horrified.

What?'' Jackson asked urgently.

"I remember there were several calls from Owen after Sarah died. I wasn't in a mood to talk to anyone. Besides, I assumed it was just about fishing. Maybe he was calling about Emily's pregnancy.''

Jackson frowned. "Are you sure?''

"Yeah. I couldn't understand why the man kept leaving messages for me.'' George slapped the table with his hand. "Jack, we've done that family a terrible injustice.''

Jackson took that news the way he had all the rest— with a blow that was threatening to overwhelm him. "I can't grasp any of this.''

George shook his head. "I know, son.''

Jackson didn't say anything else and George asked, "What are you thinking?''

"I keep wavering between anger and compassion,'' Jackson told him. "Emily had to deal with the pregnancy alone. As you said, that couldn't have been easy. She's a proud, intelligent woman.''

"Yes,'' George agreed.

"Then, on the other hand, I feel she callously gave our child away. I don't even know where my daughter was born or anything about her.''

"Why didn't you ask?''

"I was in a state of shock and…I had to get away from Emily before I said something I'd later regret.''

"I see,'' George muttered. "What do you plan to do?''

"I'm not sure,'' Jackson said, taking a swallow of coffee.

"You're not planning on leaving things like this, are you?''

Jackson inhaled deeply. "I can't answer all these questions, Dad. Give me some space."

"I always try to do that," George said in a reasonable voice.

He knew that and he was snapping at his father for no reason. There was silence for a moment, then Jackson said, "Sorry, Dad, but there's something on my mind and I can't shake it."

"What?"

"I don't want to talk about it."

"You can always talk to me."

He knew that, too. He took another deep breath. "I'm thinking of finding my daughter." The words seemed to embrace the morning air and they sounded so right, so real.

"Hot damn! Now you're talking."

Jackson tried to smile at his dad's exuberance, but his facial muscles couldn't complete the task. "She has Talbert blood in her veins and she deserves to know that, and I deserve to know where she is and that she's happy." He wasn't sure of much, but he was sure about that.

"Did you talk this over with Emily?" George asked.

Jackson fingered his cup. "No."

Silence. Then George plunged on. "Do you plan to?"

"I'm having a hard time thinking about Emily."

"Well, son, much as you want to deny it, you're not blameless in this."

Jackson sucked his breath in sharply. He'd never expected to hear those words from his father—the same words Emily had used. But it was the truth, and it burned through him like a wildfire, searing nerves that were already frayed and weak.

"Don't you think I'm aware of that?" he shot back.

"I'm just saying there has to be a good reason for what she did. Find out what it is, then do something about it."

"Dad, you make this—"

"Talk to Emily," George broke in. "Then find my granddaughter, because I won't settle for anything less."

Jackson lifted an eyebrow. "Your granddaughter, huh? All of a sudden this is about your granddaughter."

Without missing a beat, George replied, "You're damn right it is."

Jackson shrugged. "Well, whatever we call her, she's probably happy and with a loving family. She may not even suspect she's adopted."

"And it could be just the opposite," George said solemnly.

Jackson squeezed his eyes tight at the agonizing thought.

"You have to talk to Emily. The way to find your daughter is through Emily."

"Dad." Jackson sighed in irritation and sipped at his coffee.

"Last night you were glad enough to see her," George reminded him.

"That was last night."

"How did you leave things?"

"Not good."

Silence ensued again.

George watched his son closely. "I raised you better than that."

Jackson's eyes slammed into his father's, demanding an explanation.

"I raised you never to judge anyone unfairly," George said quietly. "And you're judging Emily."

Jackson got to his feet and carried his cup to the sink. His father was correct, as always. He was judging Emily, something he had no business doing. He didn't know what had happened back then and he'd never bothered to go and find out. He didn't have a right to anger or much of anything else. It took two to create a baby, and he had to take responsibility.

His father was making him think, opening his eyes, and what he saw disturbed him. At the moment, he could only deal with the pain inside him, but he had to face the consequences of his actions—then and now.

*He was not blameless.*

"I didn't say that to hurt you," George said anxiously.

Jackson glanced up as the morning sun made its appearance. "I know, Dad," he told him. "You said it to make me think—like you always do."

George breathed a long sigh. "Then you'll see Emily."

"I don't have much choice, but I've got some thinking to do first."

George walked over to the cabinet and pulled out a frying pan. "How about a big breakfast?"

Jackson smiled as the muscles in his face relaxed. "I could use one of your artery-clogging meals."

"Watch your mouth, my boy," George said in a teasing voice, then in a more serious tone, he added, "I'm just saying one more thing and this is strictly an old man's observation. You never cared for Janine the way you cared for Emily."

"Dad," Jackson said impatiently, but he suddenly realized that was probably true. He had loved Emily, like he'd told his dad, truly loved her with all the enthusiasm and honesty of youth.

"Something good will come of this. I feel it," his father was saying. "Soon, I hope, I'll be able to take my granddaughter out there—" he pointed to the lake "—fishing. I'll teach her to bait a hook and show her how to use a rod and reel. I'll tell her about her grandmother..." His voice cracked on the last word.

Jackson swallowed hard at the pain in his father's voice, and they embraced. "Now, don't go getting your hopes up. Remember she'll be eighteen years old and I doubt she has much interest in fishing."

"Doesn't matter. Something good will come of this. Mark my words," George mumbled.

Jackson didn't agree, didn't argue, didn't speak. All he felt was a pain as intense as when his mother had passed away and he was struggling to stay afloat and keep everything in perspective—his emotions, his life…and Emily.

EMILY WOKE WITH a throbbing headache, but she hadn't had any dreams. That was a relief. She managed to dress and get to work on time. If anyone noticed her hollow-eyed appearance, nothing was said. She went through the routine of her day, trying not to think, trying only to concentrate on her patients, but at the oddest times she'd hear Jackson's voice and feel like bursting into tears. She didn't—she was too professional for that—but it was a struggle all the same.

By the end of the day, she knew what she had to do. She was going home—as she'd promised Becca. She needed to get away, to see her parents, see Becca, and get a different slant on things. Her emotions were close to the breaking point.

She met with Dr. Freeman, who would oversee her patients while she was gone. She hadn't had more than two days off in years and decided to take ten. She wanted to be home for Becca's prom. That would cheer her up.

Stopping by the post office, she arranged for her mail to be collected. She also had the newspaper stopped. Then she drove to the condo and packed. Within an hour, she was headed for Rockport, Texas, where she was born and raised.

She tried to keep her mind a blank but couldn't. She kept seeing Jackson's face and hearing his cruel words. Would he ever understand? She doubted it, because *she* had a hard enough time understanding it. Until she found some sort of forgiveness in herself, she couldn't expect Jackson to calmly accept her actions.

The drive was long and peaceful, and as soon as she smelled the saltwater, she knew she was home. Copano Bay greeted her, and when she drove over the bridge into Rockport-Fulton, she felt a sense of belonging. Water stretched out in all directions, a sight she'd seen every day of her life until she was seventeen—until she was banished from home. A flash of loneliness stabbed her.

As a child, she'd practically lived on the water, going with her dad when he took people out fishing. Other days it was just the two of them searching for the best fishing spots. She'd been happy and carefree, without a worry in the world. Then she turned thirteen and started to develop a figure. All of a sudden, the men looked at her differently, and her mother noticed. Rose refused to let Emily go with her father when other men were along. Emily recognized that this was the beginning of a lot of changes in her life and the start of her mother's domination over her.

She wiped the memory away. Turning off the highway, she drove toward Fulton Beach to be near the water. She kept driving along the edge of Aransas Bay until she saw the small yellow-and-white house with the yellow cottages behind it. *Home.* She was home. With that feeling, a sense of dread prevailed. It happened every time she came here and that was probably never going to change. She just had to overcome it.

She pulled behind her dad's truck and got out. The melancholy sound of seagulls filled the air and the cool breeze from the water touched her skin. These were familiar sensations she associated with home and childhood.

Walking toward the front door, she heard raised voices—her mother's and Becca's. Emily drew in a deep breath, opened the door and stepped inside. Rose sat in her recliner, an angry scowl on her face. Her dark hair was now almost completely gray, and her blue eyes dimmed with pain and age. Becca paced back and forth, waving her arms in her usual spitfire manner, her dark eyes brimming with resentment. Another argument. Emily braced herself.

Her father stood in the kitchen doorway with a solemn expression on his tired face. His hair was also gray, and his daughters had inherited his dark eyes.

The loud voices immediately stopped and Becca flew across the room into Emily's arms. "You're home, Em. Thank God you're home." Becca kissed her and Emily kissed her back. This was why she came—to feel this closeness that only sisters could experience. Becca needed her, and as long as she did, Emily would continue to return home.

"You didn't say you were coming, Emily Ann," her mother said in a critical tone Emily knew all too well.

"Nice to see you," her father put in, but there were no hugs or kisses or the love they once shared as a family. In her parents' eyes, Emily had done something unforgivable. It had been more than eighteen years, and they'd never recovered from their disillusionment.

Emily cleared her throat and sat on the old beige sofa beside Becca. "I took a few days off and decided I'd come for a visit."

Rose pointed a finger at Becca. "Because she called you, didn't she? You wouldn't come home for any other reason."

Before Emily could answer, Becca jumped to her feet. "So what if I did? You're driving me crazy. I'll soon be eighteen and you still treat me like a little girl."

"Don't talk to me in that tone of voice," Rose threatened.

"Or what?" Becca asked sharply. "You'll take away my privileges? Ha!" Becca threw back her head and laughed a sarcastic laugh. "*What* privileges? I have to be home at ten. You monitor my dates. I can't have new clothes or go anywhere, and on and on it goes. I'm like a prisoner."

"Go to your room!" her mother shouted. "I'm tired of arguing with you."

"You bet I'm going to my room and I'm packing and getting out of here. Not even Em can stop me." She ran down the hall and slammed her door.

Her father disappeared into the kitchen as he always did—anything to avoid a confrontation. Rose reached for the oxygen mask that lay in her chair. She held it to her mouth and took several deep breaths. Emily could see she was having difficulty breathing.

She got up and took her mother's pulse. It was racing, but Emily felt sure she was just agitated, and in a moment she'd calm down.

"You okay?" Emily asked softly.

Rose removed the mask. "I can't deal with your sister anymore. She's wild and out of control."

Emily bit her lip and knew she and her mother had to talk—a long-overdue talk. The only person out of control was Rose. How could she make her see that?

She pulled up a chair and sat next to her and had to fight the urge to hold her hand. She held the hands of many of her patients while she talked to them. It made them feel as if they were important to her, and it made Emily feel closer to them. But with her mother it was a different story. When Emily was small, she was held, kissed and loved, but now things were so different. These days her mother rarely touched her and Emily felt as if she was tainted...tainted because she'd gotten pregnant out of wedlock.

That was the dread about coming home—experiencing this coldness from her mother, and her father, too. Though her father was never as outspoken as Rose, it was there in his eyes...the disappointment. And that broke her heart.

## CHAPTER FIVE

"WE HAVE TO TALK," Emily said, trying to keep the pain from ruling her emotions.

Rose removed the oxygen mask. "About what?"

"Becca."

"I wish you'd stop calling her that. Her name is Rebecca."

Emily inhaled deeply and ignored the criticism. Emily had started calling her sister Becca when she was a baby, and now everyone did. Her mother had always hated that, but this wasn't about Becca's name.

"She'll be eighteen soon like she said—a grown woman, able to make her own decisions."

"She's immature, irresponsible and—"

Emily broke in. "She is not."

Rose's eyes narrowed. "You're not around all the time. You have no idea what she's like. When you're here, she's on her best behavior. Other times she sneaks out to be with Tommy Wilson. He's a football jock with long hair and an earring. He's only after one thing and she can't see that. She's—"

"Stop it," Emily interrupted harshly. "Can't you see what you're doing?"

Rose frowned severely, but she didn't answer.

Emily went on. "You're making Becca pay for my sins. You're afraid the same thing will happen to her that happened to me."

Rose compressed her lips into a thin line, still not answering.

"Please don't do that," Emily begged. "Becca is not me. I was weak as a teenager, but she's strong. Surely you can see that?"

*Strong enough to stand up to you and I wasn't.*

When her mother remained silent, Emily took another approach. "She's in there packing. Is that what you want?"

"She won't go anywhere," Rose replied stubbornly. "Especially since you're here."

Emily felt as if she was butting her head against a brick wall. Nothing was getting through to her mother—nothing. She decided to try yet another tactic.

"Becca will graduate soon. Why don't you let her spend the summer with me?"

Rose eyes widened fearfully and she took a couple of breaths from the mask. "No," she finally said. "This is her last summer at home and she needs to get a job to help pay for college."

Emily started to say that she'd pay for Becca's college, but she knew her mother didn't want to hear that. Rose resented the influence Emily had on Becca's life, but underneath Emily could see that her mother was afraid of losing Becca. Even though they argued all the time, Rose was scared to death of losing her youngest daughter.

Emily's tone softened. "Becca's going to leave home. You have to face that. Besides, you're always bickering. That's not good for your health. It's not good for anyone."

"Stay out of it, Emily Ann," Rose warned.

The younger Emily would have acquiesced immediately, but the older Emily did not. She got slowly to her feet. "No, I'm not staying out of this. I'm not letting you punish Becca for my mistakes."

Rose's eyes grew enormous and she reached for the oxygen mask again.

"I'm taking Becca to Corpus tomorrow to buy her a dress—and she's not coming home at ten o'clock. It's her senior prom and she's going to enjoy it."

"Is that it, Emily Ann?" Rose asked cryptically. "You didn't get to go to your prom, so you want to live it through Rebecca. Well, that wasn't my fault. It was yours."

Anger simmered through Emily's body and she had to restrain herself from walking out the door and never coming back. But she couldn't keep avoiding the issue. "Yes, it *was* all my fault and I've paid dearly for it. A day doesn't go by that I don't regret giving up my daughter."

"And, of course, you blame me," Rose bit out.

*Yes, yes, yes.*

Emily had to take a calming breath. She couldn't talk about this with her mother. All they did was blame each other, and the truth was they were both to blame. The bitter aftertaste of that left Emily cold and drained. Why had she come home?

*For Becca.*

"I'm not arguing with you about the past," she said stoically. "There's nothing either one of us can do to change it. Right now, I'm just worried about Becca."

Rose looked at her closely. "You can't make up for your mistake by spoiling Rebecca."

"I'm not trying to do that," Emily denied, and had to get away from her mother before she said something she'd regret. She whirled around. "I'm checking on Becca."

As she walked down the hall, she thought her mother was probably right. She bought things for Becca, indulged her because she couldn't do those things for her own daughter. She came to an abrupt halt as the truth hit her.

She had lost her daughter forever, and now she'd lost Jackson—again. She staggered under the pain, but she couldn't deal with that. She had to think about Becca...the only bright spot in her life.

She tapped on her sister's door and went in. The dresser drawers were open and Becca was haphazardly throwing clothes into a small suitcase on the bed.

Emily stared at the pile. "I don't think they're all going to fit."

"Don't try to stop me, Em," Becca said, adding a couple of sweaters to the stack.

Emily moved some clothes aside and sat down. "It'd be a shame to miss the prom, especially since you're nominated for prom queen."

"Doesn't matter," Becca muttered under her breath.

Emily watched her bent head for a second. "You're not seriously thinking about leaving me here *alone* with Mom, are you?"

The words had the effect Emily was hoping for. A grin spread across Becca's face and she plopped down beside her. "No, I wouldn't do that to you," she said with a laugh. "I wouldn't do it to Dad, either." She quickly sobered. "But Em..."

"Don't worry," Emily said. "I told Mom I was taking you to Corpus tomorrow to buy a new dress and that you weren't coming home at ten."

Becca scooted back on the bed in excitement. "You did? What did she say?"

"Let's just say she's aware of what's going to happen and I'll be here to make sure it does."

"You're staying until next Saturday?" Becca asked eagerly.

"Yes, I wouldn't miss seeing my baby sister on this special day."

Becca threw her arms around Emily. "I love you. I couldn't survive without you."

Tears stung Emily's eyes. She needed to hear that... desperately. It gave her the strength to go on.

When Becca drew back, Emily tucked strands of hair behind Becca's ears. "I think we need to get this cut." Becca's hair fell halfway down her back.

Becca made a face. "Tommy likes my hair like this."

"And we have to talk about Tommy."

"Jeez, we're not gonna talk about sex, are we?"

"Should we?"

"Why? Is there something you want to know?" Becca asked smartly, then burst into giggles and pointed a finger at Emily. "You should see your face."

Emily couldn't resist a smile. "You're incorrigible."

"That's how I've managed to live with two sticks-in-the-mud."

"Don't talk like that."

Becca hung her head. "It's not that I don't love them— I do. I just have a problem dealing with Mom's views and her outlook on life. She thinks I'm wild and some boy will get me—" She stopped and stared at Emily. "You know."

"Yes, I do." *All too well.* "That's why I want to talk about sex."

"I'm not having sex, if that's what she told you. Other girls are, but I don't feel right about it...yet."

Emily felt a moment's relief, but she had to talk to Becca about other things. Unpleasant things. She had to tell Becca about the past. That would be hard...so hard. Becca had always looked up to her, thought she did nothing wrong. Now Emily's own words would tarnish that image; it would take everything in her to expose her true self. She'd told Jackson, so telling Becca should be easy and it might help her understand their mother's fears. The revelation would cost Emily more than she wanted to dwell on. She had to do it regardless.

"I'm glad to hear that, but—"

Becca cut in. "I know all about the birds and bees. Remember you gave me that book when I was twelve? We discussed it at length."

"But we never talked about protection."

"Every girl knows about protection," Becca told her. "Besides, I'm not stupid enough to have unprotected sex."

"I want you to realize that when you do make the decision to…to get involved, it comes with risks and responsibilities. Sometimes protection doesn't work and you have to be prepared for the consequences."

To Emily's horror, tears ran down her cheeks, and she quickly brushed them away.

"Em, what is it?" Becca asked worriedly. "You're crying."

What was wrong with her? Emily chastised herself. She seemed bent on a course of self-destruction. She'd told Jackson because she'd convinced herself that he needed to know and it had backfired. But then, what had she expected? It would've been best if he'd never known. Now… No, she wouldn't do this to herself anymore. She *had* to face the past and not let it destroy her. And she had to tell Becca.

It might be another bad decision, but she'd take that risk. When Becca heard about Emily's past, she'd understand why their mother was so strict and so scared of her getting pregnant. That could only help. Her mother wouldn't approve; she was well aware of that. Rose had said long ago that it was a secret no one should ever hear. Emily had made a mistake and it was best forgotten. But it wasn't. Rose was using Emily's past against Becca, and Emily had to put an end to that.

She turned toward Becca. "I have to tell you something, and it's very difficult."

"Are you pregnant?" Becca asked in a whisper.

Emily shook her head. "No."

"I didn't think so. You being a doctor and all."

She reached for Becca's hands and held them tight. "There's a secret I'm going to tell you, but it's between you and me. Okay?"

"Okay. I won't tell a soul," Becca promised.

"When I was seventeen, a young man came to the coast to go fishing, and he was handsome and charming and I fell head over heels in love with him."

"Oh, good, a love story." Becca slid closer.

How Emily wished it was. A love story with a happy ending…

"I was going through a difficult time because I'd just discovered Mom was pregnant and I wasn't taking it too well."

"Why?" Becca asked. "Didn't you want a sister?"

Emily swallowed. "I guess I was very immature for my age because all I could think about was myself and the embarrassment Mom's pregnancy was causing me." It hurt to say the words, and for a moment she didn't speak. In a low voice, she continued. "Up until that time, I was a perfect daughter. I never did anything wrong. But I changed overnight. I started staying out late, dating guys Mom and Dad disapproved of. I rebelled every chance I got. Then I met this man and I rebelled even more."

"Gosh, that doesn't even sound like you," Becca said.

"I was very different back then and I'm only telling you now so it'll help you understand why Mom is the way she is."

"What happened with the man?"

"When his fishing trip was over, he went home."

"Were you...lovers?"

Emily took a deep breath. "Yes, we were lovers." She tried to go on but found she couldn't. The next words were locked in her throat. She licked dry lips and forced the words out. "After he left, I found I was...pregnant."

Becca eyes grew big with disbelief. "No way."

"Yes, I was and it devastated our parents. I finally realized what a fool I'd been. Mom was struggling to carry you and I added the burden of my own pregnancy. It was a very trying time."

"I can imagine. I'll bet Mom went right through the roof."

"Something like that," Emily admitted. "So do you understand why she's so paranoid about the same thing happening to you?"

"Sort of," Becca answered slowly, and Emily could almost see the questions running through her head. Questions she didn't take long to voice. "Mom made you have an abortion, didn't she?" Her voice held derision.

"No," Emily replied.

"You miscarried?"

Emily shook her head as her stomach knotted tight.

"Then what happened to the baby?"

Emily met her puzzled gaze. "I gave her up for... adoption."

"No way." The disbelief intensified, then realization dawned. "Oh, no! Mom made you give away your own baby."

Emily gripped Becca's hands. "I was a grown woman and I had choices to make and I made some wrong ones. Wrong for me, anyway." She paused, shaking her head. "It was a horrible, horrible time and I can't explain the anguish of those days. I was young and foolish, but that doesn't suffice…nothing does. The pain never goes away. It's always with me.''

"Oh, Em.'' Becca wrapped her arms around her and they held each other. ''I'm so sorry.''

Oh, she needed this. Someone to hold her and to understand and not condemn her. It felt so good and now she'd have the strength to deal with the days ahead. They talked for a long time and Emily poured out her heart in a way she never had before.

Finally Becca asked, ''Did you ever tell the father?''

Emily told her about Jackson and meeting him again.

"And he had the audacity to judge you?'' Becca said angrily. ''I'd love to slap his face.''

Emily smiled at Becca's loyalty. ''I'm not sure he judged me,'' she replied. ''He was just upset. It had to be traumatic finding out about a daughter he never knew he had.'' For some reason, she didn't want her sister to think badly of Jackson.

"You're defending him,'' Becca said in shock, then her eyes narrowed on Emily's face. ''You're still in love with him.''

Emily opened her mouth to protest, then shut it quickly. ''That's absurd.'' The words erupted spontaneously from her lips. She refused to even think such a thing.

"No, it's not. You're—''

"Becca,'' Emily pleaded. ''Don't.''

Responding to the tone of Emily's voice, Becca immediately backed down.

Silence followed.

"I have a niece,'' Becca said almost to herself. ''And she's about my age.''

"You were born in June and *she* was born in August.''

"We would have grown up together…been the best of friends,'' Becca said confidently.

"Yes." Emily blinked back tears. She couldn't say another word.

"Don't cry, Em," Becca said quietly.

"I'll never see her," Emily murmured with an ache in her voice. "I'll never see her face."

Becca put her own face in front of Emily. "You can see *me*. I'm always here."

Emily brushed away a tear and smiled slightly. "And I love you more than I can say, and tomorrow I'm buying you the most expensive dress we can find."

Becca grinned. "Planning on testing Mom's blood pressure, are you?"

"Why not, little sister? We're due to have some fun, and tomorrow you and I will do just that."

Becca drew back at the light in Emily's eyes. "I've never seen you like this."

Emily felt giddy and young again, and all because Becca hadn't condemned her or looked at her with disgust. This was the first time she'd even allowed herself to believe she could be forgiven for the past. Forgiven and loved again. That was silly and she knew it; nonetheless it was the way she felt.

"Becca." Emily became serious. "I have to put the past behind me and find a happy medium with Mom. I need your help to do that. I need you to be more understanding and patient."

"I'll try," Becca whispered.

"That's all I ask."

Arm in arm, they returned to the living room.

AFTER JACKSON LEFT his father's, he went to his apartment and fell into a deep, restless sleep that was filled with dreams of Emily. When he woke, she permeated his mind, his body and soul. He'd said he didn't want to think about

Emily and yet he couldn't *stop* thinking about her. He raised himself to a sitting position as he remembered the Emily he'd once known. There was something different about her, something fresh and exciting. The first time he saw her shining, wholesome face he was enraptured. And when he looked into those dark, sultry eyes, he felt as if she'd reached inside him and touched a place no woman had ever touched before—his heart. He could almost recapture that feeling and it caused so many other emotions to surface.

*He wasn't blameless.*

He took a shuddering breath as the truth of that struck him. He took another long breath as he admitted to himself that he'd taken her love in selfish haste and hadn't given any thought as to how that would affect her after he'd gone. The fact that he'd *planned* to go back didn't matter. He should have been more considerate of her eighteen years ago. And last night…

He'd told Emily he had to get away from her. That was true. If he'd stayed, he would've said things that couldn't be retracted. He hadn't wanted to do that, and he now knew why. He couldn't hurt her. To his shock, he realized that Emily had captured his heart years ago, and no woman had done that since. He'd had affairs, even married, and yet no one affected him the way Emily had. Why, then, hadn't he gone back? Why?

The question tortured him, forcing him to delve further into his soul. He had been young and in torment over his mother's illness. His life had taken a downward spiral; nothing had mattered but his own pain. He'd told his father that he'd loved Emily and he meant it. Once, he thought nothing would keep him from her, but he'd been wrong. Their love had been shattered by the frailty of human life.

That didn't excuse his behavior. It just made him see more clearly that he was not blameless.

He drew his knees up and remembered Emily as she was long ago—laughing and delightful and loving, except when she was around her mother. Then she became solemn, almost stoic, and he'd seen the immense power Rose wielded over Emily. But it hadn't kept their love from developing into something profound. On the beach, away from her mother, they talked, confided in each other. Laughed together. Fell in love. He'd learned everything about Emily, and he knew she wasn't heartless, quite the contrary. She wouldn't have given their child away... unless...unless she was coerced. *By her mother.*

He got out of bed in a quick jerky movement and started to pace around the room. As his father had said, he'd judged Emily without hearing the whole story. He should have asked questions. He should have consoled her. It must have been agonizing for her—scared and unable to reach him and then having to face Rose. What had he done? He should've stayed last night; maybe they could've talked things out. Instead he'd run like the young fool he'd been years ago.

Damn. Damn. Why? Why had he done that? Because he couldn't face his own weakness. He wasn't blameless, but he had blamed, judged and condemned her without even knowing it. He'd done it because she'd given away their child and he took that as a sign that she hadn't loved him or the baby. There it was, plain and simple. The deep pain in his heart had driven him out the door. He still cared for Emily. Years had not diminished his feelings, and now that he was thinking more clearly, he understood that Emily hadn't given up their child without pressure.

He stopped pacing and stared down at himself. He still had his clothes on. He hadn't even bothered to remove them when he got in. He had to shower and change. He had to see Emily. He had to hear her story and, this time, he'd listen with an open heart. The first thing he'd tell her was that he was sorry he hadn't come back as he'd promised. Then he'd explain that he intended to take responsibility for his thoughtless actions. But most of all, he wanted to make this right with Emily. He prayed she'd understand his reaction, but then he remembered that shattered look in her eyes. His heart constricted with a new kind of pain. Would she forgive him? He didn't know, but he had to find out.

As he hurried toward the bathroom, the phone rang and he swerved to pick it up. "Hello."

"Jackson, what the hell happened to you?" Colton's voice came through loud and angry. "You were supposed to talk to Conley."

Jackson sat heavily on the bed. He'd forgotten all about Conley. "I'm sorry, but I've had a family crisis that's just about wiped me out."

"Is your dad okay?"

"Yeah, it's something entirely different. I'll explain later."

"Conley's due here in about half an hour and I'm not sure how to handle him."

Jackson grimaced, not wanting to go into the office. He wanted to go to Emily, but he had to take care of business first. "I'll be there," he said without enthusiasm.

A long pause. "Are you sure?"

"Yes, I'll come. I just need to get dressed."

"Thanks, Jackson." He could hear the relief in Colton's voice. "We'll talk when you get here."

"See you then," Jackson said, and hung up.

He lived in an apartment about ten minutes from his office; that was the reason he'd chosen it. It also had a pool, tennis courts and a gym, which added to its appeal, but he never used any of them. He worked all the time. He was a workaholic…just like Janine had called him in one of their bitter arguments. Of course, he'd called her the same thing. But *his* life was going to change. He now had something else on his mind, something besides work.

*Emily.*

*He had to see Emily.*

# CHAPTER SIX

THE NEXT MORNING was Saturday and Emily planned to sleep in, but she was awake at six, as always. Old habits were hard to break. She crawled out of bed, careful not to wake Becca, but nothing less than a bomb exploding would do that. Becca was curled up, her dark hair tumbled over the pillow. Asleep she looked just like the little girl Emily couldn't wait to get home to see. She was almost grown now, and Emily hoped she made better choices than her bigger sister had. She would, Emily thought with confidence, because she was sensible and well-grounded. But then, she reminded herself, she'd been exactly the same way. She shook her head. It didn't matter. She intended to be here for Becca, trying to help her through these difficult years with their mother. Becca deserved her support. And now that Emily had told her about the past, Becca was better equipped to understand Rose.

Emily slipped on a pink silk robe over matching pink pajamas and headed for the kitchen. She felt much better today. Telling Becca her secret had lifted a burden from her and she could handle Jackson's anger on a new level. She wasn't letting him drag her into despair, into misery and pain. She'd been there and she wasn't going back. But she did wonder about Jackson and how he was and if he'd calmed down. She wished she could talk to him again, try to explain, but he didn't want to see her. She was sure of that, and it was probably just as well, she told herself. Still, that didn't relieve the pain in her heart.

As she neared the kitchen, she heard raised voices—her parent's.

"We have to do something," her mother was saying.

"Just leave things alone, Rose," her father replied.

"That's your solution to everything," Rose shouted. "But I can't do that. I'm scared."

Emily walked into the kitchen and everything became very quiet. Her mother busied herself at the stove and her father buried his face in the newspaper.

Were they talking about her? Her immediate reaction was no, they were arguing about Becca. Rose wanted Owen to do something, and Owen refused to interfere. Her father was a meek, docile man who wasn't much good with words or with people. Fishing was his great passion and he indulged it to his heart's content. That was the only time Emily remembered seeing him truly happy.

"You're up early, Emily Ann," her mother said.

"I'm always up early," Emily answered, reaching for a cup and filling it with coffee. She sat beside her father at the table.

"Going fishing today?" she asked.

The paper lowered a fraction. "Yeah, I got a man coming at seven. He wants to catch some redfish."

"Since you know all the best spots, that shouldn't be a problem." She sipped her coffee.

The paper lowered completely. "Sometimes it has a lot to do with the weather," he said, eager to talk about fishing. Emily suddenly realized that was the only thing they ever talked about. When it came to everyday problems, her father shied away. She'd really needed him eighteen years ago, and he'd done the same thing. It was as though he couldn't make himself believe she was pregnant, so he did what he had to—or what her mother told him to do. Emily groaned inwardly. She had to stop blaming her parents. It was her fault...her own fault.

"I'd better get moving." Her father's words broke into her thoughts. "I've got to get bait and gas up the boat." He stood and grabbed his baseball cap from the table. "See you later." With that he disappeared out the back door.

"Where's Rebecca?" her mother asked.

"She's still asleep."

"I won't have her lying in bed until noon."

Emily glanced at her mother. "It's not even seven in the morning, and it *is* Saturday."

"She needs to be out looking for a summer job."

Emily took a deep breath. "I told you, I'm taking her shopping today."

"She doesn't need—"

Emily held up a hand. "Don't start."

"You can't come home and spoil her. I have to deal with her when you're gone."

"Let go, Mom," Emily said softly. "Becca will be gone soon enough. Try to enjoy these last months with her."

Rose twisted her hands. "I lost you. I can't lose Rebecca."

Emily was shocked at the heartfelt revelation. Her instant response was to comfort her mother, to say she hadn't lost her at all, but in truth she'd be lying. Their relationship had changed drastically the day her mother had said, "You have embarrassed and shamed your father and me, Emily Ann, something I thought you would never do. For your sake and ours, you have to give the child up for adoption. It's the only option you've got."

After that, it was a steady barrage of the same thing and in the end she'd done exactly what her parents had told her to—still the dutiful daughter. Now Rose was feeling a sense of loss concerning Rebecca because she was grown up and would soon be leaving home. That Emily could reassure her about.

"Mom…"

"Don't say a word," Rose said emphatically. "You've made it very plain how you feel." Before Emily could respond, Rose went on. "You blame us, but we were only thinking of you and your future. You wanted to be a doctor ever since I can remember, but with a baby, you would never have gone to college or med school. You'd be stuck in some dead-end minimum-wage job."

*But I would have my daughter* was all Emily could think.

Through the agonizing thought, she heard Rose asking a question, "How many times did you call that boy?"

"I lost track," Emily murmured.

"And he never answered any of your calls. He didn't want to talk to you, and George Talbert wouldn't even talk to Owen. They made it clear they weren't willing to take responsibility."

Emily frowned. "Dad called Mr. Talbert?"

"Yes, and he got the runaround. They said Mr. Talbert wasn't taking calls. Owen left messages, but he never called back. We don't have to wonder why, do we?"

Emily was aware why Mr. Talbert hadn't called back— the same reason Jackson hadn't. Mrs. Talbert had died and they wanted to be left alone to deal with their grief. At the time, nothing else had mattered. Emily now understood that, but she wouldn't tell her mother because then she would have to explain she'd seen Jackson again. That would only cause more problems.

Emily took a calming breath. "I'm tired of talking about this. I wish I could come home just once without all this rehashing of the past."

"Me, too," Rose muttered. "And just once I wish you wouldn't undermine my authority with Rebecca."

Emily bit her tongue until she thought it would bleed, but she wasn't rising to the bait; she knew exactly what her mother was doing. She was applying pressure, hoping Emily would back down and support her strict rules for Becca. But that wasn't happening.

Emily got slowly to her feet. "As I told you last night, Becca is not paying for my mistakes. She has a good head on her shoulders, and I trust her."

Rose snorted. "You don't even know your sister. The time you spend with her, you spoil her rotten and indulge her every whim."

"Mom." Emily sighed irritably.

"No, you listen to me," Rose continued. "I have preached and preached to you girls about boys, and neither one of you has heard a word I've said. So go ahead, buy her a new dress, indulge her, but whatever happens will be *your* responsibility."

Emily nodded. She refused to react to her mother's accusations and threats. They were only saying things to hurt each other, and again Emily questioned her decision to come home. It always renewed the pain. Why did she think it would be different this time? She didn't; she knew better. She'd come home for Becca. She had to keep reminding herself of that.

As she walked to the door, her mother's words followed her. "Wake your sister. I'm making pancakes. Your favorite."

Emily had the urge to laugh. Pancakes would make all the heartache go away. They would sit down as a family and talk companionably and enjoy them. Oh, yeah, that sounded as plausible as aliens landing on their roof, but appearances were important to her mother and they would pretend. Then Rose could tell her friends that her daughter had come home and what a good time they'd all had. Her mother lived in a false world of her own making. That didn't concern Emily anymore. What did concern her was Becca, and she'd do anything to keep peace for her sake— except bow to Rose's demands or accept her unreasonable rules.

IN LESS THAN THIRTY MINUTES Jackson was in his office and it didn't take him long to soothe Mr. Conley.

Later, Colton said, "How do you do it? A few words from you and Conley's like a docile teddy bear. With me, he was a roaring lion, demanding instead of listening."

Jackson smiled at his friend, whose long blond hair curled in all directions. That was the problem. He looked more like a rock star than a computer genius. Jackson had experienced the same reaction when he first met Colton, but he'd found him to be intelligent, responsible and trustworthy. When Clay, Colton's brother, had decided to sell his share of the company, Jackson had been skeptical, but everything had worked out, and he and Colton had become fast friends. Jackson trusted him completely. It took their male clients a while to respond to his boyish charm, but once they did, it was smooth sailing. And the women— they all loved him. There were never any problems with female clients.

Jackson riffled absently through his stack of messages. "Get the hair cut."

Colton groaned. "Don't start with my hair."

The long hair had been an issue from the beginning, but Jackson deferred to a man's right to look the way he wanted. "You asked, and I'm telling you. Older clients balk when they see long curly strands on a man. They figure he's either a would-be hippie or some kind of heavy-metal rocker.''

''Jackson—''

''I don't want to talk about your hair,'' he broke in. ''That's your business, anyway. I've got something important to tell you.''

He told him about Emily and his daughter, and Colton's eyes grew wide. ''You have a daughter?'' Colton breathed incredulously.

''Yes,'' he admitted, liking the sound of that more and more. ''And I'm flying back to Houston as soon as Nancy can get me on a flight. I need you to handle things while I'm away.''

''Sure, no problem. I'll put my hair in a ponytail or something.''

''Yeah,'' Jackson said teasingly. ''That'll help tremendously.'' He stood and handed Colton his messages. ''You take care of these. I've got to pack. I'll check in every day.''

Colton took the papers. ''Okay. Gosh, you have a daughter.''

''Yeah, it takes some getting used to,'' Jackson admitted. ''I'll talk to you tomorrow.''

Before he could reach the door, Colton asked, ''Did Janine get in touch with you?''

Jackson turned with a frown on his face. ''Janine? My ex-wife?''

''Yeah.''

''No. What the hell did she want?''

''Well, she came in on Tuesday looking for you. I told her you wouldn't be back until Friday. She returned yesterday and was a little upset to learn you weren't here. She asked me to give you a message.''

''And?'' he prompted.

"She said she needed to speak with you as soon as possible."

"Really? What about?"

"She didn't say. She just said it was important."

Jackson's frown deepened. His first impulse was just to leave and worry about calling her later. He and Janine had parted on amicable terms and she had remarried. He hadn't talked to her in months, but if she'd said it was important, then he had to call. He glanced at his watch. Damn. It seemed that circumstances were conspiring to keep him away from Emily.

"Did she leave a number?"

Colton sifted quickly through the messages in his hand. "Yeah, here it is." He handed the slip of paper to Jackson, then walked out.

Jackson called his ex-wife; he reached her office, but she was in court. He left a message on her voice mail, saying he'd be out of town for a few days, but if it was important she could reach him on his cell phone. He gave her the number and hung up.

For the life of him, he couldn't figure out why Janine wanted to talk with him. She was a corporate lawyer, ambitious, driven and fixated on success. At first he was attracted to that, but later it began to wear very thin. Janine had never touched him deep inside, the way Emily had. If she had, he'd still be with her today. It felt good to admit that Emily had such power over his emotions. He had blocked it from his mind for years, until this morning, in fact. But now…

An hour later, Jackson was on a plane to Houston. Once he'd landed, he rented a car and went straight to Emily's condo, but she wasn't home. It was Saturday, so where could she be? At the hospital? Out doing errands? He should've called, but he didn't know exactly what to say. He had to see her face-to-face.

He had no choice but to wait. He thought he'd go insane at the wasted time, but then he saw her neighbor drive up and Jackson got out of his car and went over to her. She was an elderly lady, and she seemed a bit frightened at the sight of a strange man approaching.

"I'm looking for Dr. Cooper," he said immediately, hoping to reassure her.

She relaxed visibly. "She went home. She left yesterday."

"Thank you," Jackson replied, and ran back to his car.

So Emily had gone home to Rockport. He wondered how often she did that and what kind of relationship she had with Rose and Owen. Considering what had happened, it must be strained.

He stopped at a gas station to buy a map and tried to figure out the shortest route to Rockport. Highway 59, he decided, which should get him there in a little more than three hours. As he drove, he went over and over what he was going to say to her, wishing they'd had this talk in Houston. With her family around, it would be much more difficult, but that didn't deter him. The Coopers probably hated him, but he didn't care about that, either. He was seeing Emily. She was the only one who could stop him.

EMILY AND BECCA SPENT the day shopping. By three o'clock, Emily's feet ached and she began to despair of ever finding the right dress. Then they saw it in a shop window—a whisper of pink, made of the finest silk. It was strapless with a straight, floor-length skirt, and a slit that ran up one side to above the knee. A beaded short-sleeved jacket went with it. There were also beads on the bodice. The dress was lovely, and from Becca's reaction, Emily

knew she liked it, too. The price tag was the only draw-
back, but she couldn't resist. The dress fit Becca perfectly
and Emily bought it without question.

As she waited for Becca to change, she thought about
her own daughter. Was she getting ready for her prom?
Did she have someone to buy her a beautiful dress? Emily
prayed she did and that she had a loving mother who supported her and was always there for her. She bit her lip to
choke back the emotions swelling in her throat, but it
didn't help.

*No, no,* she screamed inside. *She's my daughter. I love
her. She doesn't need anyone else.*

Hysteria was threatening her composure, and she pulled
herself together. She couldn't keep doing this to herself.
Her mother was right—although she couldn't admit it to
Rose. She spent money on Becca to ease her own guilt,
but nothing would ever take away the enormous burden
she carried. Becca's bright smile made a difference,
though. Yes, it made a great difference.

It was after six by the time they reached home. Becca
ran to her room to change into the dress to show her parents. She came back twirling round and round in the pink
silk—except she'd forgotten the jacket. Rose's mouth fell
open at her daughter's naked shoulders and exposed leg.

Rose glared at Emily in outrage. "She's not wearing
that! She looks like a slut."

Tears welled up in Becca's eyes and Emily went to her
side. "It has a jacket. She just forgot to put it on," Emily
said, and whispered to Becca, "You'd better have forgotten, because if you did it on purpose, I'm going to strangle
you."

Becca charged back to her room and came out with the
jacket on.

"See," Emily said. "It looks nice."

"It doesn't look bad, Rose," Owen put in.

"No." Rose shook her head. "She's not wearing it. It's too skimpy for a girl her age."

"Rose," Owen pleaded, to no avail.

"I said she's not wearing it, and that's final. You know how she is. As soon as she's out the door, the jacket will come off and she'll do what she pleases."

"Mom, this is really too much." Emily spoke up, trying to keep her temper. "All young girls wear strapless dresses these days."

Rose pointed a finger at her. "This is *your* fault. You spoil her, then she's uncontrollable."

"Stop it, stop it!" Becca screamed at the top of her lungs. "Em bought me this dress and I'm wearing it. I don't care what you say. And if you keep on, I'll just move out. Ginger's mom said I could move in with them."

Emily gaped at Becca. She had never mentioned this and Emily wondered if this was true or just an attempt to get back at Rose. She had a suspicion it was the latter.

Rose reached for the oxygen mask, gasping for breath. Emily started to go to her, but then she didn't. Rose only needed to calm down.

Finally Rose removed the mask and looked helplessly at Becca. "You talked to Ginger's mother about moving out?"

"Yes," Becca answered defiantly. "And I'll do it, too. She's a nice lady and she trusts Ginger."

"She's been married three times and she works in a bar," Rose told her in a belligerent tone. "I'd die before I'd let you live with that kind of woman." Rose reached for the mask again.

"She's not a saint like you are, but—"

Emily walked over and put her arm around Becca's

shoulder, stopping her in midsentence. "That's enough," she said mildly.

Becca stomped her foot. "She makes me want to scream, pull my hair out, do something violent. I can't take anymore. I—"

The ringing of the doorbell startled everyone. After a moment, Owen opened the door and Emily's world came crashing down around her feet. Jackson stood on the threshold looking nervous and devastatingly handsome in jeans and a cotton print shirt. Her stomach churned with a gut-wrenching cry. *Jackson is here.* He'd come back. That could mean only one thing. He wanted to talk about their daughter.

"Mr. Cooper, I'd like to speak with Emily, please." When she heard his deep voice, her heart began to race and her palms to sweat.

"Oh, my God," Rose cried, staring at Jackson, finally recognizing him. She turned to Emily. "What's *he* doing here?"

Emily couldn't say anything. She was gazing wordlessly at Jackson, hoping he'd decided to forgive her.

Rose noticed the look. "You've been seeing him behind my back, haven't you? I thought you had more sense than that."

"Who is he?" Becca whispered in her ear, but Emily was frozen somewhere between the past and the present, and nothing registered but the pleasant memories that floated through her mind—Jackson smiling at her, stealing kisses and loving her until nothing else mattered.

"Tell him to leave, Owen." Her mother's voice cut into her like a knife, jerking her back to reality.

"No." Emily found her voice and walked to the door.

"Emily Ann," Rose called in a threatening voice, but Emily ignored her.

"I'll talk to him," she told her father, and he moved aside with a worried frown.

Emily stepped onto the porch, closing the door. Her nerves glowed like fireflies as she watched him. She felt as though they were kids again, wanting so much and not knowing that wants were accompanied by responsibilities. They were adults now and responsibility lay heavily upon them. She could see that in his eyes. The anger and disgust had been replaced with a desire for answers.

"Why are you here?" she asked even though she knew. She had to say something to ease her jittery nerves.

"To talk. I need to talk to you." The words came out in a rush.

She needed that, too, but with her mother acting the way she was, Emily had to acknowledge it wasn't the right time.

"I can't at the moment. Things are rather…tense, as you probably heard."

"Yes, your mother hasn't changed much over the years." Jackson grasped a little more of what she must have gone through when she discovered she was pregnant. He cursed himself again for not being there for her at that difficult time.

"I have to deal with my family first."

"I understand," he said, to her shock. "I'll get a room over at the Holiday Inn and wait for you."

"Jackson…"

"We have to talk in private, Emily. Surely you can see that."

"Yes." She'd already made that decision, but she had to talk to her mother before she could do anything else.

Would Rose always rule her life? No, she told herself firmly, but she did have obligations she couldn't ignore. "I'll come as soon as I get free."

With that, Emily turned and went back into the house, ready to face another ugly scene, but this time she would tell her mother the truth. There would be no more secrets. Jackson knew, the way he should have years ago. She had to make this clear to Rose, prepare her for what might lie ahead—what Jackson might choose to do.

Even Emily didn't know what that was.

## CHAPTER SEVEN

EMILY ALMOST RAN into Becca when she entered the house. "Em, come quick! Mom's having trouble breathing."

Rose lay in the recliner gasping for each breath. "Can't… breathe…can't…"

"Shh," Emily said as she took her pulse. "Save your strength." Rose's heart was racing alarmingly. "Becca, get her heart medicine."

In a second Becca was back with a small bottle. Emily removed a pill and placed it beneath her mother's tongue. "Relax and try to breathe normally. Just relax," Emily coaxed. She motioned to Becca. "Get my medical bag."

After Becca had brought the bag, Emily removed her stethoscope and listened to Rose's heart. As she expected, the heart rate was already slowing down to a normal beat.

She looked at her father and Becca, who were waiting anxiously. "She's fine now. Stress brings on these spells." She paused, then added, "I need to talk to Mom alone."

Owen headed for the kitchen.

Becca hesitated. "Are you sure?"

"Go to your room. I'll talk to you in a minute." Emily's voice was unyielding and Becca didn't argue.

"Jeez, what did I do?" she grumbled as she obeyed.

Very deliberately, Emily took her mother's hand and held it. "I'm going to talk, and I want you to listen. Okay? Without interrupting me."

Rose nodded.

Emily told her about meeting Jackson again and about the reason he hadn't come back, and finally she confessed that she'd told him about their baby.

"Why, Emily Ann?" Rose asked, her voice barely a whisper. "Why would you tell him now?"

"Because he's her father and he has a right to know."

"But what good will it do?"

Emily looked down at her mother's frail hand in hers and knew she was lying. That had to stop. She had to stop lying to herself and to Rose. "The truth is, I told him for purely selfish reasons—my own selfish reasons."

"What are you talking about?"

She gripped her mother's hand. "Ever since I gave her up for adoption, I've had these dreams where she's running away from me. I try to catch her so I can see her face, but before I do, I always wake up. I've never seen her face and I never will. I've never held her or touched her and…" Her voice trembled on the last word.

"Oh, Emily Ann, I never realized it affected you so deeply," her mother cried with heartfelt sympathy, and Emily soaked up her compassion.

"Mom." Her voice was incredulous. "I gave away my child. A child I carried for almost nine months. A child I talked to every day of that time, telling her how much I loved her and so many other things. When she was taken from me, I felt an emptiness and a loss that's never been filled, and I don't think it ever will be."

Silence followed.

"And, of course, you blame me," Rose said quietly. Just like that, the old Rose was back.

Emily drew a hard breath. "I wish I could say that I didn't, but I'd be lying. Part of me will always blame you for the pressure, but in the end it was my decision and I didn't have the strength to stand up for myself or my daughter.''

Silence again.

"How is seeing Jackson Talbert again going to change that?''

Emily thought for a minute. "I'm not sure it will, but I have this need to share her with Jackson. He loves her as much as I do and he's feeling the same emptiness and loss.''

Rose's eyes opened wide. "You think he loves your baby?''

"Of course'' was her immediate response.

Rose squeezed her hand. "Don't fool yourself about this man.''

"I'm not. We were only together a little while, but I feel as if I know him better than anyone.''

"You're romanticizing the situation when it was sordid and—''

"No.'' Emily stopped her. "We were in love and our daughter was a result of that love.''

"You're fooling yourself,'' her mother repeated.

Emily patted her hand and got to her feet, not wanting to argue. "If I am, that's okay. I'm thirty-five years old and capable of making my own decisions and mistakes. I can handle whatever lies ahead.'' She looked at her mother. "I'm going to have a talk with Becca, then—''

Rose sat up straight. "Why do you need to talk to Rebecca?''

"Because I don't like her attitude or the way she talks to you.''

Rose relaxed somewhat. "I told you she's out of control.''

"I don't agree with that, but I do have a few things to say to her.''

As she turned away, Rose asked, "If I asked you not to see Jackson Talbert again, would you listen to me?"

"No, Mom, I wouldn't." She glanced back. "This is my life and you have to let me live it—my way."

Rose gave a long sigh of regret.

BECCA SAT IN THE MIDDLE of the bed brushing her long hair when Emily entered the room. She had changed out of the prom gown and now wore a baggy T-shirt.

"Is that him?" Becca asked excitedly. "Is that the father of your baby?"

"Yes," Emily answered, not seeing any reason to deny it.

"Wow, he's handsome."

Jackson had always been handsome and charming and everything she'd ever dreamed of in her girlish fantasies. She shook the image from her mind.

"I don't want to talk about Jackson. I want to talk about you."

"Jeez." Becca scowled, lowering the hairbrush. "What did I do?"

"I want to believe you wore the dress out there without the jacket because you were in a hurry, but I'm beginning to think you did it on purpose because you knew how Mom would react."

Becca didn't say anything, just hung her head.

"And I don't believe Ginger's mom said you could move in with them. You know how Mom feels about that woman and you only said it to upset her. Didn't you?"

"Maybe," Becca mumbled, fiddling with the hairbrush.

"Why did you do that? Don't you care about Mom's health? Stress brings on the spells with her heart."

"I'm sorry."

"Then stop trying to get your way in everything and show a little respect."

"Okay," she muttered, then asked, "Are you gonna take the dress back?"

Emily breathed deeply. "No, you can keep the dress, but I don't want you to use me as a wedge against Mom, and I don't want to hear any more talk about running away or moving out."

"But she makes me so angry."

Emily sat on the bed. "She makes me angry, too. I guess we'll have to learn to live with it, because she *is* our mother and deserves our respect."

"Yeah," Becca agreed, glancing at Emily. "You're not mad at me, are you?"

"No, I'm just tired of all the arguing."

Becca threw her arms around Emily's neck and hugged her. "I couldn't stand it if you were mad at me."

Emily stroked Becca's hair. "Apologize to Mom and let's try to have some harmony in this house." She stood. "I'll talk to you later."

"Where are— Oh, you're going to see him."

"Yes, I am."

"Wow," Becca breathed dreamily. "Just think, after all these years, you meet again. It's *so* romantic." Her voice suddenly changed. "But Mom's not taking his appearance too well."

"I'll handle Mom."

"Okay."

As Emily walked out of the room, she was no longer thinking of her mother but of Jackson. Talking to him would take all the tact she possessed. What she said would either fuse the past to the present or split the two apart forever, and she would never hear forgiveness from Jackson's lips. And she needed that…desperately.

JACKSON PACED BACK AND FORTH, repeatedly glancing at his watch. Where was she? It had been more than two hours. Why wasn't she here? Had she changed her mind? The questions went around and around in his head until he thought he'd go crazy. He picked up the phone to call the Cooper house, then put it down. He had to be patient, he told himself, but patience wasn't something that came easily to him.

He threw himself down in a chair. He had treated her shabbily and she deserved better than that. She definitely didn't deserve his anger. He berated himself as he'd done for hours now. All those years ago, he should've been there for her. He should've come back, or at least called, but he'd selfishly gone on with his life. He didn't understand how he'd done that, especially since he'd loved her so much. Of course, his mother's death had knocked him for a loop and he wasn't thinking rationally. That was the excuse he kept making for himself, but the real truth was slowly emerging. He'd been scared, scared to death. He had loved his mother and he never wanted to have those deep feelings for anyone ever again. Because when you lost that person, the pain was too great. As long as he didn't feel, he couldn't hurt. So, like a coward, he'd put Emily out of his mind.

He was so engrossed in his own misery that he didn't hear the first tap at the door. At the second tap, he was instantly on his feet and he yanked the door wide. Emily stood there looking tense and tired, but she was a beautiful sight to his eyes. ''Come in,'' he said quickly.

Emily took in the room at a glance—a suite actually, with a bedroom and sitting room. She wondered why he needed all this space.

''Nice accommodations,'' she said as she took a chair.

It was a stupid remark, but she had to say something to still the butterflies in her stomach.

Jackson sat opposite her on the love seat. "It was all they had available. Tourists are already coming to Rockport."

"Yes, I'd forgotten. Peak season is starting. Every place will be busy until after Labor Day."

The silence stretched, and for a few minutes, neither said anything else.

Emily was the first to speak. "You wanted to talk?"

Jackson moved to the edge of his seat. "I do, but I'm not sure where to begin. I guess before I do anything else, I should say I'm sorry."

She swallowed the lump in her throat, trying not to read too much into that. "For what?"

"For getting angry and leaving so quickly when you told me about the baby."

"I'm sure it's a normal reaction when you're told something like that."

"No," he denied. "Anger is never normal. I just had a hard time dealing with the news."

"Well, it was an honest reaction." She tried to keep her voice neutral.

"I suppose, but I didn't stop to think about the reasons behind your actions. All I could think about was myself, *my* feelings, and I had to get away." He took a breath. "After some soul-searching, I see things more clearly. I didn't come back the way I promised. I didn't do *anything* I promised. So I don't have a right to anger or anything else." He paused. "But I would like to hear what happened to make you do something so drastic, and I'd like to hear about our daughter. I don't even know when she was born."

"August 15," she said in a voice so low he had to strain

to hear. "My parents sent me to live with my great-aunt in San Antonio. That's where she was born." Her eyes met his. "The same time you were there, starting your company."

"Oh, my God."

"When you told me that in the restaurant, I couldn't believe it. I waited and waited for you to come back, and all along you were so close...but so far away."

"Oh, Emily..."

"Why *didn't* you come back? Why didn't you?" The cry came from the deepest part of her soul. She hadn't even realized she'd spoken the words aloud until she saw his devastated face.

Jackson's tongue suddenly felt too big for his mouth and he couldn't speak or swallow. He was locked in a void of pure agony—the agony he'd caused her.

"If you'd loved me, you would've come back." The words seemed to emerge of their own volition. She wanted to stop them but couldn't.

"I loved you more than any woman I've ever known," he said softly, aware of the bitter aftertaste in his mouth. "After we left Rockport, you were all I could think about. That night I couldn't sleep. I just kept remembering how you felt in my arms and I was so sure I'd never lose that feeling. But I did. When my parents told me about my mom, I became dead inside and I couldn't feel anything except the grief. I'm sorry, Emily, but that's the truth."

She bit her lip to keep it from trembling. "I know, I shouldn't have brought it up again." She knew he was sorry and she understood about the past, but she supposed she had to hear him say it again.

"You have to tell me what you feel. We have to be honest with each other," he said next, and he was right. "Emily, I—"

She held up her hand to stop him. She had to tell him everything now or she wouldn't be able to. "When I discovered I was pregnant, I was terrified. I left messages for you, but you never returned any of my calls. I know now that you were dealing with a lot of pain, but it doesn't change what happened." She paused for a second.

"When my mother found out, she was like a madwoman, ranting at me and calling me names. She said I'd shamed and disgraced the family. She became so upset the doctor insisted she stay in bed. He told us there was a danger she might lose the baby if she didn't calm down. The news hit me hard. I had problems with Mom's pregnancy, but I didn't want her to lose her child. After my parents talked, Dad agreed with her and said I had to give the baby up for adoption. Mom couldn't handle the stress, and it was the only thing to do. I nodded in agreement because I couldn't cause them any more pain. But I couldn't say the words. They made all the arrangements and I lived in a world that didn't seem real. I just existed, going through the motions. After graduation, my dad moved me to San Antonio."

She looked down at her clasped hands, the words coming easily now. "My aunt was a religious person and she quoted scripture to me every day so I could repent of my sin. I stayed in my room most of the time, feeling banished by everyone I loved. Except my baby. When she kicked, I knew she was alive and that meant that I was, too. I never really accepted the fact that I'd have to give her up and in the end that made it much harder."

Jackson got up and knelt on the floor by her chair. He had to be close to her because he was feeling such intense pain.

"Becca was born the first week in June, and I wanted to go home to be with them, but my parents wouldn't let me. They were afraid someone might see I was pregnant. The birth weakened Mom's heart and her baby was weak, too. I worried and worried about them until I made myself sick. Finally Dad called and said they were better and that he'd soon take them home. It was a big relief. I don't know what I would've done if anything had happened to Becca.''

She inhaled deeply. ''The stress took its toll on my body and my baby came early. Things happened so fast, it's hard to recall that part. All I remember is a cold, sterile hospital room and the pain—excruciating pain that racked my body. And the tears…tears because I was all alone. Then I heard her crying and for a few minutes everything seemed fine, until they whisked her away to her waiting…parents. I screamed and begged, but nothing helped. The nurse said I'd done the right thing and these emotions would pass, but they haven't. I hear her in my dreams. I see her in my dreams and I ache to hold her, but I never will. I don't deserve to.''

''Emily, Emily,'' Jackson whispered, and unable to resist, he wrapped his arms around her.

She melted into his embrace, needing his comfort more than she'd ever imagined.

''That's not true,'' he whispered into her hair.

She pulled back and dried her eyes with the back of one hand. ''Yes, it is,'' she whimpered. ''I gave our child away. You have cause to hate me and every—''

Jackson cupped her face in his hands and looked into her watery eyes. ''I don't hate you. When you first told me, I was hurt, but now I understand that I have to accept part of the blame. It takes two to create a baby and it takes two to handle the responsibility, and I didn't. I want you to know I deeply regret that.'' When she didn't respond, he said again, ''I don't hate you. Please believe me.''

She blinked back tears. ''I know that adoption is right

for some girls, but it wasn't for me. I should've tried harder to keep her. I... How do I stop hating myself?''

He wiped her tears away with his thumbs. ''I'm not sure, but I have an idea.''

His gentle touch sent a warm current through her body, chasing away the cold. ''What?'' she managed.

Jackson took an audible breath. ''We find our daughter.''

She drew away, a frown on her face, as if she didn't understand the words.

''Listen to me,'' he said. ''We have a daughter. Don't you want to see her to reassure yourself that she's okay and with a loving family?''

''Yes,'' she murmured. She used to dream about finding her, and now Jackson was voicing something she dared not let herself believe—that she could actually see her child.

''Then let's do it.''

She put a hand to her head, which was beginning to throb. For years she'd fantasized about this and she still had the same doubts. ''I don't think I can.''

''What do you mean?''

She clasped her hands and tried to explain. ''If I see her, I don't think I can walk away. I can't let her go again. It would kill me.''

With his finger, Jackson lifted her chin, forcing her to look at him. ''She'll be eighteen in August and probably getting ready for college. Any way you look at it, we won't be a big part of her life—that's the sad fact. She's already grown, but we'll know where she is and that she's well and happy.''

''We'd be disrupting her life, causing her a lot of pain. I can't do that to her. I can't hurt her again.''

''Emily, Emily.'' Jackson rested his forehead against

hers and tried to understand what she was feeling. "Ever since I've cooled down, it's all I can think about, and I believe you want the same thing. So what's holding you back? I can't do this without you."

She felt his breath on her cheek and heat rose up in her so strongly that it shocked her. It had been years, but her body remembered everything about him—his scent, his touch, his sensitive hands. She didn't know why she was feeling such things when her mind was in chaos, but Jackson had always had that effect on her. Somehow, he could make her feel good about herself. She didn't think that was possible...now.

From somewhere deep in her heart, she found the words she needed to say. "I'm scared. I'm so scared she'll hate me like I hate myself."

"That's a chance you and I both have to take."

She shook her head, still not convinced. "I don't know." A sliver of hope shot through the doubts and fears, and she had to ask, "Where do you think we should start?"

"At the beginning—with the agency that handled the adoption. And we'll talk to your parents."

Emily closed her eyes tight in pain. "They'll hate this, especially my mom."

"Do you care?"

"No," she answered in a flash, and opened her eyes. She had just told her mother that she was old enough to make her own decisions and handle the consequences. And she meant every word. This choice was hers—hers and Jackson's. Did she have the courage to do it?

The answer to that question was a resounding *yes*. Her heart began to race at the mere thought of seeing her daughter. For a moment it was so overwhelming that she had trouble breathing, but despite her euphoria, she had to establish one stipulation.

"Promise me something," she said in a firm voice.

"Anything."

"If we're lucky enough to find her, promise me that if she's happy and with a loving family, we won't disrupt her life. We'll walk away."

"I'm not sure I can do that," he admitted honestly. "A moment ago you said you couldn't, either."

"That was the weak me. I was thinking about myself. The strong me is thinking about her and I can't survive hurting her. Just seeing her face and knowing she's okay will be enough for me."

"Are you sure?"

"No," she said with a catch in her voice. "I'm not sure about any of this. All I know is that I have to see her."

Her pain twisted his insides into knots and he realized he'd do anything she wanted. "I promise," he said softly. "And I won't break this promise, but you have to help me be strong…like you."

She smiled slightly. He thought she was strong when in reality she was a mass of quivering nerves.

His gaze was riveted on the smile that lit up her beautiful face. Other emotions, basic and primal, stirred inside him. Her dark eyes were warm and glistening with so many feelings that screamed for sustenance…sustenance that had been deprived for way too long.

Without a second thought, Jackson touched his lips to hers. Her sweetness and softness was just as he remembered—and more. She affected his senses like no woman ever had.

His caressing touch and clean, male scent evoked memories of passionate nights. Happier times. Times she would never forget. Times she wanted to— Her thoughts stopped as she allowed herself to renew that bond. Her tongue met his and a hot ache curled through her. When his mouth opened over hers, she met his passion with a fervor of her own. They needed this, the intimacy, the closeness, to ease the hurt and anguish. For that moment they lost themselves in feeling.

The ringing of the phone shattered the mood and Jackson slowly drew away. They stared at each other a long second before he stood and answered the persistent phone. She heard him say, "Hi, Colton," and everything after that went over her head as she caught sight of herself in the mirror on the wall. Her hair was mussed, her lipstick smeared and her blouse askew. The sight was like a bolt of electricity to her brain. What was she doing? She was letting her emotions control her like she had years ago. She couldn't do that again. She had to be in control; that was important to her. She had to look toward the future, and all she could see there was an unidentifiable face. Until she saw that face, she couldn't let herself be swayed by inner yearnings that had nothing to do with the future.

She was an adult now and she had to admit the truth. She was attracted to Jackson, just as before, and he seemed to feel the same way, but now it was fueled by a love they shared for their child. *That's all it is,* she told herself. *That's all it is.*

Jackson hung up the phone and saw her worried expression. His heart seemed to tighten. She was regretting the kiss—that was all too clear. He'd kissed her outside the restaurant, but it wasn't like this. They had put their hearts into it and it felt so right. At least to him. To her, it was obviously something else.

He inhaled deeply. "That was my business partner." When she didn't answer, he added, "I'm sorry." It occurred to him that he was saying this a lot. With reason.

She tucked her hair behind her ear in a nervous gesture. "What for?" she asked, but she didn't have to. She knew he was feeling the same things she was—a sense of being overwhelmed by events and grasping at emotions that weren't real.

*Then why did it* feel *so real?* She ignored that voice inside her.

Taking a long breath, she tried to speak, but Jackson placed a finger over her lips. "Shh," he whispered. "I didn't want to rush you, but here I am doing exactly that. My only excuse is the effect you have on me…. But we can't think about ourselves right now. We have to think about our daughter."

"Yes," she agreed wholeheartedly, but she needed his closeness to get through the days ahead. She wondered if he had any idea how much she needed him and how much she feared that need.

# CHAPTER EIGHT

EMILY AND JACKSON TALKED until after midnight and Emily found it hard to leave him. She enjoyed talking about their daughter, telling him the few little things she could. Their child had been a symbol of the love they'd once shared and she had carelessly let it go. That was the reason she'd been so tortured all these years. But she felt Jackson understood now and that liberated her in so many ways. She could face the future with him by her side. She didn't want to analyze her emotions any further than that because she was so exhilarated, she didn't trust her own perceptions.

She'd come home with such a heavy heart, but now she felt free and light, and it was all because of Jackson.

After Emily left, Jackson couldn't even think about sleeping. He felt terribly alone without her, so he walked across the highway to the beach. He sat on one of the park benches and watched the moonlight as it played tricks with the water. Condos in the distance beckoned with bright lights, but all he could see was Emily's face. They had a daughter and now they'd find her…together. Emily had forgiven him, which lifted a weight from his shoulders. He could face anything as long as he had her. That thought rocked him. In a matter of a few days, she had become the center of his world. Everything else had shifted in importance and his whole perspective had changed.

He could see that she was both frightened and elated at

what was happening between them, and he intended to take it slow and give her all the time she needed. The days ahead wouldn't be easy. Finding their daughter would be an enormous task, but he was determined that they'd succeed.

Emily had to talk to her parents; that was the first hurdle. Jackson wanted to be with her, but Emily insisted it would be better if she talked to them by herself. She was right, but he didn't want her to endure that unpleasantness alone. There'd be a big scene, he was sure. Rose Cooper would be against the idea, but he trusted Emily to persuade her.

He leaned against the bench, resting his arms along the back, and let the soothing sounds take him away. The water lapped against the shore, and the smell of saltwater brought him memories of Emily. The few times they'd made love, the same sounds, the same scent had surrounded them. Their daughter had been conceived in the easy-flowing rhythm of the night. Suddenly he buried his face in his hands and prayed for the strength to help Emily—prayed they could find their daughter so they'd remember that time with love and happiness.

ALTHOUGH IT WAS LATE when Emily reached her parents' home, lights were still on. Her heart sank. She hadn't wanted to talk to them until morning, but it was just as well, she told herself as she entered the living room. They had to know what she was planning to do and she needed their help.

The TV was on and her father was asleep in his chair, but her mother was wide awake, her eyes on the door, and they seared right through Emily.

Emily laid her purse on the coffee table and perched on the edge of the sofa. Her father stirred and sat up.

"What took so long?" Rose asked in a tight voice.

"We had a lot to talk about," Emily replied, trying to remain composed and not lose her temper at her mother's obstinate nature.

"Like what?" Rose shrilled. "Like how he deserted you when you were pregnant?"

Emily bit her lip to keep words from tumbling out.

"Calm down, Rose," Owen said. "You'll make yourself sick."

Rose took several gulps of oxygen from the mask. "Are you planning on seeing him again?" she finally asked.

Emily met her mother's eyes squarely. "Yes."

Rose clenched her hands. "No, you can't! He'll only hurt you."

Emily got up and went over to her mother, kneeling by her chair. "As I told you earlier, I'm old enough to make my own decisions."

"But Emily Ann—"

"Don't try to talk me out of it," Emily said. "My mind is made up and nothing you say will make any difference." She took a shaky breath. "Jackson and I have decided to find our daughter."

The color drained from Rose's face. "What?" she choked.

"We're going to find our daughter," Emily repeated.

Rose had to take several draws on the mask. "What good will it do? It'll just cause you and the child more pain. Is that what you want?"

"What I want is to see my daughter. I have to see her face. Please try and understand."

"That's selfish," Rose said harshly. "You'll destroy the life she has, because of your selfish needs."

Emily shook her head in despair and slowly got to her feet. "I need your help." She wouldn't give up. She had a mission and her mother wasn't dissuading her with guilt or threats. "Tell me the name of the agency that took my baby."

Rose glared at her. "I refuse to get involved in this. That man has filled your head with nonsense and you can't even see it."

Emily sighed deeply and turned to her father. "Tell me, Dad." Owen looked away and she knew he wouldn't go against her mother's wishes.

"Fine." She wheeled toward the hall. "I remember names and I can put it together."

"Emily Ann," her mother called.

She came to a sudden halt.

"You'll regret this."

Emily didn't answer, just headed to Becca's room. As she opened the door, she saw Becca dive into bed. She'd been listening at the door.

Becca lay curled up with her back to her, as if she was asleep.

"I know you're awake," Emily said as she fell onto the bed fully clothed. She was mentally and physically exhausted.

Becca sat up. "Aren't you gonna put your nightgown on?"

"In a minute."

"Are you really gonna search for your daughter?"

"Yes."

"Wow, then this Jackson guy isn't so bad?"

"No, he's actually quite wonderful."

A slight pause, then Becca asked, "Are you sure, Em? I mean, he hurt you once."

Emily turned to look at her sister in the darkness. The moonlight shone on her face, her long, gleaming hair. "I'm very sure Jackson won't hurt me again."

"Jeez, your voice sounds all mushy like you're still..."

The unfinished sentence hung between them, and Emily didn't feel the need to acknowledge it. What she and Jackson were feeling was personal and private, and she'd only talk about it with him.

She didn't have to worry; Becca was quickly on to something else. "Mom's about to have a heart attack."

"Mom will be fine," Emily assured her. "Once she realizes she can't browbeat me again."

"What happened to all the harmony we're supposed to be having?" Becca asked in a teasing tone.

"It was blown to hell in a short second."

Becca laughed.

Emily touched her soft cheek. Becca was so intense, so excitable. She wondered if her daughter was like that. Would she have that same enchantment, that same... Her throat closed up and she thought her heart would burst with the gravity of not knowing.

*But she would.*

*Soon.*


"WHAT ARE WE GOING TO DO?" Rose asked Owen after Emily had left the room.

"Nothing, we're doing nothing" was Owen's response.

"How can you say that?"

"Because it's out of our hands now."

"It is not! If you'll talk to her, she'll—"

"No," he interrupted tersely. "I'm not talking to Emily. I did that years ago, and I promised myself I wouldn't do it again. I supported you when you said she had to give the child away, even though I felt it was wrong. I was the one who took her to San Antonio to live with that awful aunt of yours, and I was the one who was there the day she had the baby. I saw all the pain she was suffering. I didn't do anything then, and I'm not doing anything now."

"Don't you understand what's going to happen?"

"Yes, Emily will find her daughter, and I think it's long overdue."

THE NEXT MORNING Emily was up early. She showered and dressed, then packed her suitcase. She spared Becca a glance as she tiptoed out of the room. They had said their good-byes the night before, and Emily had given her the name of the hotel where they'd be staying. Still, she experienced a sense of guilt at leaving her alone with their mother. But Becca gave as good as she got, and at times she instigated most of the "getting." Becca could take care of herself; Emily was well aware of that. At times, she felt as if she should protect her, but in truth Becca didn't need her protection. Emily now had to think about herself and her child. The thought was intoxicating and she sensed she was on the threshold of something significant, something she had no control over. All she had to do was to take the next step, the step that would carry her into the realm of the future.

She found her parents in the kitchen and she told them she was leaving. They didn't say a word, for which she was grateful. She couldn't stand another scene. Walking out of the room, she felt that at last she was leaving her childhood behind.

She drove straight to the hotel and knocked on Jackson's door. He opened it immediately. "Hi," he said, smiling, and her heart turned over. He was so handsome in his dark slacks and light blue shirt, his hair still damp from his shower. She ached for all the years they'd been apart. She didn't know what tomorrow would bring, but today they were bonded together in a single goal: to find their child.

"Come in," he said, walking back into the room and

putting toiletries in his suitcase. "I just got off the phone. Hope you're all packed."

"Yes," she replied, but he caught the hesitation in her voice.

He turned to her. "Emily, what is it?"

She was amazed that he could glimpse the pain inside her. She was trying so hard not to reveal it, not to think about it. "It's nothing, really. I just had a bad argument with my parents last night."

"I'm sorry."

"It doesn't matter."

"Yes, it does because it upsets you."

"I'll get over it and now I have something to look forward to."

"That's right, and we don't need your parents' approval to do this. All we need is the name of the agency they used." He snapped his suitcase shut.

"They didn't give it to me," she admitted quietly.

He swung around. "What?"

"They said it would only cause me and my daughter more pain, and they wouldn't do it."

Jackson ran a hand through his hair. "Damn, I didn't expect this, but we'll manage. You know the name of the hospital in San Antonio, and we'll take it from there."

"Yes, and that summer I heard my aunt talking to them about a Miller or a Seals agency. It has to be one of those."

"We'll find them," he said, and grabbed his suitcase. "We'd better get moving." They'd made the plans last night. There was no direct flight from Corpus Christi to San Antonio, so they decided to drive. Jackson had a rental car and they would return it in Corpus Christi, then use Emily's car for the trip. As they reached the door, he called, "Wait."

She looked at him.

"We can't go."

She frowned. "Why?"

"We can't go until you smile. I'm not going anywhere while you've got that somber expression on your face."

Her lips twitched, and he touched them briefly with his. "That's better. Much better."

It was, and all her anger at her parents disappeared for the moment. She felt relaxed and ready to confront whatever lay ahead—with Jackson beside her.

The time passed quickly, and before she knew it, they were halfway to San Antonio. She was content to let Jackson drive, enjoying the rare experience of being a passenger. They talked about any and everything. She particularly loved hearing about his dad and aunt Maude. She remembered George Talbert as having a great sense of humor, and Jackson's aunt sounded like one of a kind. They were a close-knit family, and Emily envied that. Her mother controlled their family, which meant closeness was something they avoided. Closeness and honesty...

When they arrived in San Antonio, Jackson drove directly to their hotel on the River Walk. There was a convention in town and rooms were scarce, but Jackson had booked one over the phone the night before. The hotel was upscale and very luxurious—but as soon as Emily entered the room she saw there was only one bedroom with a king-size bed. They were supposed to have a two-room suite.

Jackson noticed it immediately. "Damn," he said. "I'll see what the hell happened."

He picked up the phone and talked to the desk clerk. Hanging up, he turned to her. "This is all they have. There was a mistake with the booking. What do you want to do?"

She shrugged and sat beside him on the bed. "It doesn't

matter. I think we're adult enough to handle this.'' All she could think about was being wrapped in Jackson's arms and feeling those raw, pagan emotions he engendered in her. She couldn't believe she was feeling this way, especially after she'd convinced herself last night that their emotions were fueled by the past.

''I'll sleep on the sofa,'' Jackson offered, although that was the last thing he wanted. He wanted to be with her, wanted it desperately, but it had to be her choice.

Emily stared at the small sofa, then turned to him, a light in her eyes he hadn't seen in a long time. ''You and I have never slept together in a bed.''

The words came from a place deep in her heart, a place she'd kept hidden and closed for so many years. She was tired of denying what she felt. She wanted to be with Jackson, and she didn't need an excuse for that. She was a woman now and she was able to embrace everything that meant—even the consequences.

He watched her closely. ''You mean...''

She got to her feet. ''Why don't we get something to eat and we'll discuss it later?''

''Okay,'' he agreed, and cursed himself for not being more persistent in finding rooms. He didn't want her to feel uncomfortable or awkward. Whatever happened, he wanted it to happen naturally.

Emily had found the phone book and was thumbing through it. ''There isn't a Miller or a Seals agency. Now what?''

''In the morning, we'll start at the hospital.''

''I guess that's the only thing to do. We don't need to check birth records because I know that adoptive parents always file an amended certificate and all original records of the birth are deleted. Except I think the original certificate is sealed in Austin. If all else fails, we might be able to get a court order to see it.''

''That would be our last resort,'' Jackson said, ''but with luck, all the information we need will be at the hospital. Now, let's find some food and enjoy the sights of San Antonio.''

They ate at a restaurant on the famous River Walk along the San Antonio River. Jackson had steak and she ordered fish. They sipped good wine and enjoyed the sights around them. They visited quaint little shops as they walked along the river. Jackson even talked her into a boat ride. She laughed and joked and forgot she was a professional doctor with a reputation to uphold. For those hours, she also forgot about guilt and regret. All she could see was herself in Jackson's eyes and the woman she could have been and the woman she wanted to be.

They slowly made their way back to the hotel, arm in arm. Riding up in the elevator, Emily felt as if she were flying and nothing was going to bring her down…nothing.

Jackson had been with other women before, and more than once he'd believed himself in love, but those emotions were pallid compared to what Emily awakened in him. She opened his heart, and all he wanted to do was love her, protect her, share every aspect of experience with her. Emily's dark eyes carried him away to another time, another place, and he felt the same as he had then. Loving and needing her at the same time, and not wanting to hurt her.

When they entered the room, Emily sank onto the sofa and kicked off her shoes. She curled her feet beneath her and nestled in the cushions, feeling pleasantly exhausted.

Jackson took his keys, wallet and change from his pockets and placed them neatly on the dresser. He then removed his belt and coiled it, then laid it beside his other things.

She watched his sure, methodical movements and realized Jackson was an orderly person. She was, too. They had so much in common....

"Do you want the shower first?" he asked, staring at the lovely lines of her face, wanting to touch her so badly he ached.

"No, I'm too comfortable to move."

Jackson disappeared into the bathroom and soon she heard the steady running of water. The sound lulled her into drowsiness. She thought about his smile, his energy, his kindness and sensitivity. As a teenager she'd recognized that he possessed those traits, and now, as an adult woman she knew it beyond any doubt. Through all the bad times she'd tried to convince herself that she hated him for deserting her, but she'd never really achieved that. Last night after they'd kissed she'd had second thoughts—but only because of fear. She made a decision; she wasn't going to stop living just to avoid getting hurt.

Jackson came out of the bathroom, tightening the belt on his terry-cloth robe. Emily was asleep, her head tilted back on the sofa. Her face had a contented, peaceful look. He sat beside her and had to resist the urge to touch her; instead he watched her sleep. If this was all that happened tonight, he was satisfied. They were slowly bridging that gulf between past and present, and he could wait. As long as she was with him, he could wait.

Emily awoke feeling serene and happy. She found herself looking into Jackson's green eyes and experienced a moment of pure joy. She'd been dreaming about him and it probably showed on her face, and she didn't bother to hide it.

She sat up and brushed back her dark hair. "I fell asleep."

"Yeah," he murmured, not able to take his eyes off her.

"How long have I been out?"

"An hour or so."

They stared at each other, and at his warm gaze something unfurled inside her—desire, fresh and urgent. She hadn't felt this passion for Glen. And she *wanted* passion. Oh, yes, she wanted it all.

She leaned over and kissed him. At her touch, blood rushed hotly through his veins and he kissed her back. He drew her close and she wrapped her arms around him. Their tongues twined together, as they renewed an old passion that had been dormant for too long.

He was hungry for her and couldn't get enough. He pulled her closer, trying to soak up every nuance that was her. Her sweet fragrance filled his senses and he wanted to absorb her pain and heartache, but most of all he wanted to erase any separation between them. He wanted her close to him, as close as they could get.

Emily's head was spinning and a strong, smoldering need pooled deep in her belly. "Make love to me," she breathed into his mouth.

"Are you sure?" he asked raggedly as he kissed the corner of her mouth, her cheek, her neck.

She tipped her head back and whispered, "Yes."

His lips explored the curve of her neck and shoulder, then moved lower. "I don't want you to regret this tomorrow."

She gasped as his lips found her sensitive breast. "Stop talking, Jackson."

His fingers unfastened the rest of the buttons on her blouse and deftly unsnapped her bra. In a second they were gone, allowing him free access. Delicious shudders jolted through her as he licked and teased her taut nipples. She didn't remember reacting this powerfully to his touch before, but she must have. Perhaps she'd just tucked it away in a secret place. But now the pleasure was sharp and intense and totally enslaved her.

Her hands were at work on his body, too, easing away the robe to explore his shoulders and chest and the swirls of dark blond hair. Her hand drifted lower and she realized he didn't have anything on beneath the robe. She ran her finger over the length of him and he groaned and captured her mouth.

Somehow her slacks and panties were removed and their naked bodies fused together. Jackson stood with his body and mouth locked tight against hers. With a slow, sensuous turn and a few steps they fell backward onto the bed. Jackson rolled her over and stared deep into her eyes. "I don't have any condoms," he muttered hoarsely.

"It's okay," she managed to say. "It's not my fertile time of the month."

"Good." His lips found hers again, then traveled moistly down her body, caressing, teasing erotic places. When he touched her intimately, she cried out. The pleasure was so great that for a moment she thought she'd pass out. Then Jackson parted her legs and entered her with a sureness that thrilled her.

Her tight muscles enclosed him, and unabated gratification coursed through him. His quick thrusts brought Emily's hips off the bed as she met his passion and demanded more. They weren't teenagers experimenting with sex, they were adults with mature desires and compelling needs. As Emily soared to heights she had never reached before, she knew she loved him. She always had.

Jackson exploded into so many pieces he thought he would die from the ecstasy of it. The young Emily had been timid and shy, but this Emily was a woman who completed him, who matched him in passion and in potential. Not that the young Emily hadn't. It was just so…different now. So explosive.

A long time later, Jackson raised his head from the hollow of her neck and gazed down at her, their sweaty bodies still welded together. "Wow" was all he could say.

She smiled, a beautiful smile that touched his soul. "Have I improved?" she asked wickedly.

"Yeah, and I didn't think that was possible."

"Oh, Jackson."

He kissed her softly, gently, then pulled the sheet over them.

"No regrets?" he had to ask as she drifted off to sleep.

"No regrets," she murmured, and she knew there never would be. No matter what the future held, she would cherish this moment.

# CHAPTER NINE

THE MORNING DAWNED bright and clear. Emily stirred and encountered a male body against hers. A smile spread across her face. Jackson. What a night! It was everything she'd remembered and so much more. He was exciting and considerate and knew how to touch her to make the blood sing in her veins. The smile disappeared as something occurred to her. She hadn't told Jackson she loved him. Why? She should've, but then, he hadn't said the words, either. He had to say them first. She didn't know why she felt that way, but suspected it had something to do with the past and his not coming back when she needed him. And that feeling was embodied in fear—fear of getting hurt again. She had told Becca that Jackson wouldn't hurt her and she believed it. So, why the doubts? She knew the answer. Their future relationship hinged on finding their daughter. If they didn't, then… She didn't want to think about that.

She had decided she was going to experience life and, yes, love, and enjoy this time with Jackson, whatever happened.

Jackson stretched and sat up. His blond hair was tousled and he had a growth of beard, yet he'd never looked more handsome. A warmth spread through her lower abdomen and all rational thought simply melted away.

Jackson glanced at his watch. ''My God, it's almost nine o'clock.''

"What?" That couldn't be true. She never slept that late.

He turned to look at her and his heart constricted with so many emotions. First among them was love. He loved her so much and he was afraid to tell her. He didn't know why; he just couldn't repeat the mistakes of the past. Years ago he hadn't hesitated to express his feelings, but it was different now. So many things were standing in their way. But once they found their daughter and the past was resolved, he could tell her. That would make up for his desertion and earn her forgiveness. Was that how he felt? It must be or he would grab at everything he was seeing in her eyes. He wanted to experience last night all over again, but he vowed to take it slow. For her and for him.

He crawled out of bed. "We'd better get dressed, have some breakfast and head over to the hospital."

A moment of loneliness engulfed her, but she watched unashamedly as he strolled naked into the bathroom. His body was beautiful, lean and muscled. He must work out, she thought idly, and it occurred to her that she knew very little about Jackson or his life. But she knew all she needed to know for now.

She got out of bed and began her preparations for the day. In less than twenty minutes Jackson was ready, but it took her longer. While he waited, she heard him on the phone talking to his father and to his business partner. Again she envied that closeness with his father. Evidently Mr. Talbert was very curious about his granddaughter. He had a right to be, and Emily wondered if her daughter would ever know she had an extended family who wanted to love her.

When Emily came out of the bathroom, Jackson caught his breath. She wore a sleeveless forest-green dress that clung to her. It had tiny pearl buttons down the front, and she'd placed pearl studs in her ears, which were hard to see because her shining hair was loose around her shoulders, but he noticed them. He noticed everything about her.

He grinned. "It was worth the wait."

She slipped on the matching jacket and picked up her purse, trying to keep her pulse from racing. They had breakfast in the hotel, then drove to the hospital. It was the same cold, dark structure she remembered, and for the first time she realized how hard it would be to go back into that place.

As if sensing her nervousness, Jackson took her hand as they entered the building and she couldn't have loved him more.

They were stonewalled at every attempt to gain access to the records—confidentiality, patients' rights and so forth. She told them they were *her* records and she therefore had a right to see them. She was then informed she'd have to go through another office, sign release forms before anything could be done, but the woman who handled medical records was out and wouldn't be back until tomorrow. Emily was so frustrated she wanted to scream. Then it hit her and she didn't know why she hadn't thought of it before. She went straight to the hospital administrator, introduced herself and explained that she wanted to see her records. The administrator was cooperative; within minutes they were directed to a warehouse that housed old files. She had a release of information form in her hand, giving her access to her own medical records.

Jackson was impressed with her efforts and determination. The warehouse was about two miles from the hospital, and soon they found themselves wading through row upon row of patients' files. The clerk showed them to the year they were looking for. They searched until Emily thought it was fruitless, and then—suddenly—she saw her

name on a tab. As she removed the file, her hand began
to tremble. Jackson took it from her. Emily peered over
his arm as he read. All the facts were there: her name, date
of birth, height, weight and medical information. Her eyes
were riveted on the one fact her heart yearned to see—
*delivered baby girl; weight five pounds, one ounce; length,
nineteen inches.*

"She was so small," she murmured with a tremor in
her voice. "I never knew she was so small. Oh, Jackson."

He closed the file and pulled her to him, kissing her
hair. "Don't do this to yourself."

"I can't help it," she sniffed. "She was so tiny, and
she needed her mother."

He swallowed twice, trying to speak, but he felt her pain
because it was his own.

He drew back and looked into her sad eyes. "You can't
fall apart on me. We have a long way to go." He was
trying to be lighthearted, but they both recognized that
nothing would ease the turmoil inside them.

"Come on," he said. "Let's take this to a desk so we
can read it more thoroughly."

They found a table and sat down, then read through the
file several times, but there was no mention of an adoption
or an agency.

"That can't be," Emily cried. "There has to be more
information."

Jackson motioned to the clerk and she walked over. She
was a woman in her fifties with short graying hair and a
stout body. "Could you help us with something, please?"

"I'll try."

Jackson pointed to the file. "Emily Ann Cooper gave
birth to a baby girl and gave it up for adoption, but there's
no record of it here."

"There should be, but since the adoption was so long

ago it might've been handled differently. Sometimes an adoption agency will have the information sealed to safeguard the child.''

*Safeguard the child. Safeguard the child.* From whom? *Me.* She knew the answer immediately and Emily wanted to lash out so badly that she had to clench her hands into fists. There was no need to safeguard her child. A sob rose up in her throat and she had to remind herself that this woman had no idea what she was going through; it wasn't her fault.

''I see,'' Jackson said. ''That relieves the hospital of all liability.''

''You got it,'' the woman answered, and started back to her desk.

''Wait a minute,'' Emily called.

The woman glanced back.

''If the records were sealed, wouldn't the fact that the baby was given up for adoption still be in the file?''

''Yes, in most cases it is'' was the response.

Emily bit down on her lip to calm her agitated nerves, then asked, ''Have you ever heard of a Miller agency or a Seals agency?''

The woman shook her head and hurried off. That made Jackson suspicious. He had glimpsed something in her eyes that bothered him.

They made copies of her file. Emily wanted to keep the information close to her. It might be all she ever had of her daughter.

ON THEIR WAY OUT, Jackson stopped by the clerk's desk. ''Mind if I ask how long you've worked here?''

''Over twenty years,'' the woman replied.

She would've been around when their daughter was born. Did she know something? He let it go—for the moment. "Thank you for your help," he said as they walked away.

In the car, Emily asked, "Why did you ask her that?"

"She seemed rather nervous when you inquired about the adoption agencies."

"She did, didn't she?" She tried to remember what the woman had said. She'd answered quickly and moved away without even giving the names any thought. Turning in her seat, she asked, "Could she possibly be hiding information?"

"I'm not sure. We need to think about this and plan our next step."

"Oh, Jackson." She leaned her head against the seat. "This is so frustrating. The name of the agency should have been there. I've worked in hospitals long enough to know that."

"Yes, it should," he agreed, glancing at his watch. "Hey, it's almost five o'clock. We've been at this all day and we haven't even had lunch."

The noise in her stomach reminded her of that. The day had gone so quickly that she hadn't thought about food— only about finding her daughter.

Jackson parked the car in the hotel garage and they strolled over to the River Walk for a meal. Jackson noticed that, despite her hunger, Emily wasn't eating. She was pushing her food around with her fork. The day's events had been hard on her.

He reached out and covered her hand with his own. "We'll find her," he said softly.

"What if we don't?" she asked, and couldn't keep her voice from trembling. "What if the trail has been so thoroughly erased that we never know where she is?"

He squeezed her hand. "It doesn't matter. Because I won't stop looking. Not ever."

She knew that. Jackson was as committed to this as she was. After all, he'd been the one who'd suggested doing what she hadn't even dared to consider all these years, afraid to let herself think she could see her daughter. Now she'd gotten her hopes up and she was feeling a sense of disappointment at not being able to locate the information they needed.

Jackson couldn't stand to see her like this. He got to his feet and pulled her up. "Let's go for a walk."

They strolled along one of the many walkways. It had grown dark, and a Tejano band was playing somewhere. The party atmosphere was infectious, but Emily couldn't release the ache inside her.

To her confusion, Jackson strolled out to a street and hailed a cab. Soon they were whizzing through the older streets of downtown San Antonio.

"Where are we going?" she asked without much interest.

"Just wait and see" was his reply.

The cab stopped in front of a tall brick structure. Jackson took Emily's hand and they walked through the swinging glass doors to the elevators. In a matter of seconds, they were on their way to the thirtieth floor, which turned out to be the roof. Emily caught her breath as she gazed out onto a spectacular view of San Antonio.

"It's beautiful," she breathed, not able to take her eyes off the lights that lit up the town.

Jackson slid his arms around her waist from behind. "I started my business on the second floor of this building, and any time the pain of my mother's death and my worries about all the debt I'd taken on got me down, I'd come up here and just enjoy the view. Staring at the vastness of all this made my problems seem insignificant, and after being up here, I could deal with my life a little better."

"And you thought this could help me cope, too?" She knew that was why he'd brought her here, to help her put what she was feeling in perspective. It had. Just the fact that he cared so much lifted her spirits immeasurably.

"Is it working?" He nuzzled her neck, and lovely, tender emotions surrounded them.

"Yes," she said.

They stood like that a long time, Jackson's arms around her, her back against his chest....

Gazing into the distance, she asked, "When you were up here, did you ever think of me?" For some reason, she had to have an answer.

"Yes," he replied without hesitation. "I used to wonder where Rockport was from here. I finally figured it had to be southeast."

"Did you think of coming back?"

"As I told you, when I got home that was all I thought about. But my mother's illness shattered everything inside me that was of any value. After that, I forgot about you and everything else. Gradually your memory seeped through the agony, but I still couldn't function enough to do anything about it."

His words flowed over her and amazingly they didn't hurt. They were the truth.

"I'm sorry," he whispered, his voice filled with regret.

"It's all right. I just had to ask."

He understood. She had a need to know if he'd used her without caring about her. "We came to Rockport that winter for a reason," he said. "My mom had started chemo treatments and she didn't want me to be there because they'd told her it would make her ill for a while. She wanted Dad to talk to me, to soften the news, but he saw how happy I was with you and he couldn't do it."

She remembered his telling her that in the restaurant,

and it raised another question. He'd already told her but she had to ask again. "Did you say you loved me so I'd have sex with you?"

"God, no." His arms tightened around her. "I loved you and I meant everything I said, but after watching my mother die in such pain, I couldn't deal with anything, especially my feelings for you. I was practically out of my mind, crazy with grief. I wasn't sure I was even going to survive."

*Why didn't you come to me? Why didn't...*

She'd already asked him that question, too. She had to let it go. Her thoughts stopped suddenly as something occurred to her. If he *had* called and told her about his mother, what would she have done? At seventeen, she was not equipped to handle such a tragedy. She wouldn't have known what to say or do...but she did now.

She turned in the circle of his arms and held him tight. "I'm sorry about your mother."

"And I'm sorry for all the pain I've caused you."

She nestled her head under his chin, letting his words heal so many wounds.

He breathed in the fragrant scent of her hair and knew they'd reached a milestone—they were getting past forgiveness.

He kissed her gently and whispered, "Let's go back to the hotel."

She nodded in agreement.

When they entered their room, they did the same as they had the night before. Jackson emptied his pockets, and she curled up on the sofa, rubbing her feet. Jackson sat down, too, and took over the task. He massaged her feet with slow stroking movements.

She rested her head against the sofa and sighed in pure pleasure. "Oh, that feels wonderful."

As he touched her, his blood ran hotly through his veins, making him aware of how much he wanted her. His hand slid up her calf to her thigh, and she sighed more deeply.

"That's not my foot," she said with a laugh.

"I know," he replied huskily, his eyelids at half-mast. He disposed easily of her panty hose, slip and panties, then turned his head to capture her open mouth.

They were hungry for each other, and she trembled with a need that surpassed anything she'd ever felt. Their tongues searched and tasted until their remaining clothes became an unwanted barrier. Frantically they stripped away the garments. He suckled and tasted her breast and her hands urgently explored the taut muscles of his chest, and lower. He groaned as her hand closed around him. Unable to withstand the exquisite torture, he swung her up in his arms and carried her to the bed and covered her body with his in slow, languorous movements. She let out a deep moan at the erotic sensation and gripped his shoulders as he entered her in need and sustenance. She rocked her hips to meet each driving thrust. She felt wanton and shameless, but so right, so perfect, that she cried out his name as pleasure coiled and jerked through her.

Jackson lost control the moment she met his kiss with a fervor that ignited everything he felt for her—now and then. Last night had been magical, and tonight was thrilling in a way he'd never experienced before. Her femininity, her beauty, her eagerness incited, aroused and satisfied him so completely that he lost himself in her and the intense pleasure that racked his body.

Later, he couldn't move, speak or do anything but hold her in the aftermath of shattering, true emotions. The words *I love you* hovered on his lips, but he wasn't sure she was ready to hear them. He would wait, but he didn't think any moment could get more perfect than this.

Languid and complete, Emily lay not wanting to think, only to feel and savor their glorious union. *I love you, I love you,* ran lazily through her mind. *I'll always love you.* But the words never left her mouth. They only comforted her as she drifted off to sleep in his arms.

THE RINGING OF THE PHONE jarred them awake. Sleepily, Jackson reached for it.

"Hello," he muttered, then pushed up on his elbow. "Yes, she's right here."

With a frown, Emily took the receiver and glanced at the clock. Five thirty. Who'd be calling at this hour? Apprehension shivered across her skin.

"Hello," she said.

"Em, you have to come home." Becca's frantic voice shrilled in her ears. "Mom had a bad spell and the ambulance just took her to the hospital. I'm scared. I don't know what to do."

"Calm down," she said. "I'll be there as soon as I can."

"I'm sorry. I know—"

"It's all right. Don't worry. I'll call the hospital in a little while to see how she's doing and then I'll call you back."

"Okay."

Hanging up, she let out a long sigh.

"Evidently your mother's ill," Jackson said, watching the troubled emotions on her face.

She looked at him and touched his face lovingly. "Yes, they've taken her to the hospital and Becca's afraid." She stroked his chēek, his chin. "I've got to go home."

He kissed her forehead. "I understand."

"It's just…" She hesitated, and he knew what she was worried about.

"I'll go with you," he offered. "We've waited this long to find our daughter, we can wait a few more days."

"No." She shook her head. "I want you to stay here and keep looking. With any luck, I can be back in a couple of days."

Now that they'd started their search, he didn't want to stop, but he wanted to be there for her. He didn't want her to face anything alone, ever again. Realistically, though, Rose wouldn't be pleased to see him, so his being there might actually make matters worse.

"Okay," he agreed. "I have a few more things I want to check."

"I wanted to be with you to help do those things. Now I can't." Her voice sounded like a hurt little girl's and she didn't really know why. She didn't want to leave, but she had no choice.

"Look at it this way," he said encouragingly. "When you go home, your mother might be willing to tell you the name of the adoption agency. We desperately need that information."

"Yes, she might." She sat up, and the sheet fell away, exposing her breasts. Something kicked inside him and he had to avert his eyes.

She crawled out of bed and picked up their clothes that were strewn on the floor. He couldn't keep his eyes from straying to the perfection of her body. Her hips were slim, her buttocks slightly rounded. She didn't look as if she'd ever had a child, except for her breasts. They were fuller and his hands ached to stroke, caress and...

She straightened from reaching for clothes and caught him staring at her. "Like the view?" she asked provocatively.

That kick inside him dissolved hotly in his loins. "Enormously," he managed to say.

She smiled. "I'd better shower and get moving." The look in his eyes had her scurrying for the bathroom; otherwise she'd never be able to leave.

Jackson jumped out of bed and began his exercises, a routine he usually did every morning, but right now he had other things on his mind. He couldn't believe how much he still wanted her. If they'd married years ago, would the passion have remained as strong? Somehow he felt it would. He'd never grow bored with Emily Ann Cooper.

While Emily showered, she couldn't stop thinking about her mother. She felt sure the attack was the result of continual agitation over Emily's searching for her daughter. Rose had brought this on herself. Why couldn't she understand how badly Emily needed to know the truth about this child?

Her mother's condition usually did not bring on a heart attack. It was painful and exhausting, and these episodes drained her body of strength. It always took her days to recover. As much as she tried to tell herself that she wasn't worried, she was. Her mother's health was deteriorating and she would never forgive herself if something happened to Rose for which she was directly responsible. They had to reach some kind of compromise...for both their sakes.

After she'd dressed in a dark-blue suit and cream blouse, she called the hospital to check on Rose's condition. Luckily her doctor was there, and Emily was able to speak with him. He said she'd stabilized and was responding to medication. He felt she'd be fine in a few days. Emily breathed a sigh of relief and called Becca with the news, saying she was on her way.

She and Jackson talked little as they walked to Emily's car. Since she couldn't get a direct flight to Corpus Christi, she decided to drive, and Jackson said he'd rent another vehicle.

She stood by her car, staring into the green of his eyes. "You'll call if you find out anything?"

"Yes," he promised her, then asked, "You sure you don't want me to come with you?"

"I'm sure," she murmured in quiet tones. "I have to do this alone. I'll talk to my mom in a rational way and maybe she'll tell me what I want to hear."

He smoothed her hair back. "I hope so."

Meeting the look in her eyes, so vulnerable, so loving, he started to ask her not to go, but of course he didn't. He couldn't be that selfish. He would miss her…terribly. Letting her go wasn't easy. It was hell.

She opened the door. "I'll be back as soon as I can."

"I know," he replied, and kissed her deeply.

They clung together for an extra second, then she quickly got in the car. *Don't cry. Don't cry,* she repeated, and forced herself not to look back. If she did, she wouldn't be able to drive away.

Jackson watched the car until it was out of sight. Only then could he walk back to the hotel. Within thirty minutes he had another vehicle. He had to resume the search for their daughter and he knew exactly where to start: the woman in the records department. She knew something and he was determined to find out what it was.

# CHAPTER TEN

ON HIS WAY TO THE HOSPITAL records building, Jackson stopped at an ATM machine to get cash. He decided that if he ran into any opposition, a little money might help overcome it. Money had a way of doing that.

He was glad when he saw the same woman on duty at the desk. He smiled at her. "Hi, I'm sorry to bother you again today, but could I have another look at Emily Ann Cooper's file?"

She raised an eyebrow. "You made copies of everything, so why would you need to look at the file again?"

Jackson had a response prepared. "Dr. Cooper took the copies and, well, for my own peace of mind I'd like to read through it again." They'd actually made two copies; his set was at the hotel, but this woman didn't need to know that.

"Suit yourself," the woman replied, and Jackson felt a moment of relief. She got up and unlocked the door to the records room, and Jackson went inside. He didn't have a problem locating the file because he remembered exactly where it was. He carried it out to the front desk.

"Do you mind if I sit here?" he asked courteously.

The clerk observed him with a puzzled look and Jackson thought she was going to refuse, but then she said, "Go ahead."

Jackson settled himself across from her desk. He wanted to talk to her and he was waiting for the appropriate moment. When he began to read through the papers again, something caught his eye.

"Could you please explain this for me?" he murmured politely.

"What?" she asked in an impatient voice.

He pointed to some numbers and letters on the bottom of one page. "What does that mean?"

Her eyes followed his finger. "Those are hospital codes. We don't use them anymore, but we did back then."

He'd figured that much, and he tried not to let the frustration show on his face. "But what do they *mean?*"

She walked around the desk and began to put files in a box. "I can't give you that information. It's private."

A sense of elation came over him. She knew something, all right, and he'd get it out of her.

"I'm sorry, I didn't catch your name," he said charmingly.

She glanced at him through narrowed eyes. "It's Agnes Snell."

"Ms. Snell, I'm trying to find my daughter. Please help me."

"I can't help you," she replied sternly, then picked up the box and carried it inside the warehouse. In a minute she was back and sank down in her chair.

Jackson reached into his wallet and pulled out some money. He laid a hundred dollar bill on the desk in front of her. "Will that change your mind?"

Her eyes brightened and he knew he had her. He just had to give her a little more incentive. He laid another hundred on the desk. "I want to know what the codes mean. That's all."

She kept staring at the money. "I'm close to retirement. I can't jeopardize that."

"No one will hear about it from me."

Still she hesitated and Jackson had to do some fast thinking. "A lot of people know about these codes, don't they?"

"Sure."

"There's no reason for anyone to think I got the information from you. Besides, I told you—I'm not talking." He paused. "Come on, Ms. Snell, help me."

In an instant he could see she'd made up her mind. One hand stretched out and snatched the money off the desk. "You won't like it," she snapped, stuffing the money into the pocket of her skirt.

He frowned. "What do you mean?"

She got up and circled the desk and studied the paper in his hand. "These codes represent the condition of mother and child when they left the hospital."

"It basically says that in the file," he reminded her.

"That's the condition of mother and child when the baby was delivered and afterward. The codes are the condition at the time they *left* the hospital. It's for hospital use only."

"And," he prompted, for he sensed a big *and* after her words.

She pointed to the first set of numbers. "That says the mother went home in good condition. The numbers at the end are the date and time she was released." Her finger moved to the next set. "That gives the same information about the baby."

Jackson stared at the dates. They were identical. They both went home the same day. He glanced up at Ms. Snell waiting for her to explain.

She raised an eyebrow. "I see you caught it."

"The mother and baby were released the same day, so what?"

"I think you're in denial. The mother and baby went home together."

Jackson shook his head. "No, that's not true. Emily was here yesterday and she doesn't have our child."

Ms. Snell reached over and turned the page and pointed to a signature. "She signed it stating that the information is true."

Jackson sat stunned and in shock as he stared at Emily's signature. He couldn't believe it. No, he *wouldn't* believe it. There had to be a mistake.

"If an adoption agency had picked up the baby, the code would be on the bottom, as would the date and time," she told him.

Something clicked in his chaotic mind. "Time—what time was the mother released?"

She looked down at the paper. "Ten forty-three."

"And the baby?"

"Ten fifty-two."

Around the same time. Mother and baby left around the same time. He shook his head to rid himself of the feeling that threatened to overtake him.

Ms. Snell walked back to her chair and sat down. "If you ask me, Dr. Cooper told you a pack of lies." She put a heavy emphasis on the word *doctor* and Jackson didn't miss it.

"She wouldn't lie," he shouted, and didn't even realize he was shouting until he heard his voice echo around the cavernous room.

Ms. Snell's eyebrows shot up in alarm, but she didn't stop. "She's a doctor and probably knows all about the codes, but she didn't say a word, did she?"

Jackson stood. "There has to be another reason," he muttered under his breath. "There has to be." His gaze swung to Ms. Snell. "Is there a Miller or Seals adoption agency?"

Ms. Snell lowered her eyes and avoided answering.

Jackson wasn't letting her off that easily. He hit the desk with his fist; papers and pencils bounced. "Answer me."

She pulled back, fear in her eyes. "I think you'd better—"

He cut her off. "And I think you'd better answer me."

"Just calm down," she warned.

"Then answer the question."

"No, there's not a Miller or Seals adoption agency that I know of."

He straightened, and knew she was still hiding something. He had to force her hand. Leaning in close, he said, "I can go to the head of the hospital and tell him that for money you gave me confidential information. That should blow your retirement all to hell—or you can tell me what you know about the adoption agency. It's your choice."

Ms. Snell drew a sharp breath. "You said you wouldn't."

"That was before I knew you were concealing a critical fact."

She twisted her hands. "It won't help you."

"Just tell me."

"It's not Miller or Seals. It was the Miller Steels Agency."

"Was?"

"They sold out years ago. It's now called The Haven."

Jackson scratched his head in confusion. "I don't understand why you wanted to keep that a secret. I'm sure it's a matter of public record."

"Because I'm too close to retirement to get involved in whatever scam Dr. Cooper is pulling. Very clever the way she couldn't remember the agency but managed to twist the names. She's not fooling me. She's only fooling you.''

"Dr. Cooper is not lying," he said tightly, "and she's not pulling a scam."

"Whatever," she snapped irritably. "Now, will you please leave my office?"

"Not until you give me the address of The Haven."

"My God!" She glared at him. "You're not planning on bothering those people, too."

"The address," he persisted.

She quickly scribbled something on a piece of paper. "They're not going to tell you a thing," she mumbled, "because there's nothing to tell." She handed him the paper. "Dr. Cooper knows where her daughter is, but for some reason of her own she's keeping the information from you."

He crumpled the paper in his clenched fist and stalked out, letting the door slam behind him.

Outside he paced back and forth by his car, too wound up to drive. Emily wasn't lying to him. He knew that beyond the shadow of a doubt. He couldn't explain the codes, but there was an explanation and he intended to find it.

He jumped in the car and headed for the address on the paper. It didn't take him long to find the four-story gray stone building. He parked in the nearby lot and made his way to the front door. As he stepped into the foyer, he came to a complete standstill. There were several girls in the lobby and several more in the adjoining TV room. They were all young, in their teens, and very pregnant. For a moment he was paralyzed by one of life's dark realities—these girls were waiting to give their babies away— like Emily had. But Emily hadn't lived here. She'd lived with an aunt.

He was staring, but he couldn't help himself. He

couldn't stop thinking that these babies had fathers, fathers who probably knew nothing of their child's existence and—he had to admit—probably didn't want to. He wondered how he would've reacted if Emily had been able to get in touch with him. Would he have been happy or upset? He couldn't honestly answer that question because he didn't know. So much had been going on in his life. Things had been so different then, but now...now he wanted his daughter more than anything in the world... His daughter and Emily.

A woman approached him. "Can I help you?"

Jackson glanced at her. She was a tall, older woman with gray hair, obviously someone in charge. "Yes, I'd like to get some information."

"Come this way," she said, and led him into an inner office. She walked to a credenza and picked up several brochures. "These pamphlets will answer all your questions." She held them out to him. "Is it a daughter or a friend?"

Jackson blinked in confusion; then he understood. She had assumed he was interested in the home for a family member. He shook his head. "No, no, you misunderstood me."

Her eyes widened. "I have?"

"Yes, I need information on an adoption that took place almost eighteen years ago."

The woman bristled. "I'm sorry. We don't divulge that kind of information."

"It's important. I have to find my daughter."

"I'm sorry, but the girls and the babies are our top priority. We do everything we can to ensure their privacy."

Jackson inhaled deeply, trying to think of a way to reach this woman. "Can you just tell me if the adoption took place? That's all I need to know. Surely that wouldn't compromise anyone's privacy."

"No, all information is private and confidential." The answer came quick and sharp.

"I could get a court order."

"Go ahead," she replied, unconcerned. "Our lawyers have blocked those before. Now, I'd appreciate it if you'd leave." With that, she turned and took a seat at a desk, her back to him.

Jackson was trying not to let his anger or frustration get the better of him when he noticed a young girl standing by a filing cabinet. She wasn't pregnant; that was the first thing he noticed. The second was that her clothes were tight and revealing, her hair bleached blond. She was chewing gum. All of a sudden she winked and smiled.

Disconcerted, he left the office. All the way to his car he thought about the odd incident. He didn't immediately know why he was so taken aback, but then he did. The girl was obviously flirting, and he'd been there, done that before, but never with a girl young enough to be his daughter. That was what threw him and he wondered if his daughter might be promiscuous. God, he hoped not.

He sat in his car for a long time, thinking, and finally decided he could use this flirtation to his advantage. The older woman wasn't letting him anywhere near the records, but the young girl might. Yes, she just might.

He waited the rest of the afternoon. The girl came out at five o'clock. She hopped into a pickup truck with a young man at the wheel. As they drove away, Jackson continued to watch for the older woman. By seven, he realized she probably lived on the premises. With a deep sigh, he started his car. He'd be back tomorrow. The woman had to leave sometime and when she did, he'd have a talk with the girl.

As he entered his hotel room, the phone was ringing, and he lunged for it. "Hello," he said, out of breath.

"Jackson?" Emily's voice came through soft and vibrant just as if she was in the room. He felt a soothing, warm sensation and lay back on the bed, letting that feeling ease away the frustrations of the day. This was what he needed. Emily.

"Jackson, are you there?" A worried tone entered her voice.

"Yes, I'm here," he answered. "How are you? How's your mom?"

"I'm fine, just feeling frustrated because I can't be with you."

He knew what *that* felt like.

"Mom is stable. They have her on oxygen and an IV and they've increased her heart medication." Emily was talking and he forced himself to listen to what she was saying instead of the tone of her voice. "Becca says she didn't eat or drink much of anything since I left and she's dehydrated. She brings all this on herself and I just..."

He heard the pain in her voice and he wanted to hold her, be with her, but could only try to reassure her. "Don't worry. I'm sure she'll get better, and I'm doing some checking on my own."

"Have you found anything?" she asked eagerly.

He paused, not wanting to tell her about the accusations of that awful woman at the records department. He'd tell her later when they were together and could sort through the inconsistencies. But he did tell her the other news. "I found the adoption agency."

There was silence for a second, then she asked in a shaky voice, "Oh Jackson, are you sure?" In that instant, if there'd been any doubts in his head, they vanished. Emily wasn't lying to him. She was as anxious to find their daughter as he was.

"Yes, but it's not Miller or Seals. It's the Miller Steels Agency."

"How did you figure it out?"

"The woman at the records office told me."

"But yesterday she said—"

He broke in. "Today she was a little more cooperative."

"How did you accomplish that?"

"I'll tell you later." *Among other things.* "I went over to the agency, which is now called The Haven, but they wouldn't tell me a thing. I'm not giving up, though. I intend to get some answers."

"Oh, I miss you." Longing filled every word.

"When can you come back?"

"I don't know. Becca's upset. She's afraid Mom's going to die and that it's her fault. And she has the prom on Saturday and I feel I need to be here for her, since Mom's in the hospital. But, but..."

"But what?"

"I want to be with you." The longing was so intense that all he wanted to do was comfort her.

"Just take care of your family and I'll take care of things here."

"Jackson."

"Hmm?"

"Promise if you find out where *she* is, you won't go there without me. Promise you won't do anything without me."

He swallowed. "I won't."

"I've waited so long to even hope and now...now..."

"We'll find her."

"You keep saying that, and I'm beginning to believe you."

"Oh, Emily." He rested his head on the pillow and closed his eyes. "This bed is gonna be awful lonely to-night." He paused. "Just keep talking to me."

He could feel her smile. "I don't think talking will be quite the same thing."

"You're right about that." His face split into a grin. Oh, he missed her, needed her. No one, not that crazy records lady or anyone else, could make him have doubts about her. He'd done that once, when she'd first told him about their daughter. He wouldn't make that mistake again.

They talked for a while longer, each reluctant to hang up. Later Jackson ordered room service. He didn't feel like dining without her.

As EMILY HUNG UP the phone, Becca strolled into the kitchen. They'd just gotten back from the hospital. Tommy had driven behind them, and Becca had stayed outside to talk to him. They were making plans for the prom. Shortly after, Tommy drove home and Becca joined Emily in the kitchen.

"Can we have pizza tonight?" Becca asked, getting a soda out of the fridge.

"No, we're not having pizza," Emily answered.

"Jeez, sometimes you're just like Mom," Becca complained. "Ginger's mom has pizza all the time, so I don't see why we can't have it once in a while."

"Ginger mom is—" Emily stopped, realizing she'd been about to criticize Ginger's mom—something her mother did on a regular basis. Maybe she *was* like her mother. No, she would never be.

"Okay, we'll have pizza," she decided in a flash.

"Oh, Em, you're the greatest." Becca beamed, and sat across from Emily at the kitchen table, sipping her drink.

After a moment, she asked, "Were you talking to him when I walked in?"

"Yes, I was talking to Jackson."

"I'll bet he's mad 'cause you had to come home."

"No, Jackson is very considerate. He understands that I need to be with my family right now."

"'Cause Mom's sick." Becca fiddled with her drink and Emily knew what she was thinking.

"Becca, you're not the reason Mom is sick. You know that, don't you?"

Becca didn't look up. "It's hard to think anything else because she tells me that all the time."

"Oh, Becca." Emily got up and hugged her. "Mom had a heart condition before you were born."

"Yes." Becca sniffed. "But I make it worse. I'm always upsetting her."

"So am I, but we can't keep blaming ourselves."

"I suppose." Becca sniffed again, then became quiet. "Em?"

"What?"

"She's not going to die, is she?"

"No, I don't think this is Mom's time to die. She'll be home soon and things will be back to normal."

"I hope so." Silence for a moment, then Becca asked, "When will you be going to see…him?"

Emily had noticed that she never said Jackson's name and wondered why. "His name is Jackson."

"Yeah, whatever," she mumbled.

Emily frowned, not understanding this attitude. "You've never met Jackson. Why don't you like him?"

"I don't like what he did to you—getting you pregnant and then leaving."

Emily cupped Becca's face and tilted her head so she could meet her eyes. "He didn't know I was pregnant and he had no reason to think that I was. We used protection, but it didn't work. Please don't judge Jackson until you get to know him. I guarantee you're going to like him. He'll spoil you rotten just like I do.''

"No, he won't," Becca said in a hurt voice. "He'll find your daughter and then you won't be interested in me anymore. You'll have *her*."

"Becca, Becca." Emily sighed, tucking Becca's hair behind her ears. She was jealous, plain and simple. She didn't want anyone to take her place in Emily's life. "You're my baby sister and the light in my otherwise dreary world. That'll never change—even if we find our daughter. She'll be almost eighteen and have her own family, but I need to see her. I have to know she's happy. Even then, I'll only be her biological mother—the woman who gave her away."

Becca's eyes grew stormy. "She'd better not ever say that to you. I'll slap her face."

Emily remembered her saying similar things about Jackson and knew that Becca just didn't want her to be hurt. She was fiercely protective, just as Emily was toward her. Despite the difference in their ages, they had a close bond.

Emily smiled into her eyes. "No, you won't. If we find her, you're going to love her as much as we do and you'll have a lot in common, being so close in age and all." Emily's voice grew dreamy. "She probably has Jackson's green eyes and my dark hair and a feisty in-your-face attitude, just like you."

Becca watched Emily's enraptured expression. "You really love her, don't you?"

"Yeah." Emily blinked back tears. "It's a mother thing, but it'll never affect the way I feel about you."

They embraced. "I know," Becca mumbled into her shoulder. "I'm just being a jerk."

Emily kissed her forehead. "Don't worry about it. Now, let's order that pizza so we can go back to the hospital." Emily walked to the phone.

"Em?"

"Hmm?"

"When I called you, he—I mean, Jackson answered the phone. Were you sleeping together?"

Emily stopped in her tracks. How did she explain this? With the truth, she immediately decided. She turned to face Becca. "I've loved Jackson since I was seventeen and I still do. We're adults, and we know what we're doing and what we want."

Becca flushed. "What's it like—sex, I mean?"

Emily thought about her answer, wanting to be truthful, yet cautious. "It can be the most wonderful, fulfilling experience if it's with someone you love. Otherwise, it's just a physical act."

"All my friends are having sex. I feel like an outcast."

"When you're ready, you'll know, and it won't have anything to do with your friends or anyone except the man you love."

"Jeez, you make it sound so special."

"It will be. Just be sure to use protection."

Becca nodded and Emily was glad Becca could talk to her. She knew Becca couldn't discuss sex or much of anything with their mother. She hoped her own daughter had someone to talk to, someone patient and understanding.

It struck her suddenly—her own daughter could be having sex. She could already be pregnant, could even have a child. She didn't know anything about her, so she had to prepare herself for anything. Her daughter was a grown woman, and for an instant, Emily was paralyzed by the immensity of it all.

## CHAPTER ELEVEN

EMILY WAS RELIEVED Jackson had found the adoption agency. That meant she didn't have to talk to Rose about it. She'd planned on doing it as soon as she reached the hospital, but after seeing her mother's condition, she'd changed her mind. Much as she wanted to find her daughter, she couldn't endanger Rose's health.

They left Rose resting comfortably. Emily's presence seemed to bolster her spirits and Emily knew why: Rose assumed she'd given up on the idea of finding her daughter. Emily didn't tell her otherwise. She didn't see the point; it would only upset her. Emily decided that what she did from now on would be her business. Her mother need not be involved. She and Jackson would find their daughter together…without interference from anyone.

That night, Emily lay curled up in bed, wishing Jackson's strong arms were around her and his hard body was against hers. That was all it was—wishful thinking. She had to stay with her family, and Jackson was busy gathering information in San Antonio. They'd be together soon but even that thought didn't ease the ache inside her—the ache of wanting his love.

JACKSON TOSSED AND TURNED. He knew the sheets had been changed, but he could smell Emily's scent, feel her presence, until the hunger in him grew to gigantic proportions. Unable to stand the torment, he got up and grabbed his laptop, determined to get his mind on other things. He went straight to the Internet, searching for information on the Miller Steels Agency and The Haven. At 2:00 a.m. he fell exhausted into bed, his head reeling from a profusion of facts, but he still didn't know if the agency had handled his daughter's adoption. The gray-haired lady at The Haven was named Mable Hale, and she was the director. The agency was known for legitimate adoptions and for the care and welfare of mothers and babies. That wasn't the information he was looking for, but it gave him an insight into the kind of place he was dealing with.

When Jackson woke up, he called Colton to check on things at the office. Everything was fine, so he showered and dressed and had breakfast, then headed for The Haven. He waited across the street…waited for the gray-haired lady to come out so he could talk to the young girl. Wearing sunglasses, he hoped Ms. Hale wouldn't recognize him if she just happened to notice him outside. Periodically he climbed out of the car to stretch his legs, walking no farther than the next intersection, all the while keeping his eyes on The Haven. He felt lunchtime was his best bet, but by two o'clock that hope faded. He strolled to a take-out place down the street and bought a hamburger and a malt, then he went back to his car and waited. A little after five, the young girl came out and got into the truck again. He was frustrated by his wasted day, but he wasn't giving up. Clearly the older woman didn't leave the building unless absolutely necessary.

He drove back to his hotel and logged on to the Internet. He wanted to find out everything he could about Mable Hale. The woman's whole life was the agency and the girls, which didn't leave him many options.

Later he talked to Emily; he hated to tell her he hadn't

found a thing, but she understood. They both knew this wasn't going to be easy.

The next morning Jackson drove to the agency and waited again. At three o'clock he was still waiting. He would wait forever if he had to. Mable Hale had to shop or keep appointments or perform some other sort of normal activity. And when she did…

His thoughts were interrupted by the sound of sirens, which grew closer and closer. An ambulance pulled into the parking lot and parked at the rear of the building. Starting his car, Jackson drove nearer to see what was happening. The paramedics jumped out and wheeled a stretcher through the back entrance. In less than a minute they rolled a pregnant girl onto the ambulance. Ms. Hale was right behind them and she got into the vehicle with the girl.

*Thank you, thank you*, resounded in his head. This was what he'd been waiting for. Ms. Hale would be gone for a while. When the ambulance entered traffic, sirens blaring, Jackson walked quickly to the front door.

As he hurried inside, he saw the blonde sitting at the desk. Yes, things were going his way.

The girl looked up and smiled. "Hey, you're back." She stood and sashayed to the counter. She was chewing gum again and wore a black miniskirt and a red tank top; her makeup was heavy and huge silver earrings dangled from her ears. She couldn't be more than eighteen.

He smiled his best smile. "Is Ms. Hale around?" he asked, just by way of conversation.

Smacking on the gum, she said, "Bridget's having her baby and she's scared, so Ms. Hale went with her to the hospital. Won't be back until later."

"Doesn't matter, I can talk to you."

"Okay." She giggled and chewed on the gum at such a fast rate it made him dizzy. "I was hoping you'd come back. We don't get many handsome guys like you in here.''

He raised an eyebrow. ''I think I'm too old for you.''

She shrugged. ''What's age? My boyfriend's only four years older than me and sometimes he uses me as a punching bag. Older guys are nicer.''

Jackson's eyes darkened. ''You stay with a guy who hits you?''

''It's better than living on the streets, and he just does it when he's drinking.''

''That's not a reason, it's an excuse, and you shouldn't stay with anyone who abuses you.'' Jackson could hear the censure in his voice and he had to back off, but it infuriated him that she didn't have more self-respect. There were probably a lot of girls like her, though, needing a home and willing to put up with anything in order to have a roof over their heads—maybe his own daughter. *Oh, God, no,* he prayed and fervently hoped she had morals and values and respect for herself.

He realized the girl was staring at him strangely and he brought his thoughts back to the reason he was here, which was hard because he'd been raised to have respect for women, and the idea of someone hitting this young girl filled him with disgust and anger. He took a deep breath and forced his personal feelings aside.

''I'm sure I sound like your dad,'' he said.

She rolled the gum around on her tongue. ''You don't look like my dad,'' she said. ''You look damn good and I bet you're *real* good,'' she added brashly, leaving little doubt as to what she was talking about. They were getting way off track and he had to turn this conversation to his advantage.

He smiled deeply. ''What did you say your name was?''

''I didn't, but if you're interested, it's Dawn Mercer.''

He leaned his elbows on the counter. "Dawn, I need your help."

Something in his voice must have alerted her, because her jaw stopped working and she took a step backward. "Hey, if it's about what you were asking Ms. Hale, you can forget it. She said no and that's final. I just got this job and I'm lucky to have it."

Jackson wasn't deterred by her negative response. He was sure he could get through to her. "This is important and I'd be so grateful.

She gazed at him from beneath lowered lids. "How grateful?"

Jackson knew it would take a lot more than two hundred dollars to get information from her. He assumed she was after money. The other possibility he didn't want to think about. Getting involved with this girl wasn't even a remote option. It was repulsive.

He reached for his wallet and laid ten one-hundred dollar bills on the counter.

The girl gasped and her mouth fell open, obviously in shock.

Jackson kept on, speaking persuasively. "This money can be yours. All you have to do is let me see Emily Ann Cooper's records."

"Gosh, I could get my own place," she mumbled. "I could go home. I haven't seen my grandma in three years."

"Where's home?" he asked.

"Lubbock."

"You can go to Lubbock and do a lot more with this money."

"Yeah," she answered, but she made no move to take the cash.

"Come on, Dawn, it's not a hard decision."

Her eyes jerked to his. "What if Ms. Hale catches us?"

"We have to hurry before she gets back. If she does, I'll take the blame. I'll say I sneaked past you or something. We don't have much time, so make up your mind."

"I don't have a key."

"But you know where the key is kept."

"Yeah," she said, but still she hesitated. Then all of a sudden she grabbed the money and went to the desk and came back with a key. "Come this way, and remember, I had nothing to do with this."

He followed her through the office and down a hall. "What year?" she asked over her shoulder.

When he told her, she stopped in her tracks and turned to face him. "Gosh, that's in the old filing room. I hate that place. It smells of dust and mildew."

"It doesn't matter," he said, almost afraid she was going to change her mind. "Just show me where it is and I'll do the looking."

She whirled around and walked to the end of the hall, where she inserted the key into a lock. The metal door swung open and they stepped inside. As the dust filled his nostrils, he sneezed. The room was as unpleasant as she'd said. Filing cabinets lined each wall to the ceiling and a small table sat in the middle. There was no outside light of any kind. The place was like a tomb, and he shook off a sense of foreboding.

A light hung from the ceiling. She reached up to pull the dangling string. "I have to be at my desk. You've got ten minutes, then you have to leave. If Ms. Hale comes back, I'll start coughing and you'd better hide until I can get you outta here."

"Fine, thank you."

"The years are on the front of each cabinet, so it shouldn't be hard to find. Just be quick."

She was nervous. So was Jackson, but he wasn't quitting now. He glanced at the years on the cabinets and kept looking until he found the one he wanted. Then he searched for the letter *C*. He opened the drawer and a mildew smell met him. The papers were yellowed as if they'd gotten wet. He shuffled quickly through the files until…he saw it—Emily Ann Cooper. Elation ran through him. Ms. Snell had been lying. Miller Steels Agency *had* handled the adoption. He yanked the file out and carried it to the table and laid it under the light. His heart raced. In a moment, he'd know who had adopted their daughter.

He peered through the contents—just two pages, mostly information about Emily. The words at the bottom of the second page had his full attention. He couldn't believe it. It couldn't be true. But there it was in bold letters: ADOPTION CANCELED.

The pain started in his stomach and spread to his heart and held it in a vise until he couldn't breathe. He couldn't do anything but stare at the words.

"No," he moaned, sucking air into his tight lungs. Something was dreadfully wrong. Now he had to find out what. At the moment, though, he could barely think. He couldn't take his eyes off the words.

The girl rushed in. "What's taking so long? You have to get outta here." She noticed his ashen face. "What is it?"

"Tell me what this means," he said in a voice that didn't sound like his. He didn't even know why he was asking the question. He knew what the words meant, but he had to hear someone say them.

She peered over his arm. "That means the mother changed her mind and kept the baby."

*Kept the baby. Kept the baby.* The words circled around

and around in his head, but he refused to believe them. He wouldn't. There had to be a mistake.

"Are you sure?" he asked.

"Yeah, there'd be lots of info if the baby was adopted."

"I see. Does a mother often change her mind?" For some reason, he had to keep talking.

"Sure, I almost did."

His eyes focused on her face. "You had a baby?"

"Yeah, when I was fifteen."

"How old are you now?"

"Eighteen."

God, she was just a kid and had already lived more than most girls.

Her words penetrated his numb mind. "When my mom discovered I was pregnant, she kicked me out. I didn't have anywhere to go. The Haven took me in, on the condition that I give up my baby. I said fine. I was fifteen and I didn't have a job or know the first thing about raising a kid, but when he started to kick and move, he became real to me and I wanted to keep him. Then I met the adoptive parents and I saw they could give him a lot more than I could."

"So you gave him away?"

"Yeah."

"Do you think about him?"

"Sometimes, but then I tell myself I gave him the greatest gift of all—a chance at a life. If he was with me, my boyfriend would probably beat on him, too."

"What about the father?"

She shrugged. "He was sixteen and refused to admit it was his. Besides, we were too young to even think about being parents. Famous last words, huh?"

The girl's words washed over him as Jackson tried to

deal with painful emotions he couldn't assimilate or understand.

*Emily. Oh, Emily. What's going on?*

"Is the child you're looking for with the mother?"

"No, that's the problem. She's not with her mother. I don't know where she is."

"Gosh, I'm sorry, but you have to leave. Ms. Hale could come back at any minute, especially if it's a long labor."

Jackson closed the file and returned it to the filing cabinet, then Dawn pulled the light string and they left. She locked the door with a final-sounding click.

As they reached the office, Dawn kept glancing toward the door. It was time to go; that was very clear. On impulse he pulled out his wallet, removed all the cash and laid it in front of her. He knew it was about eight hundred. "Get rid of the abusive boyfriend and go home to your grandmother," he said. "Lose the bleached hair, heavy makeup and tight clothes. Have some respect for yourself and you'll find a man who will, too. Don't let anyone make you believe otherwise."

With that, he walked toward the front door, hoping that wherever his daughter was, she had someone looking out for her.

"Thank you," she called after him. He heard her pick up the phone and hoped she was dialing Lubbock, Texas.

JACKSON HURRIED OUTSIDE and inhaled deeply. He needed the fresh air and sunshine, needed to be somewhere other than that gloomy place. But he still felt confused and overwhelmed, even in the bright light of day, with the busy streets around him and people who seemed to have blank faces. He was alone, struggling to make sense of everything that was happening, but all he could see were those words: ADOPTION CANCELED. Nothing else registered.

At his car, he placed his palms flat on the hood, as if he could draw from it the stability he needed. He gulped in some air and saw her face—Emily's. He could hear the pain in her voice and see the sorrow in her eyes and he knew again that she wasn't lying to him. A shuddering breath escaped him and it released the tightness in his chest. *She wasn't lying to him.* Now that he'd firmly established that in his mind, he could go on. For a moment he'd been suspended in a realm of desolation and despair, but now he could breathe again. As long as he had faith in Emily, he could sort this out. And he would. First he had to find a way to tell her, though. How did he do that?

As he drove to his hotel room, thoughts ran riot in his head. If the adoption had been canceled, why didn't Emily know? Maybe a wealthy and powerful family had adopted their daughter and they'd wanted to make sure no one could trace the child. Money talked. He'd been in business long enough to know that. If a sufficient amount of money changed hands, the records at the hospital and the agency could have been altered to suit the purposes of the adoptive parents. That was the only explanation he could think of, and if it was true, they would never see their daughter. That left a bitter taste in his mouth.

Back in his room, he paced and paced until he thought his brain would explode with so many disturbing questions. He had to talk to someone or he'd go crazy. He picked up the phone and called his father, hoping he'd be in the house and not out fishing.

When Jackson heard his voice, he experienced a moment of relief. As always, George wanted to know how the search was developing. Jackson told him what he'd found. George seemed as puzzled as he was about the information.

"I just don't understand, son."

"I don't, either, but I'm trying to piece this together because I know Emily's not lying to me."

"Sounds like you and Emily have made progress."

"We have, and if I don't do anything else, I'm going to find our daughter—for her and for all the lousy years in between. I'm just scared."

"About what?" George asked.

Jackson told him about his suspicions of a wealthy couple having all the records altered.

"I guess it's a possibility, and I've also heard about babies being sold on the black market."

"I couldn't take that," he groaned.

"You have to be prepared, son," George said. "Because it appears that something's going on that shouldn't be."

"That's what I'm afraid of." He paused. "I saw the record of her birth at the hospital, but after that, there's nothing."

"What about a birth certificate?"

"The adoptive parents would've had that changed. The original is sealed in Austin. That would probably be my next step. I'll call my lawyer to see—hey, wait a minute!"

"What?" George asked excitedly.

"If everything was on the up-and-up, there should be a record of her birth at the courthouse," Jackson said, the blood pumping through his veins with accelerating speed. "I should've though of that, but my mind's short-circuited. I'll go…" He glanced at his watch and saw it was after five o'clock. "Damn, I can't make it in time. I'll go first thing in the morning."

"Good," George said. "That might answer some of your questions."

"I hope so." Jackson echoed the sentiments. "I'll call when I can."

"Oh, Jackson," George said before he could hang up.

"What?"

"Do you mind if I tell Maudie?"

Jackson wasn't sure what to say.

"She won't tell anyone. I just need to talk to someone."

Jackson knew the feeling. "Fine, but I don't want her calling me with a lot of questions, okay?"

"I'll make certain that doesn't happen."

Jackson had to grin. His dad had as much control over Aunt Maude as he had over the weather, but she was family and would learn about this eventually. And Jackson didn't want to keep it a secret. He wanted to shout it from the rooftops.

"I'm taking her out to dinner tonight," his father was saying.

"Glad to hear that. Tell her I said hi."

JACKSON STROLLED TO the River Walk and ordered dinner at the same place he and Emily had eaten that first night. But this time, the people, the camaraderie and the jovial atmosphere left him untouched. He missed Emily and he wanted to see her and talk to her. The need was so strong he had a hard time finishing his meal.

He went back to the room and called her. It was good to hear her voice, but it wasn't enough. He couldn't tell her what he'd found out, not over the phone. He had to see her face-to-face. He comforted himself with the thought that tomorrow he might have some answers and could put an end to these unsettling events.

EMILY HUNG UP THE PHONE with a frown. Something was different. She could hear it in Jackson's voice. She couldn't put her finger on what it was, but he wasn't as enthusiastic about finding their daughter as he'd been before. He seemed resigned or disillusioned. She couldn't decide which, and she wondered if there was something he wasn't telling her. Something bad. No, she wouldn't think like that. She just wished she could be with him, but he'd said he was going to the Bexar County courthouse to look for a birth certificate, which didn't make any sense because there wouldn't be one. After that, he planned to return to Rockport. That meant he did have something to tell her. She felt an uncanny sense of dread.

Becca burst into the room, drying her hair with a towel.

"Becca," Emily complained, "why did you wash your hair? We need to get to the hospital as soon as possible. I want to catch the doctor to see when we can bring Mom home. She's responding very well to the new medication."

Becca sat at her makeup table and ran her fingers through her long, wet hair. "What's the big deal? You've been there all day, and you can call the doctor."

Emily let out a long sigh. "Don't try my patience tonight."

Becca turned to face her. "What's the matter? You seem really tense."

"Nothing." Emily dismissed Becca's question with a wave of her hand.

"You're upset," Becca insisted. "You've talked to Jackson, haven't you."

Emily glanced down at her hands and didn't say anything.

Becca got up to sit beside her on the bed. "He hasn't found anything on your daughter?"

"No," Emily murmured.

Becca hugged her. "Sorry, Em."

"It's all right." Emily brushed away a tear. "I've been praying and hoping, but I guess it wasn't meant to be."

"Sorry," Becca said again, then her face brightened,

"Oh, I forgot to tell you. I volunteered you as a sponsor for the prom."

*"What?"* Emily's eyes opened wide.

"Well, one of the sponsors has the flu and Mrs. Becker was in a panic. I told her my big sister would be glad to fill in. Besides, don't you want to see if I get to be queen?"

Emily smiled, some of the sadness leaving her. "Yes, I wouldn't want to miss that."

"Good, 'cause I also volunteered you to help us decorate. We're having it in Corpus at a ballroom because our gym's too small."

"Becca!"

"Well, Mom and Dad don't like to do those kinds of things and I thought you would."

"I need to spend this time with Mom. That's why I'm here instead of with Jackson."

Becca's face fell and Emily cursed herself.

"You'd do it for *her,*" Becca mumbled.

Emily didn't have to ask who she was talking about. She knew. Becca was becoming very jealous of Emily's daughter—a daughter Becca felt was threatening their relationship.

Emily smoothed the wet strands of her sister's hair. "I'll do it for you, too."

"You will?" Becca asked hopefully.

"Yes, and Saturday when we get your hair done for the prom, we're getting it cut."

"Ah, jeez, Em. You're taking the fun out of it."

Emily smiled into her gorgeous eyes, knowing that no matter what happened she would always have Becca. She just wished Becca wasn't so jealous of her daughter. The odds of finding that elusive daughter were getting slimmer and slimmer. She quickly suppressed the sobs that welled up in her throat.

## CHAPTER TWELVE

JACKSON DIDN'T SLEEP MUCH. He was too nervous. He was up at dawn, ate breakfast in his room, then went for a walk. After that, he headed for the courthouse and waited for it to open. If their daughter was adopted, there'd be no record of her birth, except in her adoptive parents' name. He had to see if there was a birth record under *Baby Girl Cooper*. If not, he'd know with certainty that something underhanded had happened.

The woman at the desk was very polite and immediately directed him to someone else. Jackson thought this would be another runaround, but when he told the second woman what he wanted, she smiled and asked how he was related to the person on the certificate. He told her he was the baby's father. She said she'd need some identification. He wasn't surprised because he'd researched it on the Internet and knew exactly what the procedure was. They didn't give information out freely. He showed her his driver's license, his social security card and a copy from the hospital records that identified him as the father. She inspected the papers and said it would take a while, but she would get it. Jackson stood at the desk tapping his fingers impatiently, then stopped doing that, and started to pace. He couldn't be still.

When he saw the woman coming toward him with a piece of paper in her hand, his stomach tightened painfully and his breathing became labored. She had something—that meant...

She handed him the paper. "I'm sorry it took so long, but the child's name is on the certificate and I had to make sure I had the right one."

He stared at the birth certificate and everything in him shut down. He couldn't speak or move, he just stared at the names on the paper. *Mother: Emily Ann Cooper. Father: Jackson Scott Talbert.* Seeing his name on the legal document made it all so real—so agonizingly real. He had a daughter, and her name was... As he read the name, the numbness exploded into a dire awakening that chilled his whole body. It couldn't be. How could it?

"Sir? Sir?" He realized the woman was talking to him.

He blinked and tried to focus. "Yes?"

"Are you all right?"

He nodded, but he knew he wasn't. Things would never be right again. How could that be the name on his daughter's birth certificate? Was it a coincidence or something else? Did Emily know? Had she given their daughter this name? He should've asked her. Dammit, he should have asked, but he'd just assumed she hadn't named their baby. So many questions charged through his head. Still, he had a feeling that Emily didn't know about any of this. That it would be as much of a shock to her...

Jackson glanced at the woman. "Can I have this?"

"Once you pay the fee, it's all yours," she replied.

He laid the money on the counter. "Thank you," he said hoarsely. He walked away, the birth certificate clutched tightly in his hand.

He sat in his car and tried to make sense of what he was reading. He'd guessed that something underhanded had happened with the adoption, but he'd never expected this.

How long he sat there he didn't know. He couldn't stop

looking at the paper and he realized he had to show it to Emily. Maybe she could explain, but again he had the sinking feeling that Emily was in the dark. That worried him.

Before he told her, he had to have more facts. He didn't want to upset her needlessly. The name could be a fluke. There had to be an answer that would explain everything, and he knew the truth lay in Rockport. How could he get the information he needed? The courthouse would only release information to a close relative or... He hurried back to his hotel and called Colton.

"What's up?" Colton asked.

"I need the name of the private investigator who helped you get the goods on that girl who claimed you were the father of her child."

There was a long pause. "What are you talking about?"

"I need a private investigator and I don't have a lot of time. You gonna help me or not?"

"Slow down and tell me *why* you need an investigator."

Jackson told him what he suspected and how he needed someone to get records from the courthouse in Rockport.

"Damn, Jackson, I'll call him, but I doubt he can do it on such short notice. He runs a ranch outside San Antonio and he only leaves for special cases."

"I'll pay whatever he asks," Jackson said. "Just talk to him."

"I will, and I'll get back to you."

"Do it now. I'll be waiting."

Jackson paced his hotel room, constantly glancing at his watch. If the man refused to do it, he supposed he could get someone else. But Colton had liked the investigator and said he was honest and straightforward. That was the type of person Jackson wanted. Someone he could trust.

The phone rang and he yanked it up.

"You're in luck—he'll do it," Colton said. "His name is Ethan Ramsey and he'll be calling you in a few minutes."

"Thanks, Colton." Jackson heaved a sigh of relief. "How did you get him to agree?"

"I used the old Prescott charm and, of course, he's a friend of the family."

"Thanks again. I owe you for this one."

"Yeah, and I'm keeping a list."

Jackson could hear laughter in his voice; he needed Colton's sense of humor right now. He was wavering between insanity and hysteria.

"Jackson." Colton was calling his name. "I hope it turns out the way you want."

"I'm not sure about anything. I'm in a state of shock."

"Good luck, and call if I can do anything else."

Jackson hung up and paced again, waiting for the phone to ring. When it did, he took a couple of deep breaths before he answered it.

Ethan Ramsey had a strong, masculine voice and Jackson immediately liked the sound of him—direct and to the point. Jackson told him what he wanted, and Ethan said it shouldn't be a problem. They arranged to meet at the Aransas County courthouse in Rockport in three hours.

Jackson quickly packed and checked out. He left San Antonio at eleven-thirty and was in Rockport before three. The urge to call Emily was strong, but he had to wait. He had to have final proof.

A white Chevrolet pickup truck drove up beside him and a tall man wearing a cowboy hat and boots clambered out. From what Colton had told him, the man had to be Ethan Ramsey. He walked with a slight limp; Jackson knew he was an ex-FBI agent who'd been shot in the line of duty. He was a well-decorated law officer, another reason Jackson trusted him.

Jackson got out and they shook hands. He felt the calluses, which probably epitomized Ethan Ramsey—a man unafraid of hard work and unconcerned about appearances.

They talked for a moment, then Ethan went into the courthouse. He was out in fifteen minutes, shaking his head. The document Jackson wanted wasn't there. Frustration overwhelmed him, but he wouldn't give up. There had to be proof, but where? Ethan said he could go to Austin next week and check the records, but first he suggested they look in Corpus Christi, since the towns weren't that far apart. Jackson was eager to try anything.

Forty-five minutes later, Jackson watched Ethan walk into the Nueces County courthouse. He leaned against his car and waited, hoping Ethan would find something to explain their daughter's birth certificate. When Ethan came out carrying papers, Jackson's heart raced into his throat.

Ethan handed him a piece of paper. "I think this is what you need."

Jackson carefully read the birth certificate. It was just as he suspected, but it still didn't make sense. "Yes, but..."

Ethan passed him another document. "This might help clarify it."

Jackson's hand shook as he read it. "Oh, my God, this explains everything." He swallowed. "How did you get these?"

"I showed the county clerk my identification and told her about the case I was working on. Usually when you're up front with people, they respond in kind. When I saw the first document, I asked for the other, and bingo—there it was. That's the only way the scenario you described would make sense."

"Thank you," Jackson said. "I couldn't have done this

without you. You can't get information unless you're a close relative or an investigator.''

"It keeps people honest," Ethan replied. "If that's all, I'll drive back to my ranch."

"Yes," Jackson said in a daze, holding out a check.

Ethan shook his head. "No, thanks, Colton's taken care of everything."

Jackson frowned. "But he shouldn't have. This is—''

"Don't worry about it." They shook hands and Ethan Ramsey walked to his truck.

Jackson just kept staring at the papers. *Proof.* He now had conclusive proof and it would devastate Emily. How did he tell her? Oh, God, how did he tell her this? He had to find her as soon as possible.

He called the hospital and spoke to Owen, who said she'd gone with Becca to do decorations for the prom. He told Owen he'd call her later. He drove back to Rockport and checked into the Holiday Inn and ordered a bite to eat. Later, he lay on the bed staring at his daughter's birth certificate. It was real. *She* was real…now—and she had a name. He wanted to call his father, but he had to tell Emily first.

He called her again, but Owen said she was still with Becca. He wanted to go and find her, but he didn't trust himself…not yet. Instead, he went for a walk on the beach.

WHEN EMILY GOT IN, Owen told her Jackson had called. She phoned the hotel in San Antonio right away and was informed that he'd checked out. That meant he was on his way to Rockport and could arrive at any minute. She waited and waited, which was pure torture. By midnight he still wasn't there. Where *was* he?

She finally went to bed. When she woke up, there still was no sign of Jackson. She began to get an uneasy feeling. Unable to just sit around, she went to the hospital, leaving a message for Jackson if he called or came by the house. She didn't want to miss him.

Emily's time was running out. She had to be back at work next week and they weren't any closer to finding their daughter than when they'd started. Why hadn't Jackson called back? And why wasn't he here this morning?

Rose was eating breakfast when she walked into the room. The color was back in her cheeks and she had far more energy. The new medicine was working; in fact, her doctor had promised she could go home the following week.

"Emily Ann, I'm so glad to see you," her mother said. Rose's disposition had improved tremendously and they could actually have a conversation without getting into an argument.

"How are you feeling?"

"Much better." She nibbled on a piece of toast. "Especially since you've given up on that awful idea of finding your daughter."

Emily sat in a visitor's chair close to the bed. "Why was it awful?" she couldn't keep from asking.

Rose stopped eating. "Because it's too late. She's grown and has her own life now. Finding her would only hurt her—and you. It's best to leave it alone."

Emily took a long breath. "I can't," she said truthfully. "Try to understand that."

"I wish I could." Rose pushed food around on her plate. "But that Talbert man has put these ideas in your head."

Emily stood and reached for her mother's hand. On impulse she kissed it. She felt Rose stiffen. "I love him, Mom. I've always loved him."

"You don't mean that!"

"Yes, I do, and you'll have to accept him as part of my life."

"Emily Ann…"

"No." Emily held up a finger. "Just be happy for me. That's all I want from you."

Rose stared down at her food and didn't say another word, which Emily took as a good sign.

"I can't stay long," she said, changing the subject. "I've got to help Becca get ready for the prom. I'm taking her to have her hair cut."

"She's very picky about that hair," Rose mumbled.

"I know, but it needs a trim."

Rose glanced at her. "Rebecca says you're going, too. That you're filling in as a sponsor."

"Yes, and I'll take pictures so you can see everything."

There was a pause, then Rose said, "I'd like that." Emily sensed she was going to say something completely different—something about Emily missing her prom and how it was her own fault. The fact that she didn't voice her opinion meant things were continuing to improve.

When Jackson woke up, it was noon. He stared at the clock, thinking it *had* to be wrong. But it wasn't. He hadn't slept much the last few nights and it'd caught up with him. Damn, damn, damn. Emily was probably wondering what had happened to him.

He called her immediately. She answered on the first ring, and he melted into her voice, needing her more than he would've thought possible.

"Jackson, where are you?" she asked anxiously. "I've been so worried!"

"In Rockport. At the Holiday Inn."

"Oh, I wish I'd known. I'm sorry I wasn't here last

night, but I waited and you never called back. I didn't know what to think.''

"I fell asleep,'' he admitted. "I didn't wake up until just now.''

"I couldn't imagine where you'd gone after leaving San Antonio.''

"That shouldn't be too hard to figure out, Emily. I'll always come to you. You can count on that from now on.''

"Oh, Jackson.'' Her insides quivered at the promise in his voice.

Giggling voices interrupted the wonderful moment.

"Who's that?'' Jackson asked.

"Becca and her girlfriends. I'm taking them to get their hair and nails done for the prom.''

"Oh,'' Jackson replied, feeling as if he was never going to get a moment alone with her. "When can you come here?''

"I don't know. Becca volunteered me as a sponsor, so I have to go to the prom. Now I don't want to. Oh, Jackson, I have to see you.''

When she mentioned the prom, he heard an eagerness in her voice. She'd missed her own prom and all the delightful things a girl experiences in her senior year. Maybe he could make a small part of that up to her.

"How would you like a date?''

"What?''

"I'm offering my services as an escort.''

"Jackson, do you mean it?''

"Of course. It seems to be the only way I'll see you tonight.''

He heard a bubbly laugh and he knew it wasn't Becca. Emily was happy. For tonight they could both be happy.

"What time do you want me to pick you up?''

"Seven-thirty.''

"I'll be there."

Before he could hang up, she asked quickly, "Do you have anything to tell me about our daughter?"

He swallowed painfully. "Nothing that can't wait."

"Are you sure?"

"Yes, Emily. We'll talk about it later."

As much as Jackson wanted to tell her, he recognized that this wasn't the right time. He wouldn't ruin this night for her...or Becca. Tomorrow they would face the cold reality together.

EMILY DIDN'T HAVE TIME to wonder what Jackson had found out. If it was important, he would've told her. Just another dead end, she thought, beginning to see that her daughter was lost to her forever. She had hoped and prayed for a miracle, but it seemed as if a miracle wasn't going to happen. In her heart, though, she would never give up and neither would Jackson.

She didn't dwell on it for the rest of the day. She needed all her energy just to keep up with Becca and her friends. After Becca's hair was cut and styled, she had her nails done. While the girls were busy, Emily slipped away to a clothing shop, hoping to find a suitable dress. She'd planned on wearing a simple outfit, but now that Jackson was taking her she wanted something special. She wanted to be beautiful, and she was as excited as Becca and her friends.

She found a deep-purple formfitting dress with a V-neck and long sleeves. It was ankle-length and had a slit up one side. As she stared at herself in the mirror, she decided it was perfect—sleek and elegant without being overstated, and it fit like a dream.

JACKSON READ THE LEGAL PAPERS once more, then he put them away...for now. He drove to Corpus Christi to buy a suit. He hadn't brought anything dressy and he knew tonight would be formal. He would make the evening special for Emily, he vowed. They would have tonight to sustain them for the heartache ahead.

As he rang the Coopers' doorbell, he was as nervous as a teenage boy. He hadn't seen Emily in almost a week and he desperately needed to be with her. When she opened the door, his breath caught in his throat. He'd never seen her like this. She was more than beautiful, she was literally breathtaking, and he couldn't take his eyes off her, from the glossy hair hanging loose around her shoulders, to the curves molded by the purple dress, to the dark sultry eyes. For a moment he felt as if he'd stepped back in time and was seeing the young Emily. But this Emily wasn't a girl; she was all woman and he loved her.

"Hi." He smiled invitingly, and her heart missed a beat. When he smiled like that, it made her senses spin wildly and her knees grow weak. She stared into his gorgeous green eyes, then took in his magnificent physique in the black suit and tie. He was handsome, compassionate, caring—everything she'd ever wanted in a man…and more.

"Come in," she said, and stepped aside, glad she could actually move because her legs were still rubbery. She collected her purse. "Dad," she called. "Jackson's here. I'm leaving." Becca and Tommy had already left for their friend Joni's house, where they'd wait for the limo that was taking several couples to the prom.

As she turned around, she saw that Jackson had a corsage in his hand and was removing it from the box. Without a word he pinned the white orchid to the front of her dress. His fingers brushed against her breast and a warm erotic sensation awakened in her. They gazed at each other, both lost in the moment and in each other.

"Emily Ann," Owen said from the kitchen doorway, and they slowly turned to him. "Hi, Jackson," he added.

"Owen," Jackson acknowledged, and as their eyes met Jackson realized that Owen knew something about their daughter. He was the one who'd picked Emily up from the hospital, so he was aware who'd picked up the baby. By the end of the weekend, they would all know.

"Make sure Rebecca behaves herself and keep a close eye on her," Owen said to Emily.

"Dad." Emily sighed in annoyance. "This is her prom night and she deserves to have some fun."

"Maybe," Owen admitted grudgingly. "But you know how your mother is, and I don't want anything to upset her."

"Yes, Dad, we're all aware how Mom is," she replied with more sarcasm than she'd intended. "I'll make sure Becca behaves," she added. "I'll see you in the morning."

"Have a good time," Owen called as they walked out the door.

WHEN THEY ENTERED the ballroom with all the glittering decorations, Emily felt as if it was *her* prom. She was floating about three feet off the floor, especially with Jackson's arm around her waist. Decorating had been a huge, time-consuming task but the place looked wonderful, with lots of fresh flowers arranged everywhere. They joined the other sponsors and were told it was their job to watch the kids and to make sure things didn't get out of control. Sponsors sat at various points around the room. Emily and Jackson were positioned not far from the stage, where a band was starting to play.

There was a decorated gazebo at the other end and several couples were having their pictures taken. Emily took out her camera, ready to get photos of Becca. She saw her some distance away, dancing with Tommy. She glanced at Jackson, who was sitting next to her with an arm around her chair.

"Isn't she beautiful?" she murmured. She wore the jacket with the pink dress, though there were lots of girls wearing strapless dresses, and Emily was proud of her. At least she was trying to do what their mother wanted. Her dark hair hung down her back in a shiny mane and it looked so much better now that the ends had been trimmed. Emily's diamond studs sparkled in her ears.

"Yes," Jackson answered. "Because she looks a lot like her big sister."

"You'll get a reward for that." She smiled into his eyes.

"I can't wait."

"You'll have to."

He groaned in answer, his hand playing with a strand of her hair.

They watched the kids dance, sitting there in companionable silence, and at times it was amusing, especially during the fast songs. During the slow songs, though, she held her breath. Some of the kids were draped around each other, a little too close for Emily's comfort. She found herself looking for Becca, but she and Tommy danced with a reasonable space between them—close but not suffocating. Maybe she *was* a little like her mother, but Emily didn't want Becca to experience life too soon, too fast— like she had.

The lights came on and the principal took the stage to announce the king and queen of the prom. Emily reached for Jackson's hand and held it tight. He winked at her nervousness.

The principal gave a small speech and read out the names of all the nominees. When Becca's name was read, her hand tightened.

"The queen for this year's prom is—" The principal opened an envelope "—Rebecca Ann Cooper."

"Oh, my God," Emily breathed, tears welling up in her eyes. Becca was obviously having the same reaction. She seemed stunned, but she was smiling widely as she walked onstage to be crowned. Everyone stood and clapped, but no one clapped louder than Emily and Jackson.

The principal called for silence so he could read the name of the king. "Thomas Lee Wilson." Applause erupted again, and Emily snapped several pictures before the lights dimmed and the king and queen returned to the floor for a special dance. Becca waved at Emily and she waved back, wiping away a tear.

"Are you crying?" Jackson asked in a teasing tone.

"No," she denied, then added, "Yes, I'm so happy for her."

"Me, too," Jackson murmured.

The boys started to cut in to get a dance with the queen, and the girls did likewise with Tommy. Emily's heart swelled as she watched Becca laughing and having a good time, and she wished her mother could see this, but then she realized Rose wouldn't appreciate it as much as she did.

Finally Becca broke away and ran over to Emily and hugged her. "Can you *believe* it, Em? Can you believe it?"

"Yes, it's wonderful." Emily gave her a shaky smile. "You're wonderful."

"Jeez, Em." Becca seemed embarrassed, which was very rare indeed.

Emily glanced at Jackson and made the introductions. "Becca, this is Jackson Talbert, and Jackson, this is my sister, Becca."

Becca smiled broadly. "Hi."

"Hi, Becca," Jackson said, also smiling. He stepped forward and asked, "May I have a dance with the queen?"

Becca's mouth fell open, and she stared at Emily, who was staring at Jackson.

"I suppose," Becca mumbled. Jackson slipped his arm around her waist and she placed her hand in his. Slowly they began to move around the floor.

Emily gazed after them in shock. She couldn't imagine why Jackson had invited Becca to dance. But then, he was trying to please her, she decided. Tommy was standing beside her fidgeting, so she asked him for a dance.

Jackson danced for a while in silence, then he said, "You're very beautiful tonight. You look a lot like your sister."

"Yeah, people always say that, but I'll never be as beautiful or smart or anything as she is. She's just about perfect."

"You love her a great deal."

Becca's eyes narrowed to mere slits. "I sure do, so you'd better not hurt her again."

"I'll never hurt Emily again," he assured her.

A smile wreathed her face.

"Why are you smiling?"

"The way you said her name—all romantic and gooey. Like you love her."

"I do," he admitted without hesitation.

"That's good, 'cause she loves you, too."

His pulse raced. "Did she tell you that?" he asked, but he didn't have to. He knew she did. She couldn't make love with him the way she had *without* love, but he needed to hear it from someone else—someone close to her.

"Sure, several times, so you'd better not hurt her," she warned a second time.

"Don't worry, and congratulations," he said as the song ended, and they returned to Emily.

Becca kissed Emily and strolled off with Tommy to dance. Emily raised an eyebrow at Jackson. "Aren't you the chivalrous one."

He grinned. "Yeah, that's me."

"I think you took her breath away, not to mention mine."

"Why?"

"I guess I wasn't expecting it."

He slipped a hand around her waist. "Here's something else you're probably not expecting. Let's dance."

"We can't," she said, and took a step backward. "We're sponsors."

He pointed to a couple. "They're sponsors and they're dancing. So is that couple over there."

Following his gaze, she had to admit he was right, but she still hesitated. He caught her hand and led her to a dark corner. "How's this?" he asked, sliding both hands around her waist and pulling her close.

As her body pressed into his, she didn't protest. She couldn't. She was starved for contact, for the touch and feel of him. Her hands locked around his neck and they moved sensuously to the beat of the music and the hunger building in them.

"You didn't go to your prom, did you?" he murmured into her hair.

"No," she replied feebly. "I didn't gain much weight with our daughter, but anyone who held me close would've been able to tell I was pregnant."

"I'm so sorry for all the pain you went through."

"It doesn't matter. You didn't know."

"Maybe," he whispered as their bodies and feet moved

in perfect harmony, "we can pretend this is your prom, too."

"I'm too old to pretend."

He drew her body tight against him, and she felt every defined sinew and muscle.

A bubble of laughter escaped her. "That's not pretend, that's as real as it gets."

He moved back half a step and looked into her eyes. "It is, isn't it?"

"Yes," she whispered.

"A moment ago when I was dancing with Becca, she warned me not to hurt you."

Emily groaned in embarrassment. "I'm sorry. She's very forthright."

"She's an enchanting spitfire."

"That's a nice way to put it."

"But she doesn't have to worry, because I will never intentionally hurt you again. Do you know why?"

She shook her head, afraid to speak.

"I should've told you in San Antonio, but I was scared and I was trying not to just grab something I wanted so badly, the way I did before. The truth is that I love you and I have through all the intervening years, through the other women, even through my marriage. During all those years, you were in my heart."

Her hands tightened around his neck and she gently kissed his neck. She wanted to say something, but she couldn't, because emotion had clogged her throat.

When she didn't speak, Jackson's pulse stopped and he had to ask, "No response?"

"I'm scared, too," she admitted honestly. "If I say the words, I'm afraid something bad will happen...."

He stopped dancing and gazed into her eyes. "If it does, we'll face it together this time."

She heard in his voice what she hadn't heard before—the promise of tomorrow, and that was all she needed. "I love you, too," she breathed softly. "I've always loved you."

Jackson bent his head and lovingly kissed her lips. Passion erupted and the kiss deepened. "Can we get out of here?" he asked in a ragged voice.

"No," she answered in the same voice. "We have to stay until the last teenager stumbles out the door, then we have to help clean up."

"Oh, God, I don't think I can wait that long."

She ran a hand through his hair. "Well, I guess it's a good thing we're adults, because we can practice that self-control we're suppose to have."

He laughed. "What self-control?"

"Shameful, isn't it?" She laughed back, and took his hand and led him over to the lights.

They stood holding hands and watching the kids. Emily was happy and content. She hadn't felt that way in a very long time. *Jackson loved her.* The thought was exhilarating and all she wanted to do was savor this moment. But something kept nagging at her, and she couldn't let it go.

"Did you find any information at the courthouse?" she asked quietly.

He started to lie to her, but he couldn't. She'd been lied to enough. He just wished they could enjoy this happiness a little while longer, but their daughter was never far from her mind—or his.

"Yes," he replied.

She turned to him in excitement. "What?"

"Let's talk about it later when we're alone."

"But Jackson—"

His finger over her lips silenced her. "Later."

"Okay," she whispered, and he felt her disappointment. He just couldn't tell her the rest, not here. He would later, though, as he'd said. He'd show her the birth certificate and pray she had enough strength to handle it.

# CHAPTER THIRTEEN

BY THE TIME THEY'D FOLDED the last chair and finished cleaning up, it was four in the morning. Becca had gone with her friends for an early breakfast. Emily felt as if she was walking on pins and needles, and she wasn't going to get any relief until she heard what Jackson had to say.

As soon as they got into the car, she turned to him. "What did you find out? I *have* to know."

Jackson started the engine and backed out of the parking spot. "Let's go for a walk on the beach," he suggested, avoiding her question.

She frowned. "Did you hear me?"

"Yes, I heard you, but I'm tired and I need to clear my head. It's been a long night. A walk on the beach. That's all I'm asking."

"Okay," she agreed slowly, but she had an uncomfortable feeling she couldn't shake.

She bit her lip all the way to Rockport to keep from asking questions. She'd be patient and wait until he was ready to talk. When they arrived at the beach, they got out and walked in silence. Her high heels kept sinking in to the sand and she couldn't continue. She whirled to face him. "It's bad news, isn't it? That's why you're stalling. She's dead or something. That's why there was no mention of an adoption in the records."

He held her face in his hands as the wind whipped

around them. He kissed her cheek and could taste the salt on her skin.

She leaned heavily into him. "Just tell me, please."

He had wanted to prepare her, but he could see it was only making matters worse. She *had* to be told, and he wasn't looking forward to this. Her world would shatter into so many pieces he didn't know if he could put it back together. He had dealt with the news for the past two days, and inside he was a mass of broken parts, but he was holding himself together—for her.

Wrapping an arm around her waist, he led her back to the car. "Okay." He couldn't postpone it any longer. "The information is in my room at the hotel."

As they drove away from the beach, he asked, "Did you name our daughter?"

"No, I couldn't. I just always called her my little angel."

She noticed his hands tighten on the steering wheel. "What is it?"

"That's what I've been calling her for the past few days. It's strange that we'd both call her the same thing."

"No, it isn't. She is our angel," she told him. "Did you find a birth certificate?" She didn't understand how he could have, but she had to ask.

"Yes," he answered quietly.

"And there was a name on it?"

"Yes."

"What is it?"

"We'll be at the room in a few minutes and you can read it yourself."

"Why can't you tell me?"

"Emily, just be patient," he pleaded, and he felt like a coward, but he didn't know how else to handle this.

"I can't…because I feel you're trying to prepare me for something bad."

He pulled into the parking lot of the hotel and killed the engine, then reached over and stroked her hair. "I don't think it's bad," he said quietly. "There are just a lot of things that need explaining."

She started to speak and he gave her a quick kiss. "No more questions. Let's look at the document and then we'll talk."

As they got out, dawn was trying to break through the dark clouds without much success. It was a foggy, misty morning, and the wind had picked up; Emily sensed a storm was brewing. But that didn't worry her—only one thing was on her mind.

Jackson unlocked the door and they entered his room. Emily didn't even notice her surroundings. Her attention was on Jackson. "Where is it?"

"Have a seat," he said. First, he had to tell her everything he'd found out.

She sat on the love seat, rigid and tense, and willed herself to be strong for whatever Jackson had to say.

He drew a chair close to her. "I didn't tell you everything I discovered in San Antonio."

She swallowed hard. "Why?"

"At first I had to understand what I'd learned, and then I knew I had to be with you. I couldn't do it over the phone."

*Oh, God. Her daughter was dead.* She inhaled deeply. "Just tell me! I can't take much more of this."

"When I went back to the hospital records office and talked to the woman there, I noticed letters and numbers on the bottom of one page. With a little incentive, she told me what they meant."

"Hospitals used to do that, but now things are more

straightforward.'' She frowned. ''I didn't notice the codes. All I noticed was her weight and size.'' Her eyes caught his. ''What did the codes say?''

Jackson took a quick breath. ''They said both mother and baby went home in good condition—about nine minutes apart.''

''The new parents picked up our daughter at the same time I left the hospital?''

''You're not following me,'' he said softly. ''The records say that the mother and baby left *together*.''

''What!'' She sat on the edge of the seat, her eyes enormous. ''Jackson, that's not true.''

''I know,'' he assured her. ''You don't have to tell me that.''

''But why? Why would the records show such a thing?''

He took her hand and held it, and the nervousness in her stilled…for a moment. ''This is where the water gets a little murky, and I need you to listen to everything and not overreact.''

She bit her lip. ''Okay.''

''I told you about the adoption agency. With a lot more incentive, I was able to go through their records.''

Her hand gripped his. ''Oh, Jackson, then you have the name of the people who adopted her.''

He took a painful breath. ''No, I don't.''

''But—''

He cut in. ''This isn't easy, so I'll just say it.'' He waited a moment. ''The records show the adoption was canceled.''

Incredulity shifted through her eyes as she tried to grasp what he'd said. She shook her head fervently. ''No, that's a lie. The adoption was never canceled. They took my baby and now they say…say…'' She couldn't go on, the words locked tight in her chest.

"Emily." Jackson called her name and she jerked her eyes to his. "Don't fall apart on me. There's more to come."

Emily suddenly remembered why she was here. "The birth certificate." She grabbed on to it like a lifeline. "You have her birth certificate."

"Yes," he said. He got up and walked to his suitcase and brought back a piece of paper, which he laid in her lap. He wanted to spare her, but there was no other way.

She stared at the name on the certificate and it didn't make any sense. A shudder rattled through her. She tried to concentrate, but she couldn't. It just didn't make sense. But Jackson would explain it. He seemed to know what was happening.

She raised her eyes to his. "Why is Becca's name on our daughter's birth certificate?"

"I was hoping you could tell me. That's why I asked if you'd given her a name."

She gave him a confused look. "No, I always called her my angel, like I said. I don't understand this."

"I didn't, either, so with some help from a private investigator I was able to get a copy of Becca's birth certificate." He laid another piece of paper in her lap.

This certificate made sense. There was Becca's name, and Rose and Owen Cooper listed as her parents. She was born June 5. Everything was just as it should be.

"I didn't know what to think, either," Jackson was saying. "Everything was getting complicated and bizarre, but I knew something was very wrong. Colton's friend, the investigator, found the one document that pulled it all together. Here it is." This was the hard part, and there was no way to soften the blow, so he placed the paper in her lap.

The words at the top of the page were definite and

shocking. *Death certificate,* it read. *Rebecca Ann Cooper. Date of death—July 19.* As Emily stared at the words, a lump grew in her throat and things started to spin out of control. No, she had to hold on. She had to figure this out. There had to be a logical explanation.

"No, no, no," she cried, shaking her head wildly. "Becca's *not* dead. She's not dead. Jackson…" She buried her face in her hands as sobs started to rack her body.

Jackson's heart tightened in such pain that he couldn't breathe for a moment. He moved to her side and folded an arm around her, knowing she wasn't allowing herself to focus on the reality behind the death certificate. "Think about this rationally," he coaxed in a soothing voice. "Our daughter has the same name as your sister and—"

"No!" She jumped up and held her hands over her ears. "Don't say it! I don't want to hear it."

She was shaking visibly and couldn't seem to stop. Jackson had opened a wound deep in her soul and the trauma was so great that nothing registered but the pain. Nothing…and she wouldn't *let* anything penetrate because what he suggested was too horrible to face.

Jackson took her in his arms and rocked her gently. She held on tight, needing the security of his embrace, the security of something real—something she could feel and understand.

"We have to talk to your parents," he whispered against her hair. "They're the only ones who know what really happened."

The words seeped into her tired mind. Yes, her parents. They would explain the birth certificates. There had to be an explanation.

She whirled out of his arms and started for the door, then suddenly stopped and grabbed the phone. Jackson didn't try to stop her. She was on the verge of hysteria;

she had to do something and he had to let her. She punched
out a number and within seconds she was talking to her
father.

"Dad, meet me at the hospital."

Pause.

"No, nothing's wrong. I just need to talk to you."

Her eyes swung to Jackson. "He'll meet us there, and
then they'll tell us what these weird documents are all
about."

He stepped close to her and cupped her face in his
hands. "Emily, love, please try to—"

"No." She pulled away. "Don't say the words. They're
not true and I don't believe them. My parents will explain.
Let's go." She wheeled toward the door before he had a
chance to take a breath, and he knew how this day would
go—hard and debilitating—but he intended to be there for
her every step of the way...no matter what.

On the ride to the hospital, they didn't speak. There was
nothing to say until she'd talked to Rose and Owen. She
clutched the certificates in her lap, glancing at them repeatedly, but she refused to think about them. She
couldn't. If she did, her whole life would explode into a
million scattered bits.

The wind grew stronger as they walked from the parking
area to the hospital, but Emily hardly noticed. When they
emerged from the elevators, her father was waiting for
them. Without a word, she handed him the certificates. His
shoulders slumped and a desolate look came over his face.

"You have to talk to your mother," he said brokenly.

No denials. No explanations. Just a sentence that told
her so much, and suddenly the lock on her mind lifted and
pieces started to filter through and she had a desperate need
to see her mother.

She took the papers and ran down the hall to her room. Jackson and Owen were right behind her.

Before she opened the door, Owen said, "Remember she's not well. Try not to upset her."

Emily sucked air into a chest that felt sore; she knew what she had to do. She gave the papers to her father again. "Let's make this as easy as we can. I just want to hear the truth. I have to know the truth."

Owen nodded and they entered the room. The lights were on and Rose was awake, sitting up in bed. She frowned at them. "Emily Ann, why are you all dressed up?" Her frown deepened as she stared at Jackson. "What's *he* doing here?"

"It's time, Rose," Owen said quietly.

"Time? For what?" she asked, clasping her hands, twisting them together.

Owen laid the papers in front of her. "They know, but they want to hear it from you."

Rose glanced at the papers, and with one hand she shoved them and they fluttered onto the floor. "No," she muttered, "I don't want to talk about this."

Emily picked up the papers and walked close to her mother's bedside. She exhaled a trembling breath. "Why is Becca's name on my daughter's birth certificate?"

A strangled cry left Rose's lips and she stared down at her clenched hands. "I told you not to do this, Emily Ann, but you wouldn't listen. You never listen to me."

"Why, Mom?" Emily persisted. Not until she heard her mother speak the truth would it be real to her.

"Owen," Rose appealed to him.

"You have to tell her," he said in his quiet voice. "She has to hear it from you."

But Rose remained quiet, and tears started to roll down her cheeks onto her hands. Emily's heart constricted, but she immediately hardened herself. She couldn't give in to these emotions. She had to insist on the truth. Clearly Rose was struggling for words and Emily decided to help her.

"My sister was born June 5 and died July 19."

"She was so tiny," Rose choked out. "I gained all that weight, but she barely weighted four pounds. Her lungs weren't fully developed and her heart had a murmur. Every breath she took was agonizing, but she kept holding on, and as each day passed, we prayed she'd make it, but…" Her voice wavered on the last word and she had to stop.

Emily reached for Jackson's hand. She needed his support or she wouldn't be able to get through this.

"She was born with dark eyes and hair." Rose started talking again. "Just like you and Rebecca. My three girls, all alike… Your baby pictures all look the same."

Rose was rambling and Emily didn't know how to stop her. She didn't even know if she wanted to—or if she could endure the truth.

"But Rebecca was different, wasn't she, Mrs. Cooper?" Jackson asked, unable to keep quiet.

Rose's eyes narrowed on him. "Rebecca's always been different."

"And you hated that, because you couldn't control or manipulate her like Emily."

"Yes, I had a hard time raising Rebecca."

"Because she was very different from you and Owen," Jackson kept on, knowing that eventually she would tell them what she'd done.

Rose's eyes didn't leave Jackson's face. "My Emily Ann was perfect, never gave me a minute's trouble until you came along. You ruined her life then, and now you're doing it again. To satisfy your male ego, you're willing to sacrifice my daughter's happiness. If you have any feelings at all for Emily Ann, you'll walk out that door and leave my family in peace."

Jackson recognized what she was doing. She was struggling desperately to keep the secret from coming out, but it was too late. "I can't do that," he said sternly. "I'm fighting to find my daughter."

"Ha!" Rose laughed cruelly. "I think you've left it a little late. Where were you when Emily Ann was pregnant? You weren't too interested in your daughter then."

"I was by my mother's bedside waiting for her to die."

Rose's face fell and she looked pleadingly at Owen. "Make him leave. He'll destroy our family."

"It's over, Rose," Owen said. "And our family's been torn apart for years. Talk to Emily Ann. She's entitled to that."

"Owen," Rose cried, but this time it didn't work. Owen was standing his ground.

Emily's hand tightened in Jackson's and she dredged up the courage to say, "Tell me the truth."

Rose looked down at her own trembling hands. "Truth is a funny thing. Sometimes it hurts and…"

"Tell me!" Emily shouted, losing control of what sanity she had left.

Rose clamped her lips together, and Jackson hated the woman for what she was doing. Surely she had compassion in that heart of hers…somewhere.

"You're hurting me, Mom," Emily said quietly. "By remaining silent, you're making it worse. Why can't you just tell me?"

A sob escaped Rose, and she clutched Owen's arm. "I…I…"

Emily knew she had to say the words because her mother wouldn't or couldn't. She exhaled a shuddering breath. "Is Becca my daughter?" she asked in a voice that sounded as if it belonged to someone else.

Jackson held his breath. He needed to hear the answer as badly as Emily did. For the past two days he had grappled with the truth, always telling himself that it was too bizarre to be real and that Emily's mother wouldn't do such a thing. But now he and Emily had to deal with whatever Rose said. They had to find a way to absorb the truth and adjust their lives accordingly.

"Y-yes...yes, Becca is your daughter." The words came out low and gruff, and Rose began to sob openly.

The words whirled around in Emily's head. Round and round, faster and faster, until the world, her very breath, hung on those words. *Becca is your daughter.* Emily's knees buckled under the force and Jackson grabbed her to prevent her from crumpling to the floor. The room kept spinning, as did the feeling in her head. Her mother's tearful face, her father's sad eyes and Jackson's concerned look all blended together in a whirlwind of emotion that threatened to cripple her. For years she had ached to hold her daughter, to see her face, and all the time her baby had been with her.... Her sister was her daughter. The wound deep in her soul tore further, and Emily cried out from the searing pain.

"No, no, no," she moaned in denial, but just as quickly she fought back, determined not to let her mother destroy her again. "Becca is my daughter," she said, and let the words soothe and comfort in a way she wouldn't have thought possible. "Becca is my daughter. The baby I gave away is Becca."

A gasp came from the doorway and Emily saw Becca standing there. She still wore her pink prom dress and her eyes were huge and bewildered.

At that moment, the little girl in her dreams turned and

Emily saw her face for the first time. She had big brown eyes and long brown hair and her face was Becca's. Becca was her daughter.

"Oh, my God," she breathed as the reality crashed into her. Emily's heart lay heavy in her chest, and a suffocating feeling came over her and she thought she was going to faint. Then Becca wheeled and ran from the room. "Becca," Emily cried, and immediately went after her, Jackson on her heels.

"Leave her alone, Emily Ann," her mother called. "Just leave her."

The words followed Emily, but she knew she would never leave Becca again.

# CHAPTER FOURTEEN

EMILY RAN INTO THE HALL, but Becca was nowhere to be found. She turned to Jackson. "Where is she? Where did she go?"

Jackson glanced at the elevators. "She didn't use the elevators, so she must've taken the stairs." He pushed a button. "We can probably catch her on the ground floor."

The elevator whizzed down, but when they reached the main floor, Becca wasn't there. They ran toward the parking area and Emily saw Becca's red Mustang speed away. Emily had given her the car for her sixteenth birthday, which had led, predictably, to a huge argument with Rose.

"That's her," Emily shouted, and they dashed to his rental car. She refused to think about Rose as they followed it out of Corpus Christi to Rockport. "She's headed home," Emily said lamely.

In Aransas Pass, Becca ran a red light. Cars honked and swerved to miss her. Jackson was forced to stop. "She's going to kill herself," Emily cried, fighting to maintain a grip on reality.

Jackson was also struggling with his emotions. He was cursing himself for not handling things better. Now his daughter was hell-bent on a collision course.

*His daughter.*

It was the first time he'd allowed himself to even think the words. He'd had the information for days, but he'd been afraid to believe it...afraid it wasn't true. It was, though. Becca was his and Emily's daughter.

The light turned green. "Where do you think she'd go?" Jackson asked.

"Maybe to her friend Ginger's. Or to Joni's or Tommy's."

They went by all those houses, but the Mustang was nowhere in sight. They drove around Rockport and every place Emily could think of and they still didn't find her.

"Let's check my parents' house again," Emily suggested. "We might've missed her."

She realized the clouds had darkened and the wind was growing steadily stronger. A storm was definitely on the way. That didn't matter. All that mattered was finding Becca.

When they reached the house, Emily jumped out and ran inside. In a minute she was back. Jackson had remained standing by the car.

"She's not there." She sighed dejectedly. "Where could she..." Her voice trailed off as she looked toward the water and the boat docks. She saw a flash of red on the other side of the pier and knew it was Becca's car. She kicked off her high heels and ran toward the docks.

Her breath was coming in gulps when she got to the car. Becca's purse and corsage were on the seat and the keys in the ignition, but Becca wasn't anywhere.

Jackson reached her side, his breathing labored. "She's not here, is she?"

"No," Emily muttered forlornly, and then she noticed the boats. Her father had two—a twenty-one footer and a twenty-three footer. The smaller boat was gone. "Oh, my God."

"What?" Jackson asked, his eyes following hers to the boats.

"My dad's other boat is missing. Becca must have taken it. There's a storm coming and she's out on the water. We have to do something. She doesn't stand a chance in this high wind."

Jackson held Emily's trembling body against his for a second, just needing her contact. "I'll go call the Coast Guard. They'll bring her back. Everything will be all right."

For that moment Emily submerged herself in Jackson, but suddenly the events of the past hour crowded in on her and she beat her fists against his chest. "No, no, it won't!" she screamed. "I should never have said I loved you. I knew something bad would happen like before, and it did. We were selfish, selfish. Now we're going to lose her. Oh, God. Oh, God. Oh, God."

Her words shocked him, but he recognized that she was on the edge and didn't know what she was saying or doing. He grabbed her hands and held them. "Emily, love, listen to me," he said, wanting to ease that intense pain inside her. "Our love is not selfish and the bad things didn't happen because of it. Pull yourself together." He took a breath. "Becca needs us. I have to go call the Coast Guard. Will you be okay?"

The wind howled with an eerie sound, echoing the turmoil in Emily, but through the fog of despair she heard Jackson's voice and she nodded her head.

*Becca needed them.*

"Yes," she mumbled, and Jackson ran toward the house.

As Emily stared out at the misty, turbulent water, thunder rolled across the black sky. The wind whipped her hair into her face and she wrapped her arms around her waist to still her fears.

It didn't work. Fear, stark and paralyzing, claimed her,

and she sank to her knees and buried her face in her hands. Sobs shook her body as she let the tears flow unheeded. She cried for all the wasted years, for the baby she'd never nurtured, and most of all for the young woman whose heart she had just broken. "Becca," she cried. "I'm sorry." The sound was muffled against her hands. Then she cried for herself and Jackson and all the pain they'd been through and the pain that was yet to come.

Fear was a palpable thing, controlling her, but she had to fight back...for Becca's sake. She got to her feet, mesmerized by the rocking of the boat as the wind banged it against the pier. To and fro. *Bang, bang.* Insistently the wind kept pounding. *Bang, bang.* The noise galvanized her into action. Becca's life was in danger and she couldn't wait for the Coast Guard. She had to help her daughter.

Without another thought, she ran to the pier, hitched up her dress and jumped into the boat. She untied it and pulled up the anchor. Taking the seat at the center console, she turned the key. The boat fired on the first try and she guided it toward open water. She hadn't driven a boat in a while, but it came back to her quickly and easily. The high waves lapped at her and at times she thought the boat would capsize, but she didn't turn back. There was a small island not far away, where she and Becca used to go to swim and escape from Rose for an hour or two. Emily hoped that was where Becca had gone and she headed directly for it.

JACKSON RAN BACK to the boat docks and his heart stopped as he realized Emily was gone—and so was the other boat. "No, Emily, no!" he cried, but he knew it was true—Emily was out in that churning water somewhere, looking for Becca.

He didn't have time to think as he saw the big Coast

Guard boat glide up to the pier. A young man leapt out and ran toward him. Jackson met him halfway, not giving him time to speak. "My daughter's out in this weather," he shouted against the wind. "Her mother went after her. You have to find them. Please."

"Slow down, sir," the man said. "Haven't you heard? There's a major storm coming. We're advising everyone to get off the water and head for shelter. It's going to hit any minute."

Jackson threw back his head. "Why the hell do you think I called you? You have to save my daughter and Emily."

Another man walked up. "We can't go out until the weather clears. It's too dangerous."

Jackson frowned at him. "Isn't that what you're *supposed* to do?"

"Yes, sir, within reason, but we're required to take precautions. As soon as we're able, we'll go after your daughter."

"That'll be too late! They'll both be...dead." The words came from deep in his soul and the two men glanced at each other.

The wind wailed and shrieked, and they had difficulty remaining on their feet. "We have to find shelter," the first man shouted. "The storm's breaking. Is there somewhere we can wait this out?"

Jackson pointed to the Cooper house. The two men started toward it, then the second one turned back. "Come on, man, you can't stay out here."

Jackson wasn't listening. His eyes were focused on the tumultuous horizon. The wind rocked his body as he made his way to the shore. The two men tried to get him to the house, but eventually they gave up and ran for cover.

Jackson watched the water as the waves crashed against

shore. A small boat was perilous in this type of wind; even he knew that. He wondered who the storm would take first—Emily or Becca. A suffocating sensation burned his throat and he brushed away a tear, then another. The wind tugged and shook him, but he kept his eyes on the water. Finally the wind made him stagger and knocked him down. He struggled to stand, refusing to move from this spot where he had last seen Emily. But the wind was stronger than his will and it roared into him, blowing him to the sand. Again he stood. It was him against the wind—something he could fight, something he could vent all his rage on. The third time the wind took him down, he stayed on the cold, wet ground. Without them, without Emily and Becca, he didn't have a reason to fight. The wind ripped and tore at him, but it was nothing compared to the pain in his heart.

THE WAVES SLAMMED into the boat and Emily feared it would capsize at any moment. The farther she went, the stronger the waves became. She was soaking wet and her body trembled, but she kept going. Relief filled her as she saw the shape of the island, then just as quickly that relief spiraled into agony. She could see an overturned boat being tossed on the water—her father's boat. Where was Becca? Oh, God, where was Becca?

She gassed the motor and jetted through a wave toward the shore with a whooshing, deafening sound. The impact jarred her from the seat to the bottom of the boat with a painful thud. Quickly collecting herself, she crawled from the boat. The high wind forced her backward and she had trouble standing. Through sheer willpower, she managed to stumble down the island shoreline. "Becca, Becca, Becca!" she screamed, but the wind took the name and threw it back in her face.

The wind grabbed her body, too, and she felt herself going down, but she scrambled to her feet, mud coating her arms, legs and face. She tried to control her breathing and the fear exploding through her. "Becca, Becca, Becca!" she screamed again. Her voice caught as she saw a figure huddled farther down the beach.

*It was Becca. She was alive.*

Emily tried to regain her balance, but the wind was too strong. On her hands and knees she crawled until she reached her. With a muffled cry, like a wounded animal, Becca clutched at her and they held on tight. Thunder rumbled and lightning cracked as the storm broke in all its fury. Wind tore at their bodies and rain pelted their heads, but they remained locked in each other's arms. Even when high waves threatened to engulf them, they didn't move as a force stronger than nature bound them together.

JACKSON SAT ON THE MUDDY BEACH, his knees drawn to his chin. The heavy rain flattened his hair against his scalp and mud caked his slacks and shirt. He had removed his jacket, but he couldn't remember where or when and he didn't care. His total attention was on the horizon as he mentally willed them to appear through the mist. He had finally found what he'd been searching for all his life— love, real love, and it had vanished before he'd had a chance to fully acknowledge it. Now he was an empty shell and he hated the storm, the circumstances and everything that had taken them from him. He thought he'd suffered when his mother died, but this…this was a pain he wouldn't survive.

"Sir? Sir?"

Jackson heard the voice, but he didn't respond. Then he felt someone touch his shoulder and he glanced up into the face of one of the Coast Guard officers. "The storm's let up enough so we can go out now," the man said.

It took a moment for the words to sink in, then Jackson asked in a desolate voice, "Do you think it'll do any good?"

"I don't know, but there's always a chance."

*A chance. A chance. A chance.*

The word propelled Jackson to his feet. If there was the tiniest possibility that they were alive, he would hang on to that. He had to. It was all he had left.

"Let's go, sir," the man said as he saw the life come back into Jackson's eyes.

They walked down the pier and boarded the big white boat. Within minutes they were sailing over the waves, looking for a sign of life.

WHEN THE RAIN STOPPED and the wind released its hold, Becca asked, "Is it true, Em? Is it true?"

From the tone of her voice, Emily knew that Becca didn't hate her. That was more than she'd hoped for... more than she had a right to expect. She smoothed the wet hair away from Becca's face. "Yes," she said, with tears in her voice.

"But...how?"

Emily swallowed the lump in her throat. "My sister, Rebecca, died July 19 and evidently Mom decided to raise you as her own."

"Why would she do that?"

"I haven't heard the whole story, yet, but we will... together."

Becca pulled back and wiped a tear from her mud stained face. "You're my mother...my real mother," she said. Her eyes grew enormous. "When we were talking in my room about your daughter and you were sad because you'd never seen her face, I said you could always look at me. And it was me. It was *me*."

Emily nodded, unable to speak at the pain in Becca's voice.

"How could she do that to us? I hate her."

Emily realized that hatred could consume her, but she knew she had to reject that destructive emotion. They'd been hurt enough, and now they had to find a common ground between hatred and love. For Becca's sake, Emily had no other choice.

"We have to talk to her—try to understand why she did it."

"I'll never understand and I'm not going back. You can't make me," Becca said defiantly.

Emily held Becca's chin in one hand. "Do you know how long I've waited to see your precious face? An eternity—and I'll never force you to do anything you don't want."

Before Becca could answer, a Coast Guard boat emerged through the mist. As it reached land, Emily saw Jackson jump out and run along the beach toward them and her heart filled with so much love.

Jackson fell down beside them and his arms encircled their two bodies. "You're alive! Thank God, you're alive," he cried.

"Yes," Emily whispered, one arm around Jackson, the other around Becca. After that, no one spoke. All they needed now was to touch and be with each other. The men from the Coast Guard stood a distance away, hesitant to intrude on this moment.

Finally the older man asked, "Does anyone need medical attention?"

Jackson glanced at Emily and she shook her head, then he stared into the dark eyes of his daughter. Becca also shook her head, but Jackson hardly noticed. This was his *daughter*. He had guessed it when he'd seen the documents. He had hoped it when he'd danced with her. And he'd grieved for her on the beach, when he thought he'd lost her. But this was the first time he allowed himself to feel the joy of knowing she was really his.

As if sensing his thoughts, Becca asked, "Are you truly my father?"

Jackson swallowed and admitted in an unsteady voice, "Yes...yes, I am."

"I don't even know you."

Jackson gently touched her soft cheek. "But you will," he promised.

Emily rested her wet head on Jackson's shoulder, and the three of them sat there savoring this moment and feeling a connection that had always been there but was now brought to light, no longer hidden from them.

"Does anyone need medical attention?" the man called again.

Jackson smiled slightly. "I think he's trying to get our attention." He looked over his shoulder. "We're fine," he called, then turned back to them. "We'd better go. They're getting antsy."

But they didn't move, each reluctant to end this time, this first time, that they were together as a family. Slowly Jackson got to his feet and offered a hand to each of them. Becca jumped right up, but Emily staggered for a second.

"Are you okay?" Jackson asked anxiously.

"I'm just sore, that's all," she said. The hip she'd fallen on when she'd jetted into shore was probably bruised, but the pain was nothing compared to the joy unfurling in her heart.

As they walked toward the boat, Emily wished that joy would last forever, but she knew they had a lot to resolve in the days ahead. She had to talk to Rose and learn how she'd accomplished the whole thing. Emily wasn't sure how she felt about it...that would come later. And Becca—she had to ask her forgiveness and prayed they could build a future stronger and better than the past...with Jackson. Somehow they had to pull their lives together and survive this nightmare.

The men hooked Owen's boat to the bigger boat, so they could carry it back to the docks. Emily knew her father wouldn't be too pleased about losing his other boat, although the men assured her they would search for it and bring it back. In all likelihood it would be unsalvageable. That didn't worry Emily at the moment; she couldn't dredge up any concern for her parents' feelings. However, she had no intention of letting bitterness and anger control their lives. She had Becca to think about. She had waited eighteen years to have her daughter and nothing would destroy that relationship. It was a vow she made to herself.

They sat together in the boat as they sailed toward home. They were wet, dirty and tired, yet complete in a way Emily couldn't explain. She would remember this for the rest of her life. It was crazy, but she felt as if she'd just given birth to Becca and they were taking her home to a new beginning...a new life.

WHEN THEY REACHED THE DOCKS, they thanked the Coast Guard officers and headed for the house. Jackson drove Becca's car to safety, and Emily and Becca walked arm in arm. As they entered the house the silence became strained and awkward.

They stood, irresolute, in the kitchen, and Emily finally spoke. "Well, I think the first order of business is to get cleaned up."

"Yeah." Becca frowned at her wet and dirty dress.

"My beautiful prom dress is ruined. Everything's ruined," she muttered hurtfully.

"Becca—"

"If you don't mind," Becca interrupted. "I'll take the bathroom first."

"No, go ahead," Emily said, and watched with a heavy heart as Becca disappeared down the hall.

Jackson gathered Emily into his arms and held her tight. She rested heavily against him, needing his warmth and comfort more than she'd ever needed anything.

"Becca is our daughter," she murmured into his chest. "I keep saying that to myself over and over, and it makes me scared...so scared."

He pulled back to look into her eyes. "Why? Why does it do that?"

"Because Becca and I have this great relationship as sisters, but now that's going to change. I hope it's for the better, but I have this uneasy feeling."

"Yes, things are going to change and *together* we'll make it better."

"Oh, Jackson." She wrapped her arms around his neck. "Right now I'm somewhere out in limbo and I hardly know what I'm feeling, but I just can't imagine... I can't even fathom why my mother would do this to me. She knew how much I wanted to keep my baby and then to..." She couldn't go on as overpowering emotions threatened her composure.

He kissed the side of her face. "We'll talk to your mother, find out all the details. Then we'll plan a future as a family—that's what I want most of all."

Emily grew stiff in his arms and fear tugged at his heart. "We have to take it slow," she said, taking a step back. He felt empty and lost and he couldn't explain it, but he sensed Emily distancing herself from him. That was stupid, he told himself. Emotions were running high and he was just misreading the signals.

But her next words didn't ease the feeling. "This is going to be very hard on Becca. I need some time with her so we can adjust to the new situation."

Jackson didn't miss that she'd left him out of this "situation" and he wondered if she had any plans for him in her future.

Before he could ask, Becca came into the kitchen wearing a bathrobe. "Your turn, Em," she said, then walked to her room without even glancing at him. The emptiness grew.

"I'll go to the hotel and change," Jackson said before his fears could completely defeat him. "I'll be back soon, and we can all go talk to your mother." With that, he walked to the door, not giving her a chance to object. He *had* to be part of their lives. God, he hoped she felt the same way.

## CHAPTER FIFTEEN

EMILY DIDN'T HAVE an opportunity to talk to Becca before Jackson was back. She was worried because Becca was acting sullen and defiant, so unlike herself. On the drive to the hospital she was quiet and that bothered Emily, too. Becca was always talking about anything and everything, but now she didn't have a word to say. The traumatic revelation had affected them all and she hoped Jackson wasn't going to rush things. She had to make him see that they had to move slowly.

When they arrived at the hospital, she didn't have time for further introspection. Outside the room Becca held back.

"I don't see why I have to be here," she said in a petulant voice.

Emily put an arm around her shoulders. Becca had on jeans and a T-shirt and hadn't bothered to even brush her hair. It hung in disarray down her back. She looked like a bad-tempered little girl who couldn't get her way.

"I told you I'd never make you do anything you didn't want to," Emily said softly, and Jackson admired her control and compassion. "So if you'd rather not be here, you don't have to, but I thought you'd like to hear how our lives got so messed up." Becca didn't respond, so she went on. "We have to find a bridge from the past to the future, and we have to do that without resentment and anger. It's hard, I know, because I personally want to break something, but for our family's sake I have to be strong and forgiving. That's the only way we can survive."

Becca shuffled her feet. "Okay, but I'm not talking to her."

Emily glanced at Jackson and she was glad he was letting her handle this. She knew it was taking all his restraint not to say something. "Fine," she answered. "You do whatever you feel is right for you."

Emily took a deep breath and they entered the room. Owen jumped up. "Thank God, you're okay. We were so worried with the storm and all." His eyes settled on Becca. "Are you okay, Rebecca?"

"I'm fine. I'm just great," she flung out, in that sullen voice she'd assumed. "I just discovered my mother is really my grandmother and my sister is really my mother. On a scale of one to ten, I'm hanging in at zero."

Jackson could see his daughter was about to fall apart. He'd thought she had her emotions under control, but clearly she didn't. He suddenly saw what Emily was talking about. They couldn't rush her. She was already overwhelmed. He felt selfish because he'd been thinking about himself, *his* feelings and a future she wasn't ready for. Instead, he had to be a father now—a real father—and help his daughter.

He reached down and took her hand. It trembled like a lost leaf in the wind in his. He was prepared for her to jerk or pull away, but she didn't. She seemed to need his strength and that gave him a good feeling. He led her to the chairs not far from the bed. He sat and she eased down beside him.

Emily saw that Jackson was managing Becca and she felt amazed at how naturally the girl responded to him. But then, he was her father and…

She couldn't think about that just now. She had to concentrate on her mother and finding out the truth. Walking to her bedside, she tried to find the right words, but decided there were no right words. "Why did you take my baby?" came out of its own accord.

Rose pleated the top of her sheet with nervous fingers. "I told you to leave it alone, Emily Ann. Why couldn't you do that?"

Emily bit her tongue and knew Rose wasn't going to make this easy. "Because I lost my child, a part of myself, and I could *never* leave that alone. It was always there in my heart, an ache, a pain that wouldn't go away. I needed to know if she was happy, healthy, and most of all I had to see her face."

Rose didn't say a word or look up. She kept twisting the sheet.

"Tell me why you decided to take my baby," Emily said again.

Still Rose didn't respond. Owen, who was standing on the other side of the bed, touched Rose's shoulder. "Stop being so proud and stubborn, and tell her what happened."

Tears fell down Rose's cheeks and she slowly began to speak. "When I was forty and I first discovered I was pregnant, I was angry. I didn't want another child. I had a grown daughter and the thought of raising a baby at my age was ludicrous. But I couldn't escape the truth. When you found out, you became rebellious and I hated the baby even more. My perfect daughter was someone I didn't know. You wouldn't listen to me anymore and when *he* came on the scene, everything went from bad to worse. I knew you were sleeping with him and I was powerless to stop it." She paused. "When he left, I was relieved and I hoped we could get our lives back to normal. But I started having problems with my pregnancy and I thought God was punishing me for not wanting the baby. Then I realized *you* were pregnant and I was filled with rage. I didn't want what had happened to me to happen to you. I'd raised you differently.''

Emily frowned. ''What are you talking about?''

''When I was seventeen, I got pregnant in high school, just like you did, and the boy wanted nothing to do with me or the baby. I didn't know what to do. Owen and I were good friends and when I told him, he offered to marry me.''

A gasp left Emily's lips. Did that mean— Oh, God, she couldn't take a shocking revelation like that on top of everything else.

Rose sensed her trepidation. ''Don't worry, Emily Ann, Owen is your father. My little boy was stillborn. You were born several years later.''

Emily let out a sigh of relief and suddenly realized what Becca was going through. Finding out you're not the person you thought you were could be devastating. She would talk to Becca about that later. Now she focused on her mother's words. ''I insisted you give the baby up for adoption because you had this brilliant future ahead of you and I didn't want you to lose that. Ever since you were a little girl, you wanted to be a doctor, and I knew if you had the baby, your dreams would be ruined. And I was angry with you for being as stupid as I was. Maybe I wanted to punish you. I'm not sure. All I know is that I thought I was doing the best thing for you.''

Emily tried to understand, but she couldn't. Nothing was making sense to her. ''Why did you decide to raise my baby when you told me repeatedly that you couldn't?''

Rose resumed making tucks in the sheet. ''When my baby died, I was severely depressed. As much as I didn't want her at first, in the end I wanted her with all my heart. I kept thinking it was my punishment for being selfish and

I just couldn't deal with her death. I never told anyone she died. I came home a week after she was born and every day I'd go to the hospital to see her. I continued to do that after her death. Instead of going to the hospital, I went to the cemetery. Since she was born in a big hospital in Corpus, no one in Rockport knew my secret. Owen said I was having a nervous breakdown and I probably was. I kept pretending she was alive, and as the birth of your baby grew near, I suddenly realized that she *could* be. I'd lost my child, but I wasn't going to lose my granddaughter. I called the adoption agency and canceled everything. Then when my aunt called and said you were in labor, we went to San Antonio. Your father took care of you and I took care of the baby. She looked so much like my Rebecca that I named her Rebecca, too. It was crazy, insane, I can see that now. But then…all I wanted was a baby.''

Emily put a hand to her throbbing head. ''I don't understand why no one at the hospital knew the adoption was canceled. The nurse who was with me during delivery knew nothing about it. She even talked about how I was doing the right thing.''

''She didn't know because I didn't tell hospital personnel until after you delivered. I just told them there wouldn't be an adoption…that we'd be taking the baby home.''

''You were there when my baby was born?'' Emily asked in a pained voice, even though she knew the answer. At the time she'd felt so alone and her parents were there all along, waiting to snatch her baby.

''Yes, I was the first one to hold her. The day you were released, I stayed in the nursery and filled out forms while Owen took care of you. I was afraid one of the nurses might say something as you were leaving, but everything went smoothly. After Owen left you at my aunt's, we took the baby and came back to Rockport. Once we got home,

I felt I'd done the right thing. She was so much like my Rebecca.''

Becca made an agitated movement. Jackson wished he could make all this go away for her and Emily, but he couldn't and he felt so helpless and angry. Angry at what this woman had done to their lives.

"But she wasn't your Rebecca. She was mine," Emily cried from the deepest part of her soul. "You knew how much I wanted to keep her. Why didn't you tell me? Why?"

Rose raised her eyes to Emily. "Owen wanted me to, but if I'd done that, you would've forgotten about your dream of being a doctor."

"You could've taken care of her while I went to school," Emily said.

"You went to school in Austin, and if I'd told you, you would've taken the baby from me. At the time, I couldn't handle that. I couldn't. I was too depressed. Rebecca was the only thing that saved me."

Emily had a hard time grasping how her mother had accomplished all this. "Didn't you need Rebecca's birth certificate for school and things?"

"I used my Rebecca's," she murmured.

"So you kept it a secret all these years and you never felt the need to tell me. Even when I was going through hell, you did nothing to help me. How can you justify that?"

"I can't, but I could see how happy and healthy Rebecca was and how successfully your career had developed. I knew I'd done the right thing for all of us, and it was—until now. If you'd just left everything alone, no one would ever have known."

"I had a right to know," Emily said in a burst of anger.

"I had a right to know my own child. Jackson had a right to know his daughter. You took that away from us."

Rose brushed at her tears. "I hope you can find a way to forgive me."

"No." Emily raised one hand, suddenly rejecting the forgiveness she'd said they had to have. "Don't ask me to forgive you. I'm so raw inside that every word hurts like hell. I'm not sure I'll ever get past that." She turned and ran from the room.

Jackson immediately went after her. Becca followed.

"Rebecca," Rose called, but Becca didn't answer or go back.

Jackson caught Emily in the hall and held her. She trembled and he held her tighter. The truth was tearing them all apart, and Jackson had a hard time controlling his own emotions. He glanced over his shoulder and saw Becca standing there like a lost soul. Of the three of them, Becca was the most affected. He and Emily had made bad choices, bad decisions, and they had to live with that. But Becca was an innocent victim.

Jackson motioned to her and she walked over and he enclosed her in their embrace. As before, on the beach, they held each other.

Finally Jackson said, half humorously, "Ready to go, ladies?"

The drive to the Cooper house was again made in silence. When they reached the house and Becca had gone inside, Emily caught Jackson's arm. "I need this time with Becca...alone. I have to talk to her."

There was that word again, *alone,* and he was beginning to hate it.

"Don't push me away, Emily."

"Jackson, please," she begged. "I'm not doing that.

Becca is filled with so much anger that she's about to explode. I have to help her through this.''

His eyes narrowed. "You don't think I can?"

She licked dry lips. "She hardly knows you. I've known her all her life, and I know her inside and out. Please understand. We have to do what's best for Becca."

"She needs both of us," he said in a patient voice, trying not to feel hurt, trying to understand.

She rubbed his face with the back of her hand. At her loving touch, he knew he'd do what she asked. He wanted them to be together, but he was realistic enough to acknowledge that it wasn't going to happen quickly or easily. Just wanting something didn't ensure that it would come about.

"Yes, she does," Emily murmured. "But as I said before, we have to go slow and I desperately need to explain my part in all this. I need her forgiveness."

Her voiced quavered and he gathered her close and kissed her. "You have tonight," he whispered against her lips.

"Thank you," she whispered back.

He got into the car and drove away. She watched until he was out of sight then went inside to talk to Becca.

She wasn't in the living room. Emily found her in the bedroom, sprawled across the bed sound asleep. It had been a long, trying day and Becca was completely exhausted. Emily quietly closed the door and walked into the living room and curled up on the sofa. She couldn't sleep. Instead, she got out the photo albums and looked through them. She had a need to see her child. There was Becca lying in a crib and Emily couldn't take her eyes off the small baby. She remembered the first time she'd held her, and how right it had felt. She'd thought it was because she'd given away her own child that she'd experienced

such closeness, but it was so much more. She turned the
pages, seeing Becca as a toddler, as a little girl, as a teenager and a young woman. A sob burned her throat and she
held the pictures to her chest as if to absorb them. She
didn't have to, though—she'd been there, through all those
years. Yet everything had changed. It was so different
now.

*Because Becca was her daughter.*

This baby, the precious baby with the big brown eyes,
was hers. Jackson had to see these, she decided, and began
to take favorite ones out of the album for him to keep. She
knew he'd want them. With the pictures around her, she
felt her eyelids begin to droop. The day had taken its toll
on her, too, and within minutes she drifted off to sleep.

ON THE WAY TO HIS HOTEL room, Jackson realized he was
hungry. He started to go back, to see if Emily and Becca
wanted something to eat. They hadn't eaten a thing all day,
but he knew they could manage on their own. He wouldn't
interrupt them. He picked up some fast food and took it
to his room.

After eating, he was restless. He wanted to be with them,
but he had to respect Emily's wishes. He hadn't talked to
his father in two days, so he called. He had to explain
what had happened. When he'd begun the search for their
daughter, he'd never imagined she'd be so close, and he
knew Emily hadn't, either. They were still reeling from the
impact. He hoped he could make his dad understand that.

As usual, George understood, but he wasn't too patient.
He wanted to see his granddaughter. He used the line about
not getting any younger, but Jackson was able to persuade
him to wait. They had to wait for Becca to adjust and they
couldn't force her. She wasn't a child anymore.

Jackson went to sleep with images of Emily in his

mind—the way she'd been in San Antonio. He remembered their happiness and their passion, their joy in each other. They would be that way again and they would have their daughter to make their lives complete. He clung to that.

OWEN ENTERED THE HOUSE and found Emily asleep on the sofa. He gathered up the pictures and laid them on the coffee table. He then got a blanket out of the hall closet and covered her. After checking on Rebecca, he went to his own room.

Emily stirred early that Monday morning and wondered who'd put the blanket over her. Her father, of course. He always used to do that when she fell asleep watching TV. God, it seemed like forever since her parents had loved her and the world was simple. Now everything was so complicated and…

The smell of coffee tantalized her senses and she realized the kitchen light was on and her father was up. He appeared with two cups of coffee and handed her one. She pushed herself into a sitting position and took the cup.

Owen sat beside her in his customary jeans and plaid shirt. He sipped his coffee, then said, "What we did was wrong. I knew that all along, but I couldn't stop it. When we lost the baby, I think Rose lost her mind and she was completely out of control. I didn't know how to help her. Your baby was the only thing that gave her a reason to live. That doesn't excuse anything or make it right. I'm just sorry for all the pain we put you through. You're my daughter and I should've stood up to Rose, but I've never been very good at saying no to her."

Emily just drank her coffee. She didn't know what to say.

"If you can't forgive us, I'll understand, but I hope that

as time goes by we'll find a way to mend the pain and suffering. We're a family and that's what a family does.''

Her father had probably never talked to her for this long about anything except fishing, which showed her how important it was to him. He was fighting to keep his family together and she was fighting to have one. Maybe there was a common ground.

''I can't live with the anger and resentment,'' she told him. ''I see it in Becca and it's destructive. I want more for Becca and myself than that.''

''Please talk to your mother again. We have to forgive and forget.''

He was right. She'd find no peace without forgiveness. Somehow, she had to forgive her mother, and she prayed that Becca would forgive her. The forgiving would come gradually; but the forgetting would be hard. Time—she needed time.

''I'll talk to Mom,'' she said quietly.

''Thank you, Emily. I know you have a good heart.'' He paused, then asked, ''What about Jackson?''

''I love Jackson and he's going to be part of my life…and Becca's.''

''I see.'' He looked down into his cup. ''Then you're going to take her away from us.'' There was sadness in his voice, but she had to persevere.

She took a deep breath. ''From now on, I will be her mother and you and Mom will be her grandparents—the way it should have been from the beginning.''

''It's difficult to change years of caring and loving someone.''

''I know, but I also know that you and Mom will try to make this easy for Becca and me.'' She didn't know any such thing. She was just hoping they wouldn't throw unnecessary hurdles in her way.

"Yes, we will."

"Thanks, Dad. I think I'll check on Becca."

"Thank you, Emily Ann. You're very gracious."

As she looked into her father's eyes, she noticed that the disappointment she'd seen for so many years was gone. In a moment of clarity, she realized it hadn't been disappointment in her but in himself. He hated what they'd done to her. That was the reason for the coolness and strain over the years. A weight lifted from her shoulders—the weight of guilt. She let out a long breath and got to her feet.

As she walked down the hall to Becca's room, she felt a sense of renewal, but she knew it would take a lot more than that.

Becca was still sprawled across the bed, her long hair everywhere, her face turned toward Emily. She sat down to study it. So many emotions filled her and it was an effort not to break down. This was her baby, her child. Why had she never suspected it? Why hadn't she recognized her own daughter? The pain in her heart wouldn't allow her to, she told herself, but at least she and Becca had always had a close relationship. The bond was there, although neither had guessed its true significance.

She concentrated on each of Becca's features. The dark hair, eyes and olive complexion she got from her, but where did she get that short upturned nose and the full lips? Emily's nose was pert and her lips more bow-shaped. Jackson didn't have that nose or mouth, either. Who—

Suddenly Becca's eyes opened and she stared sleepily at Emily. She sat up, a frown replacing the blank look. "What are you doing?" she asked in a harsh voice.

"Watching you sleep."

"Jeez, that's weird."

Emily pushed backward and rested against the headboard. "It might be, but everything's a little weird right now."

"You can say that again." Becca sighed irritably.

Sleep hadn't helped her attitude and Emily knew they had to talk—sooner rather than later. "Feel like talking?"

"About what?" Becca asked glibly.

"About the fact that you and I are mother and daughter."

"So?"

"I want you to understand my part in this."

"You already told me, remember? You said you were weak and couldn't stand up to Mom, so you gave me away. Isn't that what you said?"

Emily drew a quick breath. "Yes, I said that."

"What else is there to say?"

"Forgiveness, Becca. We need to talk about forgiveness."

Becca shrugged offhandedly. "I forgive you. Is that what you want to hear?" She moved to get off the bed, but Emily caught her hands and stopped her.

"No, I don't want to hear it in that tone of voice. I want to hear it when it comes from here." She placed her hand over Becca's heart.

Becca pulled away and fear knotted Emily's stomach, but she had to keep trying.

"We have to be able to forgive in order to go on."

Becca's dark eyes narrowed. "Can you forgive Mom?"

"Yes. I'm going to the hospital today to tell her that. I have to. It's the only way to face the future." She paused. "You have to forgive her, too."

"Okay," she mumbled unenthusiastically, and Emily knew that was as good as she was likely to get.

"Now, let's talk about the future."

Becca scowled. "What future?"

"I have to go back to my practice in a few days and I'm not leaving you here."

"What are you talking about? I've got three more weeks of school and there'll be lots of parties, plus graduation. I'm not going anywhere."

The knot in Emily's stomach tightened and she couldn't breathe. Becca had never talked to her in that tone of voice and it was getting to her, breaking down every defense, every strength she'd built up.

She said the first thing that came into her head. "Jackson and I have waited a long time to find you and—"

"Well, then go sleep with him and leave me alone," Becca snapped. She tried to jump off the bed, but Emily grabbed her.

"Listen to me, young lady. I'm not leaving you. If you don't understand anything else, you'd better understand that."

Becca clamped her lips tight in a mutinous expression and Emily knew this conversation was over—for now. She slid off the bed, saying, "Breakfast's in ten minutes. I believe you have school today." With that, she walked out the door. She had to. She was close to losing her temper.

In the kitchen, Emily had to take several deep breaths. Becca was hurting, she reminded herself; that was understandable. She just had to be patient. Becca would come around.

Becca walked into the room and sat at the kitchen table, not looking at Emily as she poured cereal into a bowl. Emily was glad Owen had already gone to the hospital. She had to try talking to Becca again.

"I've been thinking," she said as she took the chair across from her. "It would be very inconsiderate of me to expect you to pack up and leave when there's so much going on in your life at school."

"I'll say," Becca muttered, pouring milk over her cereal.

"So until school is out, I'll make the commute to Houston each day."

"What?" Becca stopped eating and stared at her with big eyes.

"I plan on being here when you wake up in the morning and when you go to bed at night."

Becca shoved back her chair and took an angry stance. "How many times have I begged you to come home because Mom was ranting and raving about something stupid and I couldn't take any more? But you always made excuses like *I can't* or *I'm too busy*. And now, all of a sudden, you're willing to come home every day for *her*. For *her* you'll come home." She screamed the last part and ran out the back door.

Emily sat there with her mouth open, not knowing what to do.

## CHAPTER SIXTEEN

EMILY HAD NO IDEA how long she sat staring into space, trying to figure out who Becca was talking about. Then she understood. Becca was talking about Emily's daughter—the girl she was so jealous of whenever they'd talked about her. Emily would come home for her daughter but not for her sister—that was what Becca thought. Becca was confused. Inside she was still Rebecca Ann Cooper, Rose and Owen's daughter. Rebecca Ann, Emily's daughter, was still an alien person to her. Becca hadn't made the transition yet, and Emily couldn't expect her to do it overnight.

*Oh, God.* Emily buried her face in her hands. She'd told Jackson they shouldn't rush Becca, but in reality that was exactly what she'd done. She was overwhelming Becca. When they started the search for their daughter, she felt she wouldn't be able to walk away from her. That was proving to be true. She wanted her daughter, but she had to stop feeling that way. Becca needed time, and Emily had to give it to her. That would be so hard—for her and Jackson.

On the beach yesterday, when she and Becca had held each other, she'd thought everything would be fine, but Becca was obviously struggling with her emotions…namely anger. She seemed angry at everyone, and she was jealous of the other Rebecca—and of Jackson. That didn't leave Emily many choices. She would now earn the title of mother. She would sacrifice her happiness for her daughter's.

*Oh, Jackson, please understand.*

JACKSON HAD BREAKFAST then paced his hotel room, waiting. By nine o'clock he couldn't stand it anymore. He had to see them. He yanked open the door and Emily almost fell inside.

"Oh!" She held a hand to her chest. "You startled me. I was just about to knock."

He took her arm and led her inside. She looked tired and upset, and his heart went out to her. "I was just going to your house." He glanced toward the door. "Where's Becca?"

"She's gone to school," Emily said, sitting on the love seat. She noticed that Jackson wore jeans and a green shirt that intensified the color of his eyes. Her heart skipped a beat, but her attraction was quickly overshadowed by other problems. "Or at least I think that's where she went. She's so angry with me, she might've taken off someplace. I'm not actually sure where she is."

"What happened?" he asked, and sat beside her.

She described their talk and what Becca had said when she'd told her about commuting to her practice. "She's confused and doesn't know who she is. She's jealous of the other Rebecca. She's jealous of my relationship with you. I have to give her my full attention to prove that I love her and that I'll never leave her again."

Jackson listened closely and each word was like a nail driven into his heart. He had to be absolutely sure he was understanding her correctly. "You're planning to commute to your practice in Houston?" It didn't sound as if there was much room for him in that scenario. As a matter of fact, it sounded as if Emily had left him out completely.

"Yes—I don't see any other way. I can't disrupt her life any more than I already have."

"And where will I be while you're working and trying to build a relationship with our daughter?"

Her eyes met his. "I'm asking for your patience and understanding. We're rushing Becca, overwhelming her, and we can't do that. We *have* to give her time. We all need time, all three of us."

"What you're asking is that I go back to Dallas and forget about my daughter," he said flatly. Unable to remain still, he got to his feet.

"No." Emily immediately denied. "I would never ask that of you. Like I said, we all need time to adjust and come to terms with this new situation."

He heard the pain in her voice and something inside him melted. He ran a hand through his hair. "God, Emily, don't—"

She broke in. "I would never try to keep you from Becca, but she's hurting and angry. I can see that, and so can you. I'm just asking you to back off…for a short while."

Jackson stared down at his shoes. He had a daughter and, whatever Emily might say, she was trying to keep Becca from him. He felt his rights as a father had been diminished by the woman he loved. He wasn't sure how to deal with that. But if this was truly what Becca needed… He sighed. Yesterday in Rose's hospital room, he'd recognized all the things Emily was talking about but hadn't wanted to face them. Now he had to.

"How long?" he asked quietly.

"Until Becca's ready to accept us as her parents."

"A week? A month? A year?"

"I can't say."

He raised his eyes to hers. "What about us?"

She glanced away. "I can't think about us."

*I can't think about us. I can't think about us.* Those words burned like a fire through his system, singeing his body with a new kind of pain.

He had to know one thing. "Is that possible for you—to forget about us?"

She clenched her hands into fists. "Yes."

"What was San Antonio? Just a romp between the sheets for old time's sake?"

"It was much more than that, and you know it."

"No, I don't," he shot back. "I was thinking of love, family and a future, but that was never part of your plan, was it, Emily? From the moment we found out Becca was our daughter, you repeatedly used the word *alone*. It might've been subconscious, but you used it. You never had any intention of letting me be part of your lives."

"That's not true," she said, trying to keep her emotions in check. She was hurting him, but she saw no other option. She just wished he'd make an effort to understand. "Besides, this isn't about us. It's about Becca and what's best for her."

"Funny," he said sarcastically. "I mistakenly thought they were one and the same." He couldn't control his anger and he hated himself for that.

Emily saw him struggling and she had to force the next words from her throat. "When we started this, you promised me that if our daughter was happy, you'd walk away. Please don't break that promise."

His eyes flew to hers. "This is completely different."

"Exactly," she murmured. "We never imagined our daughter would be my sister. For that reason, we have to stop pressuring Becca. We can't expect her to become our daughter overnight. We wouldn't expect another girl to do that and we can't expect it of Becca."

Jackson didn't say anything because he knew she was right. However, he wasn't a patient man. He was a man of action, and he preferred to simply take what he wanted. But now he would learn patience—for his daughter. Even though he was upset with Emily, he would back off and give them time, as she'd requested. It would be one of the hardest things he'd ever have to do. And it made him angrier. He *shouldn't* have to do that. He shouldn't.

Emily got up and touched his arm, and he immediately pulled free. "No, don't touch me," he said. "Right now I—" He couldn't finish the sentence, but if she touched him in any way, he wouldn't be able to do what she wanted him to—which was to walk out of their lives.

With a breaking heart, Emily realized that by saving her daughter she was losing Jackson. He was angry with her, that was very plain, and she would have to cope with that in her own way.

"I'm sorry," she said, with a quaver in her voice.

The anger suddenly erupted in him. "I wish I could believe that, but you'll be with her every day. You'll be part of her life while I'll be the father who left her—again."

"It won't be like that and—"

Jackson couldn't tolerate any more. "Just go."

She swallowed hard and walked to the door on feet that felt like lead.

"Emily," he said as she twisted the knob.

"Yes?" She turned back, hoping they could end this on a happier note.

"I won't leave without talking to Becca first. I don't want her to think I'm running out on her."

"Okay," she replied. "But be prepared for her sharp tongue and insolent attitude. She's lashing out at everyone around her."

"I think I can handle it" was the quick retort.

Emily wanted to say something else, but the words wouldn't come. *Goodbye* hovered on her lips, but she would never say that word to Jackson again.

*I love you. Please understand.*

She didn't say those words, either. Tears stung her eyes as she walked out the door. She'd just lost the one thing that gave her joy—Jackson's love. How many mothers had made this type of sacrifice for their children? Too many, she decided.

EMILY DROVE STRAIGHT to the hospital, forcing herself not to think or feel, but when she parked her car, the walls came crashing down and she cried until she couldn't cry anymore. She wiped the tears away and rested her head against the seat. In those rare moments when she had allowed herself to envision finding her daughter, she'd pictured her with a loving family. She hoped they would meet the parents; she would thank them for raising her daughter and she also hoped she and Jackson would be permitted to visit occasionally and become acquainted with her. But it had turned out so differently than she'd ever imagined. There was so much pain and heartache. Would they ever get through it?

She didn't have an answer, but for her own peace of mind she had to mend her relationship with her mother. Did she have the strength to forgive? She'd told Becca to forgive, and now Emily had to do the same. She couldn't expect forgiveness unless she was willing to extend it herself—and it had to come from her heart.

As she walked to Rose's room, she kept hearing the pain in Jackson's voice and seeing the hurt in his eyes. She wanted to turn around and go back to him, try to make things right. But she didn't know what *right* was. She had to admit she was as confused as Becca. All she knew was that she and Becca had to find each other as mother and daughter. Until that happened, there wasn't a future for any of them as a family. How would she survive these next difficult months without Jackson? She wondered bleakly if the emptiness in her heart would ever go away.

When she entered the room, she discovered her father sitting in a chair reading the newspaper. Her mother was gazing out the window from her bed.

Rose's eyes brightened when she saw her. "Emily Ann, I'm glad you came."

Owen stood. "Think I'll get a cup of coffee."

"No, Dad," Emily said. "We need to talk about this together."

Owen nodded, and Emily walked to Rose's side.

"How's Rebecca?" Rose asked before Emily could speak.

"Angry and bitter." She didn't lie.

"She's always had a stubborn streak that was hard to control. I guess she got that from…" Rose didn't finish her sentence.

"Say his name," Emily insisted.

"Mr. Talbert."

"His name is Jackson," Emily said patiently.

"Jackson," Rose repeated.

"Yes, his name is Jackson and he's Becca's father and I hope he's going to be part of our lives. Right now, I'm not sure. I'm—" Her voice shook and tears filled her eyes.

Rose reached for Emily's hand. It was the first time Rose had freely touched her in years, and it unleashed something in Emily that had lain dormant for a long, long time—love for her mother.

"I'm so sorry, my baby," Rose whispered. "I'm sorry I hurt you. I'm sorry for everything."

The years of resentment seemed to dissipate and Emily reached for her mother, and Rose held her tight, stroking her hair. She needed this more than she needed Jackson or Becca right now. She needed to feel her mother's love.

Emily straightened, but Rose held on to her hand. "I wish I could change things, baby, but I can't go back and neither can you. Please forgive me."

In that instant Emily knew she'd forgiven her mother. From somewhere in her heart forgiveness flowed easily. Maybe it was because of the word *baby*. Her mother had always called her that and now it came naturally, just like the love they'd once shared. But Emily knew that life could never be the way it used to be—too much suffering had intervened. For Becca, though, she would strive to make things better.

For the next two hours, Emily talked with her parents and she didn't hold anything back. She told them how she'd felt when she was seventeen and now. She didn't try to spare their feelings. In the end, she told them her plans for Becca. She would now be Becca's mother, but she needed their help to make the transition. Both Owen and Rose agreed to help. They just wanted to remain part of Becca's life.

Emily left the hospital feeling better than when she'd walked in. She wished her conversation with Jackson had gone as well. She'd handled it all wrong, but she hadn't known what else to do. Right now, Becca needed her full attention.

*Jackson, please understand. Don't hate me.*

She'd told her parents that Jackson was going to stay in her life. Suddenly she realized she'd forgotten to tell Jackson that. She wasn't sure it would've made a difference, though. Jackson was hurt and she was hurt, and Becca was caught in the middle. Could she find a resolution?

LATER THAT AFTERNOON, Jackson waited for Becca to get out of school. He'd found her red Mustang so he knew she was here. When a horde of kids ran from the school toward their vehicles, he watched for her anxiously. He caught his breath when he saw her standing, talking and laughing with a group of kids. One of them was the boy from the prom—the one with long hair and an earring. He wasn't too pleased about that, but then his rights as a father were just about nil. That stirred resentment inside him and he hoped he could control it.

As she walked toward her car, he thought she was going to be as beautiful as Emily, but he saw qualities from the Talbert side in her, too. Yes, this was his daughter. His heart tightened, and he quickly got out of his car and met her at the Mustang.

She frowned at him and the laughing teenager he'd glimpsed a moment ago was gone. "What do you want?"

He could see the anger Emily was talking about; she made no effort to hide it. He wanted to help her, but he didn't know where to start. Emily was right. They needed time. That wasn't easy to admit or to accept.

"I want to talk to you," he said calmly.

"Take a number. Everyone wants to talk to me," she replied sarcastically, digging for keys in her purse.

"Ten minutes—that's all I'm asking."

Still searching for her keys, she said, "If you want me to forgive you, I forgive you. I forgive everybody for ruining my life. Satisfied?"

"I'm not asking for your forgiveness."

Her head jerked up and she stared at him. "What?"

"Until I can find a way to forgive myself, I don't expect you to forgive me."

"Oh," she murmured, and he could see he'd taken the wind out of her sails—or the bite out of her words.

He noticed that all the kids had left the grounds and he pointed at a vacant bench beneath a leaning oak tree. "Let's go over there and talk. It won't take long." He walked toward the bench and Becca opened her car and threw her books and purse on the seat, then slowly followed.

Jackson sat and she sank down beside him. "I just wanted to tell you I'll be going back to Dallas."

"So?"

"I didn't want you to think I'd deserted you."

"Why should I think or feel anything?"

"Because I'm your father and I love you. That's a given. But I'm not sure I like you…just yet."

She glared at him. "Everybody likes me, and I don't care if you do or not. A guy who runs out on a pregnant girl isn't someone I want to know."

Jackson inhaled deeply. "I had no idea Emily was pregnant. I'm not going to say that if I'd known I would've come running back. My life was a mess at the time, but I'd like to think I would've taken full responsibility for you and Emily."

"Big deal."

Jackson bit his tongue, then said, "You have a right to all that anger, but it doesn't change the fact that I'm your father."

Silence.

"The important thing now is for you and Emily to have some time alone—to get to know each other."

"I know Emily fine."

"Not as a mother, you don't. Give her a chance, Becca."

Becca gazed down at the ground, her dark hair covering her face.

"This isn't easy for any of us," Jackson went on. "And

leaving isn't easy, either. But I don't know what else to do." Becca didn't respond, so he said, "If you need anything, I'm only a phone call away."

"I won't need you," she muttered sullenly.

"On second thought, I'll call you."

She glanced at him. "What if I don't want to talk to you?"

"Then just say you don't want to talk and I'll hang up. No pressure, but at least I'll hear your voice."

A puzzled look crossed her face, and Jackson reached in his pocket and handed her a card. "Here are my numbers—home, office, cell phone, and at the bottom is my dad's. If you can't reach me, he'll probably know where I am."

Her eyes widened. "You have a dad?"

"Sure do, and he's very anxious to meet his new granddaughter."

Fear flashed into her eyes and Jackson saw it for what it was—a fear of the unknown, of overwhelming events that were happening too fast for a seventeen-year-old girl.

"Don't worry," he assured her. "You don't have to deal with my family until you're ready. I promise."

"Good, because I have all the family I need."

Jackson's throat closed in pain. Her cruel words were getting to him and he had to be stronger than this. He studied her face. "You have my mother's nose and her mouth," he said quietly.

"Jeez, am I supposed to meet her, too?"

"No, she's dead. She died the year you were born."

"Oh…yeah. I remember Emily mentioning something about that," she muttered. Jackson sensed she'd wanted to say more.

Silence reigned again.

"If that's all, I've got to go. Tommy's waiting." She got to her feet.

Jackson stood also. "The boy with the earring."

Her eyes challenged him. "Yeah, you got something to say about it?"

"Enjoy yourself and enjoy life, but don't be too eager to experience it too fast. It comes quick enough."

"What kind of crap is that?" she asked rudely.

"Just a father's—"

She interrupted. "Don't say it." She put her hands over her ears. "I don't want to hear it."

He removed her hands. "I'm sorry this has caused you so much pain. You've had two parents who've loved and cared for you for seventeen years. It's selfish of me to try and snatch that away from you, and I won't." He swallowed. "But if you find there might be a place in your heart for me, all you have to do is call."

He walked to his car, got in and drove away. He didn't look back. He couldn't. His nerves were tied in such knots that one glimpse would cause him to break down. He had to resist the urge to find Emily, to see her one more time before he left. He didn't know what good that would do. They were both struggling to stay afloat in a sea of emotions that were threatening to pull them under. But, God, he needed her. Now he'd have to wait...wait to see if Emily needed him, too.

THE DAYS THAT FOLLOWED were the worst Emily had ever spent, except for the day they'd taken her baby. Becca tried her patience to the limit, but she didn't falter or give up. Rose came home from the hospital and things got worse, if that was possible. Becca was even more sullen, rude and belligerent. Nothing anyone said made a difference, and Emily began to despair of ever reaching her.

Finally she knew they needed counseling. She arranged for her parents, Becca and her to see a psychologist in Corpus Christi. Becca threw a fit and didn't show up for the appointment. Emily tried to talk to her, but she adamantly refused to have anything to do with a psychologist.

Emily talked to a friend in Houston who was also a psychologist, and she told Emily that Becca was going through a trauma; it would take her time to adjust. She told Emily not to force her, just to be patient and supportive, constantly showing Becca that she loved her. Emily went along with her advice, and she and her parents continued to see the therapist once a week in Corpus Christi. She was surprised they didn't object.

Every day she thought of Jackson and wished for his presence, but she'd made the decision to do this alone. In the turmoil of things she'd forgotten to give him the photos of Becca. She put them in an album and mailed them, hoping they'd bring him some comfort.

Emily drove the three-hour commute to and from work daily. She had talked with Dr. Bensen and explained the situation. She cut back her hours so she could get home by six, but Becca didn't care. She wasn't home most days when Emily got there. Emily then had to search Rockport to find her. An argument would ensue, although Becca always came home.

Becca wanted her room back and asked Emily to move out. That hurt. They'd always shared a room. Emily didn't say anything. She moved into the bedroom off the kitchen, the one her parents saved for tourists.

Rose and Owen were there for support, and it helped at times, but she really needed Jackson. She couldn't handle Becca. Their special bond had been irrevocably broken, and there didn't seem to be a way back.

JACKSON THREW HIMSELF into his work. He tried not to think. His only goal was to get through each day. He knew he was bad-tempered, and his staff, even Colton, left him to his own misery.

Nancy, his secretary, walked into his office one afternoon, two weeks after his return. "You have a package," she said.

"Fine," he growled, not taking his eyes off the computer screen. "Put it anywhere."

"It's from Rockport."

He raised his head and grabbed the package from his desk. "Thanks," he mumbled, ripping the paper away.

Nancy departed quickly.

There was a note attached to the front of an album. "Thought you might like these. Emily." He slowly opened the cover and his heart raced as he stared at pictures of his daughter from the day she was born to the previous Christmas. There she was in a crib, sitting on a bicycle, holding a fishing rod and standing by the red Mustang, and so many more that he lost himself in her life. His heart completely stopped when he saw what was beneath the album—a framed eight-by-ten of Becca as she was today.

Dark eyes, just like Emily's, stared back at him. He reached out and touched her precious face and felt an intense need to call Emily. He picked up the phone, then immediately replaced it. If he heard her voice, he'd be back in Rockport in a flash and he couldn't do that. He had to give them time—as he'd promised. He wouldn't break that promise.

Colton entered the office and Jackson smiled at him. Colton seemed taken aback. Jackson hadn't smiled in days.

"Want to see the most beautiful girl in the whole world?" Jackson asked, still smiling.

"Sure," Colton answered guardedly.

Jackson handed him the eight-by-ten of Becca. "That's my daughter."

"Wow," Colton said, studying the face.

Jackson flipped through the album and found the picture he wanted—one of Emily and Becca with their arms around each other. He turned it around so Colton could see and pointed to the photo. "That's her mother."

"Wow," Colton said again. "I see where she gets her looks."

"Yeah." Jackson sighed. He kept gazing at the photo. Emily and Becca appeared to be close to the same age, but they were mother and daughter. God, how he missed them.

"Jackson?"

Shocked by hearing his name, he raised his head. He'd forgotten Colton was in the room.

"I hate to bother you, but I just came by the front office and Janine is out there, asking to see you."

"Damn, I'd forgotten all about Janine wanting to talk to me. I left my cell number and she never called. Must be important, though, if she came over here on a workday."

Colton shrugged. "Must be. Just thought I'd warn you."

Almost on cue, his intercom buzzed. He glanced at Colton. "I'll handle it. Thanks."

As Jackson pressed the button, Colton walked out. "Yes, Nancy?" he said into the intercom.

"Ms. Taylor's here to see you."

"Send her in, please." He didn't know what Janine wanted, and he'd really rather not talk to her, but an encounter of some sort was obviously unavoidable.

Janine swept into his office wearing a cream suit with a short skirt and matching heels. Her blond hair was shoulder-length and her blue eyes were frowning at him.

"Where have you been? I've been trying to reach you for weeks. I thought you lived in this office. At least you did when we were together."

Jackson got to his feet and wondered how he'd ever thought he loved this woman. She was nothing like Emily and— He stopped his thoughts. "You had my cell number, Janine. You could've called me back," he remarked in a mild tone.

"I'm sorry," she immediately apologized. "I'm just feeling tense these days and I wanted to talk to you in person."

"Have a seat," Jackson invited.

Janine took the leather chair across from his desk. She crossed her legs and the sight did absolutely nothing for Jackson. Whatever he'd felt for her had died a long time ago.

"How's your father?" she asked.

"Fine," he replied. "What's on your mind, Janine?" He wanted to get this over with as quickly as possible.

She smoothed her stocking-clad knee with a nervous hand. "My life's a mess and I need help."

Jackson was thrown by the personal statement. It wasn't as though he and Janine were the best of friends or shared confidences anymore. They'd divorced and gone their separate ways.

He rubbed his chin. "I'm not sure how that concerns me."

"Oh, Jackson, just let me explain, okay? This is important."

"What is?"

"You know how hard I've worked to make partner in the law firm."

"It's been your goal ever since I met you."

"A month ago Mike Garrett made partner. I was

shocked. He's been with the firm ten years and I've been there twelve. I put in a helluva lot more hours than he does and I bring in more clients, but he made partner because he has connections and he's a man. I can see now that a woman will never succeed in this firm and I've made my position very clear. I'm leaving.''

Jackson shook his head. "Janine, I sympathize with you. I know how hard you've worked and how badly you wanted to become a partner, but shouldn't you be talking to your husband? This doesn't really have anything to do with me.''

"I need your help.''

"But I'm not the one who—''

"I need money.''

"Janine.'' He sighed.

"I need twenty thousand to open my own firm. I'll pay you back. You know I will.''

Jackson's eyes narrowed. "How does Les feel about you asking me for money?''

Janine looked down at her hands, folded in her lap.

"You haven't told him, have you?'' he guessed.

"Not yet,'' she admitted. "We spent our savings on the new house. We wanted a big place for when his kids come to visit and we wanted a pool and a tennis court for entertaining. It was extravagant, but I didn't know my career was going to fall apart.''

"I'm sorry,'' he said, and he was. Her ambitions had dictated the course of Janine's life; this failure must be harrowing for her.

She raised her eyes to his. "Please help me. You're the only person I know who's got that kind of money.''

Jackson didn't want any ties to Janine, but he couldn't say no. "I can't lend you money unless you tell Les,'' he warned.

"We've talked about the idea of me opening my own firm, but we couldn't afford to borrow any more money. Besides, this is my decision and no man tells me what I can and can't do. You know me well enough to know that."

Yes, he did. All through their marriage, she'd never wavered on any decision, especially about having children. Secretly he suspected she'd married Les because he already had kids and it wouldn't be an issue. Janine's life was her career. He'd learned that the hard way. Looking back, he could see they'd been so wrong for each other. He'd wanted a home and family and she'd wanted security. Ironically she was still fighting for security, as he was for a family. Their lives might not intersect anymore, but he genuinely wished her well.

He opened a drawer, pulled out his checkbook and began to write. "I don't keep that much money in my checking account, but I'll make sure the money's there tomorrow." He held out the check.

"Thank you, Jackson," she said as she stood to take it from him. "You won't regret this."

"Tell Les. That's my only condition," he told her.

"I will," she agreed. Putting the check in her purse, she noticed the picture of Becca.

"Who's the pretty young girl?"

Jackson took a breath and couldn't keep the words from slipping out. "My daughter."

"What?" Janine drew back in shock.

"She's my daughter," he repeated.

"A daughter? When did this happen?"

"She'll be eighteen in August. I just found out about her."

Her eyes narrowed. "Are you sure she's yours? I mean…"

"She's mine, Janine. There's no question about it."

"I see," she said, and lightly touched the picture. "The mother never told you about her?"

"No" was all he said. He didn't want to discuss Emily or Becca with Janine.

"All the time we were married, you wanted a child. Maybe if we'd known about her our marriage might have worked out differently."

It wouldn't have, simply because he didn't love Janine the way he loved Emily. But he couldn't hurt her feelings by saying that. He stood. "Maybe, but we'll never know," he murmured. "I hope everything goes well with the new practice."

"Thanks, Jackson," she said as she made her way to the door. She turned back. "I'm glad you have a daughter."

"Me, too," he said. "Goodbye, Janine." He was glad they could remain cordial.

As soon as she'd left, he picked up the album and photo. He knew someone who needed to see these. His dad.

GEORGE WASN'T IN THE HOUSE, which meant he was out fishing. He always kept iced tea in the refrigerator so Jackson poured two glasses and carried them onto the deck. He saw his father in a boat on the lake. He waved and George waved back. He heard the gunning of the outboard motor and knew he was headed for shore. Jackson went back into the house and brought out a box and set it on the patio table. He'd had Jeff, an employee, make copies of every picture in the album, knowing his dad would want them.

Jackson relaxed in a redwood chair and waited. It wasn't long before George pulled the boat onto shore and strolled to the house.

"Jack, my boy, what brings you out in the middle of the afternoon?" George called.

"Catch anything?" he asked, avoiding the question.

"Not a damn thing," George replied as he walked up the steps. He removed his wide-brimmed straw hat and sat down. "It's May and it's already hot. Guess the fish are lazy." He reached for the tea and took several swallows. "Thanks, son."

"No problem," Jackson said.

George removed a handkerchief from his back pocket and mopped his brow. "If this heat keeps up, we're gonna have one helluva hot summer."

"Probably."

George noticed the box. "What's in there?"

"Something I thought you might like to have."

"If it's more of those books on how to use my computer, I—"

"It's not about your computer." He smiled and opened the box. First he pulled out the eight-by-ten he'd had framed. "Thought you might want to see your grand-daughter," he added, placing the picture in front of him.

"Oh, oh, oh." A pleasurable moan escaped his throat. "Is that her?"

"That's Becca," Jackson assured him.

"She's so pretty and grown-up—and oh, my God."

"What?" Jackson asked at his startled voice.

"She has the Jackson nose and mouth. I wish Sarah could see this." Jackson was his mother's maiden name.

He stood and put an arm around his father's shoulder. Not wanting this to be a sad time, he pulled the album forward.

"Here she is from the day she was born."

As George studied each picture, he dabbed at his eyes

several times. "Thanks, son. This is the best gift you've ever given me."

"Better than that expensive computer you never use."

George grinned. "Much better."

Jackson felt the same way and he was glad Emily had made the kind gesture. It meant she was thinking about him. That gave him hope.

EMILY WAS AT HER WIT'S END with Becca's rebellion, and she was getting a glimpse of what her mother had gone through. While she couldn't talk to Becca, she could talk to Rose. The therapy sessions had helped tremendously. In the therapist's opinion, Rose had actually had a nervous breakdown eighteen years ago, and her guilt over making Emily give her baby up for adoption, plus not wanting her own child had driven her to it. Emily found it so much easier to understand when another person explained it, but at times it was still difficult to accept.

Becca was slowly starting to talk to Rose, which Emily saw as a positive sign. The only person Becca had consistent difficulty with was Emily, but Emily kept waiting for things to change.

One day she was about to knock on Becca's door, but stopped when she heard her talking, obviously on the phone. As she began to move away, she heard Becca say *Jackson*. She was talking to Jackson and she didn't sound belligerent; she sounded almost happy. Silently, Emily went back to her room.

How long had they been calling each other? Becca hadn't said a word, and Jackson—she hadn't talked to him since he'd left. Every day she'd waited for him to call, to thank her for the photos, but he hadn't, and she recognized that he was upset...and that he was giving her the time she'd asked for. Still, she wanted to hear his voice. She didn't call him, though, and she knew that had something to do with his not coming back all those years ago. Was she trying to punish him? The thought shocked her and she fought a wave of panic.

She loved Jackson and even subconsciously she wouldn't do such a thing. Would she? She needed him and so did Becca—that was very plain from the way she was talking to him. Emily knew she'd been so wrong when she'd insisted on this separation. Becca responded to Jackson much more than she did to her. Becca was angry with *her,* but she didn't have that anger toward Jackson.

Oh, God, what had she done? Lying in bed, she could almost hear Jackson's warm voice washing over her. It had been so long since he'd touched her and she ached for him, ached for everything she'd lost.

All she had to do was pick up the phone, but in truth she knew she wasn't ready. She had to resolve things with Becca first.

# CHAPTER SEVENTEEN

JACKSON SPENT HIS DAYS waiting for evenings, when he could talk to Becca. She had her own phone line, a gift from Emily, and he called every night when he knew she'd be there. At first the conversations were stilted and short. She never told him she didn't want to talk, though, and gradually their talks became longer.

Then one day the phone rang, and it was Becca. That was a shock, but it didn't take him long to recover. Becca wanted to let him know that she was planning to move in with her friend Ginger. She was old enough to do what she wanted and she was tired of everyone being on her case, she said. Jackson knew it was a cry for help, and he prayed for the right response.

He told her she was indeed old enough, but with age came responsibility. Was she responsible enough to be out on her own? She was quiet for a long time, then admitted she wasn't sure. Jackson let out a sigh of relief. What Becca was trying to do here was hurt Emily, and he wanted to make sure that didn't happen. Yet he had to avoid actually saying those words.

A few days later she called again. This time she said she'd decided not to go to college. She was planning to travel across the United States on a motorcycle with her boyfriend, Tommy. He had to restrain himself, but he felt it was a test—to see how he'd react.

When he didn't say anything, she asked, "Aren't you gonna try and talk me out of it?"

"Is that what you want me to do?"

Silence.

"I want you to be happy," he finally said. "If traveling on a motorcycle will make you happy, then I'll have to accept it, but I'd miss you terribly."

"You would?"

Behind the words, he heard a desperate need for love. "You bet I would, angel."

"What did you call me?"

"I'm sorry," he said in apology, not wanting to rush her. "But in my head, that's what I call you. My angel, my light at the end of a long, hard day."

"Jeez." She sighed, and Jackson waited for sharp, piercing words. They didn't come and he felt they were making progress. He hoped they were. He wanted to ask about Emily and had to force himself not to.

After that, she called on a regular basis. It was, as he'd told her, the highlight of his day. One evening he was at his father's trying to pacify George's urgent need to see his granddaughter, when she called. Jackson was startled. She never called him at his dad's. They talked for a while about school and graduation. George was cooking supper and he made some noise with a pot.

"Is that my grandfather?" she asked.

Jackson was taken aback by the question. Again he didn't want to rush her, but he wouldn't lie, either. "Yeah, he's cooking us a bite to eat and you should taste his food— Artery-clogging specialties."

Becca laughed. It was the first time he'd heard that bubbly, bright sound and it warmed his heart. "Can I say hi to him?"

He didn't answer right away. His dad had been waiting

for this moment, but Jackson wanted to be sure Becca was ready. "Okay, but Becca—"

"It's all right," she broke in. "I'd really like to talk to him."

Jackson put the phone down and turned to his father. "Someone wants to talk to you."

"If it's Maudie, tell her I'm busy." His dad was so engrossed in his cooking he hadn't even realized who Jackson was talking to.

"It's not Aunt Maude, it's Becca."

"What?" George whirled around, his eyes enormous in a pale face.

Jackson held the receiver out to him.

"It's really my granddaughter?"

Jackson smiled. "Yeah, Dad, it's really Becca and if you don't hurry, she might hang up."

George wiped his hands on a towel and took the receiver. Jackson noticed that his hand was shaking.

They talked for a few minutes, then George gave him back the phone, wiping away a tear. Jackson wanted to tell her how proud he was of her, but he didn't. He let her talk; that seemed to be the course of their conversations. Soon he hung up.

"She invited me to her graduation," George said excitedly.

"I know, she invited me, too."

George frowned. "You're not gonna ask me not to go, are you, son?"

"No," Jackson replied. "She seems to want us there, and that's good. I think she's coming around, but we still have to be patient."

George agreed, and Jackson knew his dad would do anything he had to. They both were willing to do whatever Becca needed. Jackson wondered if Emily was aware that

Becca had invited them. Surely she was, and that gave him a good feeling. He could look at things more clearly now. Emily was dealing with a lot of raw emotion and she was fighting for her daughter—their daughter. He understood that. He was just sorry he'd gotten angry with her. He missed her so much, especially at night when she was all he thought about. He was hoping that graduation would prove to be a big night not only for Becca, but also for him and Emily. And maybe, just maybe, they could talk and he wouldn't be coming back to Dallas for a while.

BY THE TIME GRADUATION came around, Emily was exhausted physically, mentally and emotionally. She didn't know how much more of her daughter's rebellious behavior she could take. Becca defied her at every turn. She stayed out late and started running with a wild crowd, but Emily dogged her every move, terrified that Becca's rebellion would drive her to make the same mistakes Emily had made.

Emily wanted to call Jackson, but again she didn't. She just kept hoping Becca's attitude would change. Then, all of a sudden, it happened. Becca became subdued instead of aggressive, although, Emily had no idea why. Becca still talked to Jackson, and Emily was tempted to ask if she'd thought about inviting him to her graduation, but she didn't do that, either. It had to be Becca's decision.

But Emily did make a decision of her own. After graduation, they were moving to Houston, to her condo. Becca took the news relatively well. They didn't even argue about it and for that Emily was grateful. She couldn't handle the commute any longer. Getting up at four each morning had taken its toll on her emotional stamina.

Her parents were worried, but she assured them they'd be okay. She knew they would miss Becca; however, a change of environment would be good for everyone. Despite the stress in the household, Rose's health had improved. Emily knew that was largely due to the fact that Becca was now Emily's responsibility, and she realized that raising Becca had taken its toll on Rose's health. Guilt had a lot to do with it, too, of course. Now that her secret was out, Rose was almost back to her old self, the mother Emily remembered from her childhood. Not only that, Rose and Becca were able to have civil conversations these days. That was the good thing that had come out of all this. Becca had forgiven Rose but Emily had to wonder if Becca would ever forgive *her*.

GRADUATION WAS A BIG NIGHT, and the place was packed. Emily wore a lavender suit and sat with Rose and Owen. She'd given Becca a gold-and-diamond watch for graduation; Becca had accepted it graciously. She didn't throw it back in Emily's face or say anything hurtful. Emily took that as a good omen for the evening.

As Becca walked across the stage to accept her diploma, Emily's heart swelled with pride. This was her baby and she was graduating. Emily fought back tears. Becca was one of the top students in her class and Emily knew that if she applied herself she could do anything she wanted in this world.

When Becca walked offstage, she waved to someone and Emily strained to see who it was. *Jackson.* Her pulse hammered rapidly. Jackson was here, and it looked like Mr. Talbert was with him. Had Becca invited them? Why had no one said anything? The evening took a nosedive and she felt hurt and left out. *Was this how Jackson had felt?* Oh, God, there was too much hurt, too much suffering, and it had to stop.

She and Jackson should be here together, sharing this

moment in joy and love, but the gulf between them seemed to be growing wider and wider.

JACKSON LOOKED ALL AROUND for Emily, but he couldn't find her. After the ceremony, Becca rushed over to them. Jackson hugged her and she hugged him back, then he introduced George. Unable to resist, George hugged her, too. Jackson held his breath, but Becca just laughed her bubbly laugh.

Jackson pulled a velvet box from his suit pocket. "Something from Dad and me for your graduation."

Becca popped open the lid. "Oh," she breathed as she stared at the gold heart encircled with diamonds.

"It belonged to my mother. I thought you might like to have it."

"Oh...it's beautiful." She glanced at Jackson. "Thank you. Put it on me, please." Becca gathered her long hair, holding it away from her neck.

Jackson took the necklace from its resting place and fastened it. She fingered the pendant as it lay just below her chin.

"How does it look?" she asked.

"Not near as beautiful as the young lady wearing it," George replied before Jackson could speak.

"Ah, jeez." Becca grinned.

People were milling around them and Jackson just had to ask. "Where's Emily?"

Becca pointed across the room. "She's over there. I guess you want to see her."

A complete change came over Becca when he mentioned Emily, and he knew things were not good between them. Nevertheless, all three of them moved across the floor to where the Coopers stood. Despite the crowd, Jackson saw only one person—Emily. She looked gorgeous, but her eyes were tired and he could see the strain on her face.

Emily saw them coming and she stared at Jackson, gazing her fill. He was so handsome in that dark-blue suit and all she wanted to do was to throw her arms around him and forget everyone else in this room. But, of course, she didn't. She politely shook hands, as did her parents.

Her cool reception threw Jackson. There was no welcome in her eyes—just hurt—and his heart sank. The evening was not turning out the way he'd hoped.

"You sure have a beautiful daughter, Emily," George was saying.

"Thank you," Emily replied courteously. "I think she's just about perfect."

"Yeah, right," Becca sighed sarcastically, and Jackson knew for sure that things had deteriorated between them. What had happened?

George was startled by Becca's tone, and Jackson started to step in and say something, but he'd promised to let Emily handle Becca. He had to keep that promise. His arms were aching to hold her, to ease the agony in her eyes, but until she asked for his help, he couldn't do that, either.

Emily heard them saying their goodbyes, but she was stuck on the outer edge of reality and she couldn't find her way back. The pain in her chest kept her hanging there, alone, with help from no one, and that was another cold truth she had to accept.

Jackson looked into her eyes for endless seconds, waiting for a sign, anything to show that she needed him. There was nothing. She seemed lost in a place he couldn't reach. It frightened him and yet he was powerless to intervene.

As Jackson and his father walked away, Emily struggled

to find her voice, but it was buried deep inside with all the hurt and pain.

*Jackson, don't go. Please come back.*

The words rattled through her throat, then sank to the pit of her stomach—a heavy weight that threatened to take her down. Through sheer willpower, she maintained her balance. But the price was way too high and she didn't know if she'd survive much more of this.

BEFORE THEY LEFT for Houston, Rose wanted to have a birthday party for Becca, but Becca adamantly refused, saying she wasn't going to celebrate her birthday anymore. They acquiesced to her wishes; Emily thought it was just as well, because soon she'd be celebrating her real birthday. That transition had to be made, but as with everything else, it had to be done with great care.

The move to Houston went smoothly until Becca saw her room. She'd always had a room in Emily's condo. During previous summers she'd spent a lot of weekends with Emily, whenever Rose would allow it. Emily had the bedroom decorated about five years ago in pink and white, and she'd recently felt it was time for a change. She'd called a decorator and most of the planning had been done on the phone. Emily had very little time, but she wanted the room ready for their homecoming. The color scheme was now cream, burgundy and deep pink. Emily hoped it would be a nice surprise for Becca; it was just the opposite. As Becca looked around, her eyes grew stormy.

"What happened to my room?" she demanded.

"I had it redecorated. Don't you like it?"

"No, I hate it," was the angry response. "I want my old room back."

Emily had to take a deep breath. "I spent a lot of money to make your room special. I thought you'd be pleased."

"Well, I'm not," Becca spat, and flung long hair over her shoulder with a shake of her head. "You did this for *her,* not me. I was satisfied with my old room."

Becca's strange words had a calming effect on Emily. Clearly, she was still struggling with her identity—not knowing who she really was and hating that Emily lavished so much attention on the other Rebecca.

She took a step toward her. "You *are* her, Becca. You're my daughter."

"No," Becca said, shaking her head again. "I *can't* be her. I'm me. You can't change me."

"I'm not trying to change you," Emily said lovingly, hoping to reach her.

"Yes, you are. You want me to be someone I'm not."

Emily fought for words to convince her; their relationship depended on it. "I love you just the way you are. I love the same little girl who mailed her tooth to me when she was five."

"Yeah, I had to because you weren't around so I could give it to you," she said sarcastically.

Emily let that pass. "I love the same seven-year-old who called me because she had a hundred-and-four-degree fever and wanted me with her."

"It was the only way you'd come home."

Again Emily didn't react. "And I love the same thirteen-year-old who called me because she had her first period and was afraid. I came home immediately to reassure you."

"Yeah, that was a shock."

"You can say all the nasty things you want, but I've always been there for you in one way or another since you were born. We have a connection, and now I treasure it more than ever."

Becca raised her troubled eyes to Emily. "You gave me

away,'' she cried, the words coming from deep within her. ''You weren't strong enough to fight for me. *You gave me away.*''

Guilt ripped through her. She gasped from the pain and struggled to keep her emotions in check—for Becca and herself. She'd been trying to talk to Becca for weeks and now that they were talking, she had to help her bridge that gap from past to present.

She let out a tight breath. ''No, I wasn't strong enough then, and I've suffered every day since for that weakness.'' She had to pause as her throat thickened. ''When I told you about my baby, I though you understood. You were very compassionate.''

''But it was *me*. I didn't know it was *me*.''

Emily had to find the words to assuage her daughter's pain without considering her own. ''I didn't, either, but I'm so glad it *was* you. At least you're not with strangers and I've always been part of your life. That I'm very grateful for.''

Becca's eyes pierced her. ''Then why do you have to study my face and look at my baby pictures over and over? I'm still Becca, and you can't find someone in me that I'm not.''

''Becca, I—''

''Don't deny it, because you act weird and do things you wouldn't normally do. Jackson doesn't. He accepts me for who I am. Why can't you? Why do you have to treat me differently?''

Intense pain gripped Emily as Becca's words slammed through her. Becca was right; she was treating her differently. *She* was the reason Becca was so confused. She could see that now. Oh, God, she was driving her daughter away! She'd asked Jackson to back off when in reality she was the one who needed time to come to terms with the new revelation in her life. She was overwhelming Becca and frightening her—exactly what she'd told herself she wouldn't do.

Gulping in air, she said, "I'm sorry, Becca. You're right, I have been acting differently."

Becca didn't say anything.

"You see, I'm fighting to keep us together, but the truth is we've always been together, so I'll stop rushing you and…and acting weird."

"Fine," Becca mumbled.

"I still have that tooth you mailed me."

Becca made a face. "It probably stinks by now."

"I don't mind." Emily wanted to sound lighthearted, although she was trying desperately not to fall apart. "And I'll have the room changed back as soon as I can."

Becca glanced around. "I guess it's not so bad. The pink was getting too girlish."

Emily bit her lip, grateful for this small concession. "Live with it awhile and then we'll discuss it."

"Whatever."

Emily wanted to hold Becca, but Becca wasn't ready for that. Still, Emily felt they'd taken a step toward the future. At least they were talking. She would hold on to that and she would stop acting *weird,* as Becca called it. That was hard when all she wanted to do was surround her daughter with love.

THEY SETTLED INTO an easy routine. Becca seemed like her old self at times; at others she was sullen or subdued, but they were coping. Emily tried to get Becca to see her friend, the psychologist, but again Becca obstinately refused.

Emily got her a job at the clinic as Dr. Hillson's receptionist. Things went relatively well for a couple of weeks, and Emily began to hope the worst was over. Then Mrs. Henry's grandson, Dylan, came to visit. Mrs. Henry was an elderly neighbor with whom Emily had always had a pleasant relationship. Becca started to hang around with him, frequently inviting him to Emily's place, where they watched TV and listened to music that got on her nerves. Emily didn't like him. He had shifty eyes and she caught him staring openly at her body on several occasions. She wanted to slap his face and tell him to leave her home— but she didn't. She and Becca were making progress and she didn't want to ruin that.

Then Becca started missing work and Emily had to talk to her, which caused a big argument, but Becca promised to do better.

Things between her and Becca were increasingly strained because of Dylan and Emily's objections to him. He was twenty-three, too mature for Becca, but Becca wouldn't listen.

The urge to call Jackson was strong and she didn't understand why she couldn't just pick up the phone and do it. She loved him and wanted to spend the rest of her life with him, yet she couldn't sink her pride enough to make the first move. Would the past never let her go?

It all came to a head one morning. Dr. Hillson's secretary called to say that Becca hadn't showed up again. Emily quickly phoned the condo, but there was no answer. She called Mrs. Henry, who said Becca had gone with Dylan to get a burger. She thought Emily knew. Emily told her to have Becca call as soon as she got back.

Emily was fuming, but she tried to see patients, tried to get through her normal routine. By two o'clock, Becca still hadn't called, so Emily phoned Mrs. Henry again. She said they hadn't come back and she was worried. She was calling Dylan's mom because she couldn't handle him. Emily told her that was a good idea.

At three Emily had had enough. She told Jean she had to leave and that she'd have to take care of the patients. Jean didn't say anything because she was aware of the turmoil in Emily's life.

When Emily entered her condo, she stood there for a moment in shock. Pizza boxes and beer cans and other trash were all over the place. The coffee table was overturned. The litter showed there'd been more than two people here today. How many?

Mrs. Henry came up behind her. "Oh, my God, what happened?"

"That's what I'd like to know," Emily said. "Looks like someone had a party. Surely you heard something?"

"Just the loud music. Dylan said Becca invited him over. I didn't know, Dr. Cooper. I'm sorry."

Emily ran both hands through her hair. "Where do you think they've gone?"

Mrs. Henry shrugged. "I have no idea, but Dylan likes beer and bars. That's why his mom sent him to live with me awhile. He had his driver's license taken away and was one step away from jail. She thought a change of atmosphere might help."

Emily let out a long breath. She'd figured Dylan had a past and Becca was no match for someone of that type. She had to find her daughter.

"There have to be a thousand or more bars in Houston," she muttered under her breath.

"I'll call his mother." Mrs. Henry headed out the door. "She might know, and she's coming to get him 'cause I'm not putting up with this."

Becca's Mustang was in the garage, so that meant she was with someone else. But who? And where? Probably with Dylan and his older friends in some bar, drinking. That answer tortured her mind. Becca was way out of her league with these people, who didn't care anything about her. The boys were only looking for a good time and Becca knew nothing about the kind of games they had in mind.

Fear gripped her—fear for Becca. She sank to the floor, her wobbly legs unable to hold her. Tears welled up in her eyes and she brushed them impatiently away. She'd cried so much in the last weeks that she wasn't going to cry anymore. She sat there feeling lost and alone.

*But she wasn't alone.*

Someone loved Becca as much as she did. Finally she knew what she had to do, what she should've done weeks ago. Why had it been so hard before? She crawled on her hands and knees and reached for the phone, pulling it down to her. Her pride, the past, nothing mattered now. She called Jackson. Pride came before a fall, they said. Well, she had fallen and she needed Jackson to pick her up. Oh, she needed him. *Becca* needed him.

JACKSON WAS LIKE A ZOMBIE as he went through the routine of each day. Colton had practically taken over the running of the company, gaining confidence and establishing good working relationships with their customers. Colton was no longer the man behind the scenes; he was out in front and relishing his new role. Jackson was glad because he was in no condition to concentrate on work. He helped when a major problem arose and tried to bolster Colton's ego, but other than that, he could have been hundreds of miles away, and he wanted to be—with Emily and Becca.

Becca hadn't called in two days and he sensed that something was wrong. He tried calling the condo, but there was no answer.

When his private line rang, he immediately picked it up and his heart twisted as he heard her voice. "Jackson, I need you. I can't do this alone anymore. She's gone and I don't know where to look for her. She's with this wild boy and..." Her words trailed away.

"Where are you?"

"At the condo."

"Hang on. I'll get there as fast as I can."

"Colton," Jackson shouted, not bothering with the intercom. Colton appeared as if by magic.

"What's wrong?"

"Call Bart. See if he's free and can fly me to Houston. I need to get there as fast as I can. Meanwhile, I'll check with the airlines."

"Sure thing," Colton responded, and disappeared into his office without another word.

The airlines didn't have a flight right away. Jackson slammed the phone down as Colton came back. "You're in luck. Bart says he was just sitting around wanting something to do."

"Great," Jackson said, heading for the door. He ran to his car. He'd waited what seemed like forever for Emily to call him, and now that she had, he wasn't going to let her down. The pain and despair in her voice got to him, and his insides roiled with fear at what lay ahead.

Fifteen minutes later, he was in the sky on his way to Houston.

*Please, Emily. Be patient. I'm coming.*

EMILY COLLECTED HERSELF before Mrs. Henry came back. Jackson was coming. She could deal with the situation now.

Mrs. Henry rushed in, waving a piece of paper. "His mother wasn't sure about the name, but she said his fa-

vorite bar was called something like this.'' She handed
Emily the paper.

She studied the names. Peek a Boob. Peek a Babe.
Babes and Boobs. *One of these or something similar* was
written at the bottom. Great, she thought sarcastically. This
would be like finding the proverbial needle in a haystack.
She grabbed the phone book. There were two clubs with
similar names and she jotted down the addresses. These
clubs were for older people who favored a risqué lifestyle.
Becca didn't know anything about such places. Emily
knew very little herself, but she was certain they weren't
for Becca.

Scribbling the addresses again on a pad, she handed it
to Mrs. Henry. ''Mr. Talbert is on his way from Dallas.
When he arrives, please give him this.''

''Don't you think you should wait for him?''

''I can't,'' Emily said, running for the door. ''I have to
find my daughter.''

Emily drove around and around, and she felt as if she
was going in circles. She'd never been in this area of
Houston and she got lost several times. Finally she located
one of the bars. As she walked inside, her skin crawled
with revulsion at the dimly lit room, the scantily clad girls
and men with leering eyes. But she forced herself to keep
looking. She sat a table and scanned all the faces. Becca
and Dylan were nowhere in sight. She ordered a beer because she was expected to order something. A man came
over and tried to pick her up. She told him she was waiting
for her boyfriend and he moved away. Clearly Becca
wasn't here, so she gladly left.

Wondering if Jackson had arrived yet, she phoned her
condo before going to the next bar. Mrs. Henry said he
hadn't. Her heart sank, but she told Mrs. Henry where she

was so Jackson wouldn't have to waste time at the first club.

She found the second place easily. She waited a few minutes, gathered her courage and went inside. This dive was worse than the other. It was filthy and full of depraved men screaming catcalls at a topless dancer on a runway in the center of the small room. One man reached up and yanked her bikini bottom and it came off. The men shouted and hooted, and the girl ran from the stage. Emily glanced around, but she didn't see Becca or Dylan. They weren't here, either.

She'd just started for the door when someone pushed a young girl onto the runway. She wore a miniskirt and a halter top. Emily froze. It was Becca. A Becca she'd never seen before. Her face was heavily made up and huge earrings dangled from her ears. The skirt barely covered her rear, and the top left little to the imagination.

Becca wrapped her arms around her naked belly and she was visibly trembling. Her eyes were glazed and filled with fear. What had they done to her child? Was she drugged?

A mother's rage ran through Emily and she pushed men aside to get to Becca. She reached up and pulled her from the runway. Sobs of terror emanated from Becca's lips and Emily had to drag her bodily to the door. She had one goal—to get her out of here as quickly as possible.

A big man with tattoos down each arm stepped in front of them. "What the hell do you think you're doin'?" he asked, his voice thick.

"I'm getting my daughter out of here," she said angrily. "She's underage, so get out of my way."

The room suddenly became quiet and the man didn't move. "I don't think so, lady. I paid that boy for this girl to dance and she's gonna dance."

Out of the corner of her eye she saw Dylan lurking in a corner and she wanted to scratch his eyes out.

"My daughter is not dancing," she repeated fiercely. "I'll refund your money."

Emily tried to get past him, but he wouldn't budge. "These good ol' boys want to see the little girl without her clothes and that's what they gonna see. Now, you can either leave or enjoy the fun." He seized Becca's arm, pulling her toward the runway. Becca made a whimpering sound and Emily went after the man. She grabbed his arm and kicked him in the shin.

"Let go of her!"

The man slapped her hard across the face. Emily tumbled to the floor. The room spun and voices were muted in her head, but she couldn't lose consciousness. She had to help Becca. She crawled to her knees and the man kicked her in the ribs knocking her backward onto the floor. Pain ripped through her, but she struggled to get up.

"You stupid bitch," the man growled, and tried to kick her again, but Becca attacked him. She punched him and kicked him, all the while screaming, "Don't hurt my mother! Don't hurt my mother!"

Through the pain and horror, Emily heard that one word *mother*. Becca had called her *mother*.

The man swung Becca up in the air and laughed at her puny struggles. Emily tried to move. He was not going to harm Becca.

"Put the girl down." Emily heard the strong voice and thought maybe she'd imagined it. The next words proved she hadn't.

"Put my daughter down," Jackson repeated. He saw Emily lying on the dirty floor, so still, and his heart split open in pain. Was he too late? Oh, God, he prayed he wasn't too late. He wanted to run to her, but he couldn't.

The man held Becca and he had to free her. He was torn between his daughter and Emily, and in that instant he knew just how Emily had felt weeks ago. Becca had to be their top priority. For the first time he understood instinctively what it was like to be a father—loving unselfishly without regard for personal feelings.

"The girl's gonna dance," the man sneered.

"On your grave," Jackson spit out.

"Says who?"

"I say, and so does the Houston police department who are right behind me. So if any of you don't want to spend time in jail, I suggest you get the hell out of here."

People scurried from the room, and the big man released Becca just as the police burst through the door.

Jackson and Becca dropped down beside Emily at the same time. "Emily," Jackson cried, lifting her head.

She moaned and he let out a grateful sigh. She was alive. Now he had to get them out of this dreadful place.

"That man slapped and kicked her," Becca said. "I think he hurt her. Em, are you okay? Please be okay."

Becca was calling her Em again. That was worth all the pain. Becca wasn't mad at her anymore. Emily could tell by her tone.

When she didn't respond, Jackson got to his feet. "I'd better get an ambulance."

"No," Emily shouted, then winced. Jackson was immediately at her side again. "Take me home. Please, take Becca and me home."

He gathered her into his arms and did just that.

## CHAPTER EIGHTEEN

JACKSON DROVE EMILY'S CAR back to the condo. She didn't know how he'd gotten here so fast and she didn't have the breath to ask. She was just grateful, so grateful. She couldn't bear to think what would have happened if he hadn't appeared.

When they got to the condo, Jackson wanted to carry her inside, but she refused. She walked gingerly into the living room and sat carefully on the sofa. Becca hovered beside her. They hadn't spoken much on the way home. Jackson was angry, Becca was upset, and she was hurting like hell. She probably had a cracked rib. She'd get it x-rayed later. Right now, she needed to talk to Jackson and Becca. She had to find out if those men had drugged Becca, but this time her concern for Becca would not overshadow her deep love for Jackson. She had to tell him how wrong she'd been, but that scowl on his handsome face stopped her.

"What the hell happened here?" Jackson asked, glancing around at the trashed living room.

Becca hung her head.

"I'll explain later." Emily looked at Becca. "I—"

"No," Jackson interrupted. He had reached his limit. They weren't going to mollycoddle Becca anymore. She needed a strong hand, and right now Jackson was in a mood to give her one. His eyes fastened on her. "Go upstairs. Get out of those clothes and wipe that stuff off your face. I want you back down here in ten minutes, then you're going to clean this place up and do some heavy-duty apologizing and mean every word of it.''

"Yes, sir," Becca replied, and ran for the stairs.

"Jackson," Emily appealed, not wanting him to be so angry with Becca.

"No, Emily." Jackson held up a hand. "I've let you handle her for weeks and it hasn't worked. Now we're going to do it my way. She's out of control and she's hurting you. I'm not standing for that."

She knew he was right—and, oh, it felt so good to have him help her with Becca. "Don't be too hard on her," she said. "I think she might've been drugged or it could have been fear. I'm not sure, but we need to find out."

"You're damn right we will," he snapped. "I'll inform the police."

"No," Emily said as he reached for the phone. "Why don't we talk to her first?"

The word *we* worked wonders. Emily was including him. On the phone she'd said she needed him and couldn't handle Becca alone anymore. He hoped that meant exactly what it implied—that they would now raise their daughter together. Even when he'd been so upset with her, he'd never stopped loving her. But he had to know how she felt.

She patted the spot beside her; even that small movement seemed to hurt "Come sit with me," she whispered. "I have to say something to you."

That look in her eyes sent his libido into overdrive and he knew he'd do anything she asked, so he had to keep his distance. He couldn't give in to her—not this time.

As he hesitated, she asked, "Don't you want to sit by me?"

"More than you'll ever know," he admitted openly.

"But if I get near you, you'll talk me into changing my mind about Becca and I can't do that. We have to be firm with her."

"This isn't about Becca. It's about you and me."

"Oh," he murmured guardedly.

"If you won't come over here, I can still talk." She paused. "I was wrong in asking you for time. Becca and I didn't need time alone. What we needed was time together. Time as a family, all three of us. I can see that now. I'm sorry if I hurt you, but I was as confused and mixed up as Becca." She paused again. "I've missed you so much. Please don't stand there forever."

Jackson didn't move. He stared into her dark eyes, seeing the future and everything else he wanted to see, but he had to be sure. "I can't," he said quietly. "I can't hold you and kiss you and then leave. I can't go through that again. The last time almost killed me."

Her eyes didn't waver from his. "I love you. I've loved you since I was seventeen and I'll never ask you to leave again. That's my promise to you."

Jackson's heart jolted at her sincerity. It was exactly what he needed to hear, but still he hesitated.

"Jackson…"

He raked both hands through his hair. "I have to know if you forgive me for not coming back all those years ago."

Her eyes still held his. "Yes, I forgive you," she replied, and she knew it was the truth.

He had to restrain himself. "Then you want the same thing I want—love, family, a future."

"Yes." She smiled. "I want that, too."

"Emily…" He was by her side in an instant and gazing into her warm, dark eyes. He drew back when he saw the side of her face. "My God, what did that man do to you?"

"Why? Is my face turning blue?"

"Yes," he answered honestly. "Let me take you to the emergency room."

"No, I'm just bruised. Nothing's broken. Maybe a cracked rib—I'll tape it later. Just kiss me. That's all I need right now."

Ever so gently he kissed her swollen cheek.

She leaned into the kiss, needing his touch, his caress, more than she needed anything. She turned her head and their lips met, softly, sweetly, then it became a kiss that swept them away with burning need. "Oh, Emily," he breathed against her lips. "How did everything go so wrong when we feel like this?"

"I don't know, but I hope it's something we can fix." She ran a hand through his hair, loving the texture of it.

"We sure can, and we begin when Becca comes down. We have to be stern with her and we have to be in agreement on that."

"I know."

They heard a door slam upstairs.

"Let me do the talking," he murmured.

"Okay," she said simply.

Jackson gave her a quick kiss and got to his feet. As soon as Becca entered the room, she began to pick up pizza boxes and beer cans. She wore jeans and a T-shirt and she looked more like the Becca Emily loved. Jackson helped her. When they'd finished, he pointed to the sofa. "Sit by your mother. I have a few things to say."

Becca meekly sat beside Emily.

"What possessed you to go to that place?" Jackson asked with as much calm as he could muster.

Becca shrugged her shoulders. "Dylan called and said he was bored and he wanted me to stay home and hang out with him today. I said I couldn't. I had to go to work.

He started calling me names like staid and Goody Two-shoes and I said I could have fun like anyone else. He came over and we listened to CDs and he called some friends. They brought beer and pizza. I didn't know they were going to do that. The girls said I needed a makeover and they did my face and lent me some of their clothes. Then the guys decided to go out and we went from bar to bar. I was scared, and I wanted to come home, but they laughed at me.'' She stopped for a second. ''Finally we ran out of money and one guy said he knew how to get some fast cash and have fun at the same time. Dylan said to do what I was told and I'd better not make a fool out of him or he'd...he'd hurt me.''

Jackson tried to suppress the rage inside him, without success. ''I'll have a talk with that young man and his parents. No one's threatening my daughter. No one.''

''Jackson,'' Emily said quietly, and that soothing voice calmed his anger.

He took a quick breath. ''Did he or anyone give you drugs?''

Becca shook her head. ''No, but they kept trying to get me to drink. I just took sips and pretended I was.''

''Do you have any idea what those guys had in mind for you?''

''Yes, and I was so scared.''

''That's good, because we learn from fear and I hope to God you've learned something.'' He took another breath, trying to maintain his cool, but the thought of what could have happened to her drove him on.

''Look at your mother's face. If your goal was to hurt her, you've succeeded. How does it feel to hurt the person who loves you most in the world?''

A sob erupted from Becca's throat. ''I didn't mean to hurt you, Em. I really didn't. I don't know why I say and do these awful things. I don't even know who I am—am I your sister or your daughter? Some days I know, but other days I get so confused I—I lash out. I'm sorry. I just don't know who I am.'' Tears rolled down her cheeks and Emily caught her face and held it.

''You're my daughter,'' she told her softly. ''You've always been my daughter.''

''Really?''

''Yes, really, and in time it will get easier, but we have to be able to talk and we have to be able to deal with the anger and resentment.''

''But it feels like it's all my fault.''

Emily frowned. ''What are you talking about?''

''When I was small and I said my prayers—'' She hiccuped. ''I used to pray that I'd wake up and you'd be my real mother and you'd take me to live with you and I'd be your little girl. Now it's come true and it's all my fault.''

''Becca, Becca.'' Emily wiped tears from her face. ''It's not your fault. Besides, I did the same thing.''

''What?'' Becca blinked.

''When I came home that first Thanksgiving, you had on a pink nightie, and when you saw me you kicked out with your feet and waved your hands as if to say, 'I knew you'd come. I've been waiting,' and I wished you were my little girl. I've wished it every time I held you and every time I saw you. There was a bond there, and subconsciously we must have sensed it. That's why we've always been so close.''

''Yeah,'' Becca agreed. ''You're my mother.''

''Yes, I'm your mother,'' Emily said with a catch in her voice.

''And Jackson is my father,'' Becca said.

Jackson had been standing apart, letting them talk, but

now he moved to sit near Becca. "Yes, I am," he said, taking her hand and holding it.

"You both must hate me for the way I've been behaving," she mumbled, her hair falling across her face.

Jackson pulled her hair back. "We could never hate you. We're your parents and that comes with unconditional love."

"I'm sorry, so sorry," Becca cried, and threw her arms around Emily. Jackson saw Emily wince, but he knew she didn't mind the pain. "I'm sorry I hurt you. I'll never act like that again. I promise. I love you."

"I love you, too." Emily kissed the side of her face. "Everything's going to be all right."

Becca reached out an arm and pulled Jackson close to them. "Yeah," she murmured happily. "Everything's going to be all right."

This was what Jackson had been waiting for, but it wasn't complete, not yet, and he hoped he wasn't moving too fast for Emily. He just couldn't be patient any longer. Looking into Emily's eyes, he spoke to Becca. "I was planning on changing Emily's last name to Talbert, and I was hoping you might like to do the same thing."

Emily was taken aback, but only for a second. She wanted them to be a family, but a small part of her wanted Jackson to ask her in a romantic setting. Then she asked herself what could be more romantic than this, holding their daughter between them? Nothing, absolutely nothing. Her heart filled with love and she waited for Becca's answer.

"Change my name to Talbert?" Becca asked cautiously.

"Yes," Jackson replied.

"I'd be Rebecca Ann Talbert."

"That's who you are," Jackson reminded her.

Becca's face brightened. "Yes, I am. I'm Rebecca Ann

Talbert.'' She glanced at Emily. "I think I'd like to have my real name."

"That would make your father and me very happy." Emily smiled, and stroked her hair. "Go upstairs and get some sleep. We'll talk again in the morning."

Becca hesitated. "Em...?"

"Hmm?"

"I really am sorry for the way I've been acting. I understood why you did what you did, but I just kept getting so confused. Even though I knew I was your daughter, I was afraid you loved her more than me. That doesn't make any sense, but I couldn't shake the feeling."

"I know, angel, and it's okay," Emily reassured her. "We've all been a little confused."

Becca smiled a genuine smile. "Are you going to call me that?"

"What?" Emily asked, not realizing she'd called her anything different.

"Angel. You called me angel. Jackson does, too."

"That's because you are our angel," Jackson answered before Emily could. "Now off to bed so I can talk to your mother."

"Will you be here in the morning?" Becca asked him.

Jackson glanced at Emily. "Yes, he will, and every morning from now on," Emily answered with a smile.

"Great," Becca said, and kissed them both. She bounced up the stairs and Emily felt the noose around her heart give way and break free.

The smile lingered on her face as she looked at Jackson. "You want to run that by me again?"

"What?" He moved close to her.

"You know."

He picked up her hand and kissed it. "Emily Ann Cooper, will you marry me?"

"In a heartbeat." She kissed his lips again and again until he captured them in a passionate vow. When he drew back, they were both breathless. She took his hand and got to her feet with a grimace.

"Emily, you need to go to a doctor."

"I am a doctor and all I need is a hot bath—and you. I want to lie in your arms and—"

"Wait." He quirked an eyebrow. "Remember we have a teenager in the house."

"That teenager will be asleep in ten minutes and a bomb wouldn't wake her."

He held an arm around her waist and they slowly made their way to her bedroom. He undressed her slowly and moaned when he saw the dark bruise on her side. "That bastard," he growled.

She kissed his chest and started to unbutton his shirt.

"Oh, Emily." He sighed with longing. "I don't think you're in any condition for this."

"I'll be the judge of that," she said lightly. In the bathroom, she turned on the tap for the Jacuzzi, then added bath salts to the water, and when it was steaming hot she stepped inside and eased down into its depths.

Jackson quickly removed his shirt, socks and shoes. He grabbed a washcloth and knelt at the edge of the tub. He stroked her body with long, sensuous movements. She closed her eyes with a wondrous sigh as Jackson's hands and the water took her away. He touched every inch of her and it was the most delicious feeling she'd ever experienced.

He lifted her from the water and toweled her dry with the same caressing motions. Sitting on the edge of the tub, he pulled her between his legs and rubbed lotion into every tantalizing, aching inch. She opened a drawer and handed him an Ace bandage. He carefully wrapped her midsection.

They didn't say a word. They didn't have to. Love was guiding their every movement.

Jackson turned down the bed, locked the door and hurried out of slacks that had suddenly become too tight. Emily slipped into bed and he crawled in beside her, gathering her close against him. She felt his arousal and her heart pounded loudly in her ears. His lips began a thorough search of all the sensitive places he'd discovered in the tub. He kissed, caressed and stroked, and her hands were equally generous with him. Their lovemaking was slow and gentle, but it expressed an urgent need that left them gasping and wanting more.

"I love you," he whispered.

Emily was drifting in a euphoric state, but she heard his words and looked into his green eyes. "I love you, too. I have always loved you and I will never stop loving you."

Jackson buried his face in the warmth of her neck, their bodies still joined, still needing that contact. Slowly he eased to the side and she nestled into him.

"How are you feeling?" he asked with concern, his hand lightly rubbing her stomach.

She ran her hands through the hair on his chest. "Happy, lethargic and very loved."

"Me, too," he whispered. "But I was talking about the ribs."

"What ribs?" She gave a bubbly laugh similar to Becca's. "They've had the Talbert touch and now I don't feel any pain."

"Oh, God, Emily." His arm tightened around her. "I don't know what I would've done if anything had happened to you or Becca today."

"It didn't. We're fine," she assured him. "We're so lucky you showed up when you did." She raised her head to look at him. "By the way, how did you manage that?

When I called the condo, Mrs. Henry said you hadn't arrived yet.''

"I called from the plane right after that, and Mrs. Henry told me where you were and what was going on. I was on a private plane owned by a friend. It was the quickest way to get here. Anyway, the pilot's a bit of a daredevil and when I told him where I needed to be pronto, he landed in a field not far from the bar. We'll probably be hearing from the Houston authorities, but I knew time was of the essence. Several cars stopped to see what the landing was about and a guy gave me a ride to the bar. I called the police from his cell phone.''

She rested her head on his chest. "It all worked out. That's the main thing.''

"I still can't understand why she'd put her life and yours in such danger.''

"Rebellion,'' she told him simply. "You've had loving parents all your life, but once you lose that anchor you're scared and you hit out at everything and hurt yourself and the people you love.''

"Even though I've had loving parents, I know what it's like to lose that anchor.'' He stroked her arm. "It's not the same thing, but the emotions are similar to what you went through with your parents—the sense of betrayal, of the support you've always counted on being taken away from you.''

"Yeah, that's why I was reluctant to discipline Becca or force her into anything. I thought all she needed was time, but when I came home and saw the house and was unable to find her, I knew I'd been wrong. What we needed was you and your stabilizing influence and guiding love.''

He kissed the top of her head. "If anything, I think she learned a valuable lesson tonight.''

"I do, too, and now she has us to help her through the weeks and years ahead."

"She sure does and—"

The phone rang, interrupting them. Jackson answered it immediately, as he was closest. She could tell he was talking to the police.

When he hung up, he said, "The cops have been trying to put this guy away for a long time, and if you're willing to testify, they think they can do it."

"You bet I will."

"Are you sure?"

"Yes," she answered confidently. "It might save another girl from going through the same ordeal."

He kissed her gently. "I'll be right there with you."

"I know," she said, and moved to get out of bed.

"Where are you going?"

She reached for her pink silk robe lying across a chair and realized her ribs weren't hurting as much anymore. Indeed, the Talbert touch was working. "I want to check on Becca—make sure she's okay."

"I'll come with you." Jackson found his slacks on the floor and hurried into them. "This is all the clothes I have. I didn't have time to pack a bag."

"I think we can find clothes for you in Houston," she teased.

"We'd better, 'cause I'm not leaving you...ever again."

They shared a lingering kiss, then walked down the hall to Becca's room.

She lay sprawled on her stomach in an oversize T-shirt. She'd kicked the sheet off and her long hair flowed across the pillows. Her shining face was turned toward them.

"She's about the most precious sight I've ever seen," Jackson whispered.

"Yes, she is," Emily agreed, and reached for the sheet

to cover her. She stared at her daughter for a moment, then stepped back into Jackson's arms.

"We finally have our child," she said in a trembling voice.

"Yes, we do," Jackson said. "And I think she knows that now."

THEY WERE MARRIED three weeks later in Rockport. Emily stood in Becca's old room at her parents' house staring at herself in the mirror. She couldn't believe her eyes. She'd mistakenly told Jackson that she'd always dreamed of walking down the aisle on her father's arm, wearing a white wedding gown. She was only half serious; it was just a girlhood dream and she'd outgrown it. But Jackson had other ideas. He had a friend in New York whose wife worked in the fashion industry. He explained that he wanted a special dress as soon as possible. Emily reluctantly gave her measurements, thinking she could find something just as suitable in Houston. Looking at herself, she was glad Jackson hadn't listened to her. The dress was one of a kind and it fit like the dream she'd always had.

It was a French-influenced design of textured roses. The bodice was strapless and the skirt slim-fitting, flaring out slightly around her ankles. The veil was layered. The whole ensemble could only be described as spectacular. Jackson hadn't seen the dress yet, but when he did she knew he was going to love it. The dress was as special as this day.

She took a picture of Becca from the dresser and smiled into the brown eyes of her little girl. She now had her daughter, and today she would marry the man she loved. *Her little girl's father.* They would unite as a family, and Emily's heart swelled with so much love and happiness.

"Oh. Oh, my."

Emily turned at her mother's voice. Rose stood in the doorway in a champagne-colored suit. Her hair was neatly done and she even wore makeup. She looked ten years younger. The stress and guilt over Becca was gone and she was experiencing a new lease on life. Already, the heart spells were fewer.

"Oh, Emily Ann, my baby, you're so beautiful," Rose murmured, walking over to kiss Emily's cheek. As she did, she noticed the picture in her hand. "You know, she's always been your daughter. Even when she was a toddler, she recognized the sound of your car, and whenever she heard it, she'd run to the front door screaming your name. I used to resent that closeness, but the therapist has helped me understand all that. I never dealt with the death of my daughter, and for a while I just…lost my mind."

Emily hugged her mother, knowing that was true. She now understood the extent of Rose's breakdown. Love had opened Emily's heart and eyes, and she could honestly say she had forgiven her mother. The heartache from the past would probably always be with her, but it didn't dominate her life or control her emotions anymore. She had too much to be grateful for.

"I know, Mom," she whispered.

"Thank you, baby. Thank you for forgiving me."

"Oh, Mom, don't make me cry. Becca has very diligently worked on my makeup and I can't mess it up."

"The limo Jackson sent is here. Hurry," Becca called from the hallway.

"I love you, Emily Ann."

"I love you, too, Mom." Emily said, fighting back tears. They embraced and neither seemed eager to let go.

"Hey, what's the holdup?" Becca asked, walking into the room.

Emily released her mother and smiled at her daughter.

As maid of honor, Becca wore a long dress of pale pink, strapless and slim-skirted like her mother's. Her dark hair was up, and pink roses adorned it.

"Nothing, angel," Emily answered.

"Wow," Becca mouthed. "Every time I see you in that dress, it just takes my breath away. When Jackson sees you, he's going to fall in love with you all over again."

And he did. Emily could see it in his eyes as she walked down the aisle. New love strengthened by the old. Love that bound their two hearts together for now and forever.

LATER THEY HAD A RECEPTION and dinner at the country club, hosted by Rose and Owen. Everyone was happy and laughing and drinking champagne, even her mother. Her father was talking and smiling more than she'd ever seen him. Her wedding day couldn't have been more perfect.

Jackson had rented a hotel suite in Corpus Christi for the night. It was the only honeymoon they wanted. They preferred not to spend time away from Becca. She'd be going off to college soon enough.

After the reception, Becca offered to show George and Maude the sights of Corpus Christi and Rockport. Colton, who'd been Jackson's best man, asked to go along, and Becca made a scornful face that Emily didn't understand. Becca didn't like Colton and she wondered why.

A few hours later, Emily was soaking in the hotel's big tub, sipping champagne by candlelight; she smiled at her husband.

He smiled back.

"Thanks for this wonderful day, the dress, everything," she said softly.

"It was my pleasure, Mrs. Talbert."

She cocked her head to one side. "Hmm, that sounds

nice, but I think I'll keep Dr. Cooper as my professional name.''

''That's fine with me—as long as you're Mrs. Talbert in your heart.''

Her eyes sparkled. ''I've always been Mrs. Talbert in my heart.''

''Have you?''

She twisted her glass. ''Well, I've wished it on more than one occasion.''

''So have I.'' He grinned. ''Happy?''

''Very,'' she whispered, and thought of their daughter. ''Did you notice Becca's reaction to Colton?''

''Like a deep freeze.''

''Yes, I can't figure out why she doesn't like him. He seems very nice.''

''He is, and all the ladies love Colton and his blond locks, so that's one less worry for us.''

''What do you mean?''

''Becca won't be falling for him.''

''I suppose, but she should at least be civil to him.''

Jackson laughed. ''Right about now, Colton's getting a good dose of Becca, Aunt Maude and Dad, and he's probably wishing he'd hightailed it back to Dallas.''

''But—''

He cut in. ''No more talk about family,'' he said. ''Let's concentrate on us.'' His foot slid between her legs.

''Oh.'' She giggled delightedly, and set her glass on the edge of the tub. She moved through the water and onto his lap, wrapping her arms around his neck. ''You want to play, do you?'' As she said the words, she moved her hips against his arousal.

''Ah,'' he groaned, and placed his glass out of reach. ''Oh, yes.'' His mouth covered hers in a heated, explosive kiss that welded them together. "I love you," he breathed in a tortured voice.

As their bodies sank into the water, she knew he did—for now and always—and nothing would ever get any better than this.

# EPILOGUE

*Four years later*

"PLEASE. STOP. COME BACK."

Two-year-old George Owen Scott Talbert paid no attention to his mother. He kept running, but Emily caught him at the top of the stairs.

She cradled him in her arms and he buried his face in the warmth of her neck. All her motherly instincts kicked in. She never tired of this feeling—loving, caring and nurturing her child. She didn't have to wonder what his face looked like. She knew every precious detail by heart. This baby she had nourished from the day he was conceived, and no one could ever take that away from her.

"Why are you running from Mama?" Emily asked gently. She'd been trying to get him to bed when he'd slipped out the door.

Scotty raised his head and stared at her with Jackson's gorgeous green eyes. "No sleep, Mama. No sleep."

Emily was baffled. Scotty was never hard to put down for the night. She smoothed his blond hair. "What's the matter with Mama's boy?"

His eyes grew big. "Part-ee, Mama. Part-ee."

She now knew what all the fuss was about. Becca's birthday was tomorrow and they were having a party. Scotty was excited about it. They'd come home to Rockport because that was what Becca wanted to do. She wanted to spend her birthday with old friends and family. Jackson and Emily had built a beach house the first year they were married and they spent a lot of weekends in Rockport.

The last four years had been the happiest of Emily's life. Becca had settled down and put all her energies into college. She'd made new friends and life was better than Emily had ever hoped. When they wanted another child, Jackson decided to stay home to take care of the baby. Up until that time, he was flying back and forth and doing a lot of work from Houston. They didn't want to be apart any more than necessary. Finally, he sold the controlling interest in his company to Colton. He maintained a small interest and his seat on the board. Emily had agreed at first, but when Scotty was born she never wanted to leave him. They had missed so much with Becca, and neither one of them wanted to miss a moment of Scotty's life. Eventually she went back to work, though, but only half days and no weekends. She enjoyed her work, but not as much as she did her family.

They bought a house in the Bellaire area of Houston and remodeled it to accommodate their growing family. It was close to the clinic, which meant Emily didn't have far to travel.

The beach house was their weekend retreat. Becca loved it here, and so did George. But Emily worried about Becca at times. It had been her own decision to go to med school. That pleased Emily, but she wanted what was best for Becca. Her daughter seemed so tired lately. Emily hated that her life was so busy, but she tried to remember what those days as a medical student were like; hard though they were, she knew Becca would manage. She also worried about the new baby and how he'd affect Becca, but Becca loved Scotty. That was plain to everyone.

Emily kissed Scotty's soft cheek. "The party is tomorrow. Tonight we have to sleep."

"No, no, Mama," Scotty shouted again. "No sleep."

Emily was debating what to do next when Jackson appeared at the top of the stairs. He'd been in his study talking to Colton on the phone. Her heart beat faster at the sight of him. They were now a family, and Jackson was the perfect father, just as she'd known he would be.

"Scotty Talbert, what are you doing still up?" Jackson teased. "You should have been in bed an hour ago."

Scotty made a dive for Jackson, who gathered him close. "Daddy, Daddy, no sleep," Scotty wailed.

Jackson lifted an eyebrow at Emily, and Emily tried to explain. "He's excited about Becca's birthday party and doesn't want to go to bed."

"Now, son..." Jackson started, but Scotty quickly interrupted him.

"Part-ee, Daddy, part-ee. Sissy."

Jackson's arm tightened around his son. "Sissy's tired. She's been working all day and now she's sleeping like you should be."

Scotty's bottom lip began to tremble and it took everything in Emily not to snatch him out of Jackson's arms.

"Sissy, sissy," Scotty cried.

Becca's door opened and she walked out, wearing one of her big T-shirts. Her dark hair, now tousled from bed, had been cut and it hung just past her shoulders. She frowned mischievously. "Who's interrupting my beauty sleep?"

Emily's heart filled with love at the sight of her daughter. "I'm sorry, angel, but we can't get Scotty down. He's worked up about your party."

Scotty wiggled out of Jackson's arms and ran down the hall to Becca. "Sissy, sissy," he called.

Becca swung him into the air, and giggles and screams erupted.

Jackson slid his arm around Emily as they watched their two children.

"Whenever I thought of having kids, I never really wanted them twenty years apart," he whispered in her ear. "But it's pretty damn good."

"Yeah." She nestled into him.

As Becca settled Scotty on her hip, she asked, "What's the matter, tiger? How come you can't go to sleep?"

Scotty clapped his hands. "Part-ee, Sissy. Cake. Boons. Pop. Pop."

"Right now Sissy's head can't take too much popping." Becca grimaced. "Want to sleep with Sissy? And when Sissy's had enough rest, we'll party all day. Okay?"

"Okay," Scotty said.

"So simple." Jackson smiled at Emily.

It was very clear that Becca and Scotty adored each other, and for that Emily was grateful. It was also clear how exhausted Becca was.

"Becca, angel, you don't have to do that. You're tired and you need a peaceful night's sleep. With Scotty, it'll be like a boxing match."

"It's all right, Mama," Becca said. "We'll be fine." She walked into her room, still carrying Scotty.

A lump formed in Emily's throat. It happened every time Becca called her *Mama*. At first the word had been awkward, for both of them, but now it was so natural. There was nothing more precious than that sound and she treasured the relationship she had with her daughter.

She turned to Jackson. "This is Becca's only weekend off for ages and she needs to rest, not baby-sit."

"Don't worry," Jackson said. "She seems fine."

"I can't help it. It's a mother thing."

He kissed her lightly. "I know. Let's check on them to make sure Scotty's not jumping on the bed and being a terrible two-year-old."

They stopped at Becca's door when they heard her voice. "You're so lucky, Scotty. Do you know that? You've had them for parents from the day you were born. It was different for me. I could be jealous if I didn't love you so much."

"Luv ya," Scotty interjected.

"Since I'm your big sister, I'm gonna give you some advice about this family and how to handle them."

"Sissy," Scotty said, and Emily could imagine him poking his little finger into Becca's chest. He loved to identify people.

"Yes, I'm Sissy, so listen." Becca laughed. "Grandpa George, he's a pushover. You probably already know that. And he'll love you no matter what, just like Mama and Daddy."

"Mama," Scotty whimpered, and Jackson had to hold Emily to keep her from dashing into the room.

"Yeah, your Mama and Daddy and mine. It used to sound strange, but it sounds right to me now."

"Daddy," Scotty said, and Jackson had to force himself to stand still.

"Now, about Grandpa Owen. He's rather quiet. You have to give him a nudge sometimes, but he'll always help you and be there for you. And Grandma Rose. That's a hard one. I hated her at times, but through it all, I've loved her and that wasn't always easy. But love is a funny thing. Once given, it never dies. It suffers through bad times, but it always survives."

"Luv ya," Scotty said again.

"I love you, too, and if I don't get you to sleep, I'm going to be in big trouble."

Scotty giggled at Becca's exaggerated tone.

Jackson led Emily away from the door and to their room. Emily brushed away a tear. "I feel as if I had a glimpse into Becca's heart."

"We did." He held her close. "*Now* do you think you can stop worrying?"

"I don't think mothers ever do that."

"Fathers, either, and I'm so proud of her."

"Oh, Jackson." She snuggled against his chest. "Life is so good and sometimes I'm afraid. I'm afraid I'll wake up in that nightmare again."

He reached for her face and held it. "That's never going to happen. We've suffered enough for a lifetime and now all we have to do is enjoy what we have."

"Yes," she said, knowing she could face anything with Jackson.

"And speaking of enjoying—" he smiled wickedly "—let's think about making *us* feel good."

She arched an eyebrow. "What did you have in mind?"

He unbuttoned her blouse. "I'm thinking of taking you to bed and showing you how much I love you."

"I already know that."

"It bears repeating," he said with a grin, marching her backward to the bed.

"Over and over." She laughed as he urged her down.

A long time later, Jackson slipped out of bed. "Come on," he said, grabbing his robe.

"What?" she asked, puzzled.

"You're not going to get any sleep until Scotty's in his bed and Becca's resting."

"You know me so well," she said with a smile.

"And don't you forget it," he returned, and handed her a robe.

Arm in arm, they walked to Becca's room. Scotty was sound asleep in her arms. For a moment they stared at the two faces, then Emily gently eased Scotty away.

"Scotty." Becca sat up, alert to any movement Scotty might make.

"It's all right, angel," Emily said. "I'm going to put him in his bed."

"Okay." She laid her head back on the pillow. "Love you, Mama, Daddy."

Jackson kissed Becca's check and pulled the sheet over her. "We love you, too, angel."

Emily bit back tears and knew that love had eclipsed the shadows from the past and the future was destined to be as bright as the stars in their eyes.

*  *  *  *  *

*Look for Becca's story in 2002!*

$\mathcal{H}$ugh Blake,
soon to become stepfather to
the Maitland clan, has produced three
high-performing offspring of his own. But
at the rate they're going, they're never going to
make him a grandpa!

There's *Suzanne*, a work-obsessed CEO whose Christmas spirit
could use a little topping up....

And *Thomas*, a lawyer whose ability to hold on to the woman
he loves is evaporating by the minute....

And *Diane*, a teacher so dedicated to her teenage students she
hasn't noticed she's put her own life on hold.

But there's a Christmas wake-up call in store
for the Blake siblings. Love *and* Christmas miracles
are in store for all three!

# Maitland Maternity Christmas

A collection from three of Harlequin's favorite authors

# Muriel Jensen
# Judy Christenberry
# &Tina Leonard

Look for it in November 2001.

PHMMC

If you enjoyed what you just read,
then we've got an offer you can't resist!

# Take 2 bestselling love stories FREE!

# Plus get a FREE surprise gift!

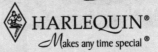

## WITH HARLEQUIN AND SILHOUETTE

### There's a romance to fit your every mood.

| Passion | Pure Romance |
|---|---|
| **Harlequin Temptation** | |
| **Harlequin Presents** | **Harlequin Romance** |
| **Silhouette Desire** | **Silhouette Romance** |

| Home & Family | A Longer Story With More |
|---|---|
| **Harlequin American Romance** | |
| **Silhouette Special Edition** | **Harlequin Superromance** |

| Suspense & Adventure | Humor |
|---|---|
| **Harlequin Intrigue** | |
| **Silhouette Intimate Moments** | **Harlequin Duets** |

| Historical | Special Releases |
|---|---|
| **Harlequin Historicals** | **Other great romances to explore** |

# CALL THE ONES YOU LOVE OVER THE HOLIDAYS!

**Save $25 off future book purchases when you buy any four Harlequin® or Silhouette® books in October, November and December 2001,**

## *PLUS*

**receive a phone card good for 15 minutes of long-distance calls to anyone you want in North America!**

## WHAT AN INCREDIBLE DEAL!

Just fill out this form and attach 4 proofs of purchase (cash register receipts) from October, November and December 2001 books, and Harlequin Books will send you a coupon booklet worth a total savings of $25 off future purchases of Harlequin® and Silhouette® books, AND a 15-minute phone card to call the ones you love, anywhere in North America.

Please send this form, along with your cash register receipts
as proofs of purchase, to:
**In the USA:** Harlequin Books, P.O. Box 9057, Buffalo, NY 14269-9057
**In Canada:** Harlequin Books, P.O. Box 622, Fort Erie, Ontario L2A 5X3
Cash register receipts must be dated no later than December 31, 2001.
Limit of 1 coupon booklet and phone card per household.
Please allow 4-6 weeks for delivery.

---

**I accept your offer! Enclosed are 4 proofs of purchase.
Please send me my coupon booklet
and a 15-minute phone card:**

Name: _____

Address: _____ City: _____

State/Prov.: _____ Zip/Postal Code: _____

Account Number (if available): _____

---

**097 KJB DAGL**
PHQ4013